Mrs. Hugh Fraser

A Diplomatist's Wife in Japan - Letters from Home to Home

Vol. I

Mrs. Hugh Fraser

A Diplomatist's Wife in Japan - Letters from Home to Home
Vol. I

ISBN/EAN: 9783337168254

Printed in Europe, USA, Canada, Australia, Japan

Cover: Foto ©Raphael Reischuk / pixelio.de

More available books at **www.hansebooks.com**

A DIPLOMATIST'S WIFE IN JAPAN

LETTERS FROM HOME TO HOME

By

MRS. HUGH FRASER

AUTHOR OF

"PALLADIA," "THE LOOMS OF TIME," "A CHAPTER OF ACCIDENTS," ETC.

WITH TWO HUNDRED AND FIFTY ILLUSTRATIONS

VOL. I.

London : HUTCHINSON & CO.
Paternoster Row ✒ 1899

AL DILETTISSIMO COMPAGNO

ME ASPETTANDO

NELLA ETERNA PACE

Two babes the mother bore at one rich birth,
Twin hearts that beat to her low notes of love,
Twin souls that leapt to each heroic call,
As generous sword to snatch the Treasure-Trove
Of hard-won honour. And our Mother Earth,
Rocking the twain in the deep rise and fall
Of her green bosom, sang proud litanies,
Promised them beauty, conquest, empire, brain and heart,
And woman's faith, and towering pride of race.
Too great to rule together, worlds apart
She set them, in the silver of the seas.
Yet heart calls heart, as erst upon the breast
That bore these glories, sovereign in their place,
The Island Empires of the East and West.

INTRODUCTORY.

IN the following letters, written during a three years'
residence in Tokyo, no method was followed
beyond the interests and the fancy of the moment; no
detailed description was attempted of Japan, her history
and her customs and her philosophies. In the times
when every foreigner saw the same sights in the Island
Empire, obtained the same stereotyped glimpses of
the people's life, and was contented with the half-
comprehended information given by his guide, it was
easy, and alas! fashionable, to describe the "toy
country" and its "fairylike" inhabitants with glib
security in large print. Those times are gone for
ever. Japan has set the doors of her secret shrines
ajar, so that we can at any rate take the first step in
wisdom, and realise how little we know. Those who,
like myself, have had the privilege of spending long
years in the country, with liberty to "visit any spot
and remain in it for any length of time," become
gradually aware of the many-sided and complex character of the people,—simple to frankness, yet full of

unexpected reserves, of hidden strengths, and dignities of power never flaunted before the eyes of the world; surprising and majestic as some of those indescribable mountain views in the central hills, where from a flowery rise in a meadow the amazed traveller finds himself on the verge of a dizzy precipice, looking out on a world where the primeval forces appear to have that moment ceased their play, where some great city of giant towers and ramparts, temples and palaces, seems to lie at his feet, overthrown and tossed upon itself as the bricks that the child builds high, and then dashes down for the joy of their fall. The Japanese scenery is often like a book of pictures. The mists rise, and show you one beauty at a time, then close in behind you. The leaf is turned, and you wonder if it was true that you saw the sun shining on a bay and little islands covered with lilies floating on its bosom. You look back, and there is only blank mist. But the scene was the truth, the mist is the illusion.

And the people have the same way of wrapping themselves in colourless conventionalities. That which you expect from them is that which they would wish to show you, and very likely all that you will ever see. But if any shared emotion suddenly draws you closer together, then the veil is rent away, you behold the springs of action, and, lo! they are those which have swayed you in the best moments of your life;

and if you are honest and humble-minded, you will say in your heart, " Brother, I misjudged thee. Perhaps thou art as near to wisdom and to love as I."

The years of my stay in Japan were those which will count in history as the first of its majority. With the proclamation of the Constitution on February 11th, 1889, Japan came of age, and assumed her full rights as a nation among the nations. The war with China in 1894 and 1895 showed that she knew how to maintain them. During the unnumbered centuries of her silent past, the two highest virtues of national life, love of country and sense of duty, had been growing, deep and strong, in the heart of the race. When the call to arms was heard, that root shot up its towering growth, and broke forth before the astonished world in the aloe flower of burning patriotism, the aloe fruit of hero deeds and hero faithfulness. The aloe dies with its rare blossom ; but not until the sword-like shoot of a new growth has given promise of its resurrection to a future glory. The thunders and acclaims of war have died away ; but the sense of shared strength and shared sacrifice, and even the memory of shared mistakes, remain. There is a new bond between ruler and ruled, between rich and poor, between the princes and the people. And should the years bring the moment back on their circling current, the Japanese people would stand again, shoulder to shoulder, to meet the shock.

Introductory

I should like to call this book a record—and an appreciation. It deals mainly with events and persons connected with the different aspects of life in the capital, in which, naturally, most of our time was passed, and which is pre-eminently the centre of Japan's vitality to-day. I have described only such places as I visited, and more especially the remote hills where we took refuge from the summer heats, and whose every turn became as familiar and beloved as the garden of my childhood. Ill health and many ties of duty generally put very long journeys out of the question ; but the faithful and patient acquaintance made with those places where my lines lay, and what I may describe as the gradual absorption of the life atmosphere surrounding me, will, I hope, make up for the fact that this work is in no way a handbook or a history, but merely a humble and faithful effort to transcribe what I have seen and learnt, and thus to bring to-day's Japan a little nearer to the understanding and sympathy of to-day's England.

The letters came to a sudden end in the early summer of 1894, when I returned to Europe—alone. In the shadow of a great grief one bright spot will stand out as long as memory lives—memory to recall the inexpressible kindness and sympathy of all my friends, European or Japanese : a sympathy so divine that it robbed sorrow of half its bitterness, a kindness so helpful and persistent that it still reaches out across two oceans to strengthen the link that binds me to the home which is home no longer. Dear people, dear kind friends, be thanked from my heart once more!

I must acknowledge my deep indebtedness to Captain Brinkley, the editor of the *Japan Mail*, for the rare and valuable information which makes it an education on Japanese subjects to read the collected volumes of his excellent newspaper. Two Japanese friends, Miss O'Yei Ozaki and Mr. Yasuoka, have given me many a quaint legend or detail of etiquette and family life, and have rendered signal help by going over these letters with me while I was preparing them for publication. As for books, the just and invaluable work of Rein has always been my companion ; the *Murray's Japan* published in 1891 was compiled by Professor Chamberlain and W. B. Mason, both profound scholars of the language and history of Japan, and is as it were a good starting-point from which to read and study in different directions ; the enchanting books of Mr. Lafcadio Hearn appeared after I left Japan, and take me back there whenever I open their pages ; and most helpful is Mr. von Wenckstern's *Bibliography of Japan*, giving four hundred pages to recording and classifying the mere titles of the books which have been written about the Island Empire.

M. C. FRASER.

THE WARREN, TORRINGTON.
December, 1898.

CONTENTS TO VOL. I.

Contents ☛

CHAPTER V.

CHAPTER VI.

CHAPTER VII.

CHAPTER VIII.

CHAPTER IX.

CHAPTER X.

Contents ☛

LIST OF ILLUSTRATIONS.

VOL. I.

List of Illustrations

xviii

CHAPTER I.

CHAPTER I.

I AM no longer homesick, so I know that the journey is nearly done, and the new country is drawing me as the sun draws the sunflowers in the old gardens at home. I am looking forward to seeing this new old friend, Japan, with the certainty of happiness which absolutely fresh surroundings always bring me; for, dearly as I love the old, I love the new still better, and can hardly imagine a care or trouble which I could not lay aside amid beautiful scenery first beheld. But I am a little afraid of Japan! I would rather not have a host of first impressions of the ordinary kind, which, as it seems to me, satisfy meagre minds, and prevent their ever really understanding new places and races. I have talked to people who had brought nothing away from Japan but the recollection of a waiting-maid and a tea-house, or one brain photograph of a short dark man dressed in unbecoming clothes. Others have seen a procession, or a dinner with chopsticks, or a missionary school, and keep all their lives one silly memory of the strangest country in the world. And—I have thought that perhaps " Little Japan " had been laughing at them ! I hope she will not laugh at me. I should like to under-

3

stand a little, to love or hate, to praise discerningly or condemn dispassionately—to make a friend, in fine.

April 30th.

I think the friendship has begun. The landing at Nagasaki and the sight of the Inland Sea have upset all my wise resolutions about first impressions. The only thing that came to me as I stepped on shore at Nagasaki was a fit of really light-hearted laughter—laughter of the joyous and unreasonable kind whose tax is mostly paid in tears. Life suddenly presented itself as a thing of fun and joy: the people, the shops, the galloping jinriksha coolies, the toy houses treated as serious dwellings by fathers of families, all combined to give me a day of the purest amusement that has ever been granted to me yet. For sixpence I would have changed places with a seller of cakes whom I met in the road. His clothes were of the impressionist kind, some rather slight good intentions carried out in cool blue cotton, the rest being brown man and straw sandals. He carried a fairy temple built of snowy wood and delicate paper, with a willow branch for a dusting-brush, and little drawers, full of sweets, which pulled out in every direction, as white and close-fitting as the petals of a moon-dahlia. All his dainty wares were white or pink, and at a distance one might have mistaken him and his shrine of sweets for a bundle of lotus blooms on two brown stems. It seemed unwise to change places with him, and might have caused confusion in the family; but I was sorry that H—— would not

4

let me buy him, pack and all, and stand him up in the
hall of the new home in Tokyo as my first curio.

And now we are in the Inland Sea; and it seems
to me that I have been taken to the heart of the country,
have seen the very essence of its beauty and remoteness,
have been set in the presence of that by which it would
choose to be judged. Our first hours were misty, and
the sea was rough ; but the mists rolled back from one
dream picture after another, and each was so lovely
that one forgot to regret the last. Of all the things
that I have seen none are so individually and weirdly
beautiful as these pine-fringed hills of Japan, with their
delicate, daring profiles rising in curves and points
that no Western mountain ever knew, crowned with
pines following each other in leisurely succession,
and holding out dark-green branches for the mists to
tear on, or coppery golden arms for the sun to strike.
The mists are not thick rolling fogs like ours ; they
wave and hang, part and cling together, curl away
from a breeze or sink back on a calm like a thousand
veils of fine gauze, each moving with a will of its own.

It was a great deal to learn all that at once, to
realise that the mist pictures of the Japanese are not
fairy dreams, but faithful presentments of nature. Yet
another and still stranger sight was in store for me.
A fresh wind came tearing down some watercourse in
the hills ; it swept under the brooding mists, and rolled
them up like a scroll ; and then—we were on a sparkling
sea, flooded with sunshine, enclosed by green mountains,
and dotted with innumerable islands. On one, just

before us, a lovely temple with a red *torii* (gate) stood right out on the flood, which bathed the feet of its sentinel pines. The deep was suddenly covered with what seemed like a flotilla of white nautilus shells, with sails all set, closing in round us with a flutter of wings, and the cool music of a hundred prows rushing through the water in the sun. Every fishing-boat from every village had put out on that liberating breeze, and the moving crowd of silver sails on the morning sea made a sight too bewildering to paint in words. The peculiar warm sheen of the junk sails, square above and round below, made in long strips, seamed and held together in a thousand lovely patterns by the interlacing ropes strained against the breeze, gave the impression of a web of silver against the blue ; and the calm majesty of the silky rush on the water's surface made me feel that our great coal-fed, screw-driven liner was a blot on the universe, and had no title to travel with that fair company.

They, indeed, took little notice of the *Verona*, and treated us with gay disdain. They pressed in on every side, till we were completely surrounded by them, thick on the tide as the white lotus blooms that smother the marble bridge in the pond of the Summer Palace. Then the wind changed, and they all floated away in a wide half circle, which became a fringe of stars on the water after the night came down.

TOKYO, *May 5th.*

I feel that the date at the head of this letter should mark an epoch in my experience ; but I am still too

6

new to these strange airs to give any clear account of what I have seen, am seeing all the time. I cannot imagine a better cure for weariness of spirit than a first visit to Japan. The country is absolutely fresh. All that one has read or heard fails to give any true impression of this vivid youngness of an atmosphere

THE BRITISH LEGATION IN TOKYO.

where things seem to sort themselves out in their real, and, to me, new values.

We reached Yokohama on the 1st, and came up here at once. As scenery Yokohama does not exist, so we will not talk about it; but Tokyo is enchanting— so far! It strikes me as a city of gardens, where streets and houses have grown up by accident—and are of no

7

importance as compared with the flowers still. How shall I describe it, so that you in Rome can see it, dear people?

As I write, here on my upstairs verandah, so wide and cool that every breeze sweeps through it from end to end, and yet so sheltered that I can wander about and work or read in absolute privacy, I am, as it were, at the heart of things; for there to my left, across the green banks of the moat, and hid in the impenetrable foliage of the gardens, is the Emperor's new Palace, which I am to see in a few days when we have our audience. It stands, as in honour bound, higher than any of the streets and buildings which lie round the first moat; but no single gable can be seen above the dark roofs of the pines, round whose red knees the smaller trees cling jealously lest any glimpse of the life Imperial reach the outer world. All round the crest of the hill run high walls, with here and there a beautiful gate. There is one, almost opposite our own, of ancient wood, soft and dull in colour, bound and hinged by sheets of beaten copper, which have taken on that wonderful blue patina that our old bronzes have in Rome. Above the gate the prophetic pines stretch their branches down to where the bank slopes away in a hundred yards of sheer green turf to the water of the moat. Here and there a pine or a cherry tree has been set, and some hang far over and dip in the water. Beneath their shade live a pair of white herons (I am sure they are royal lovers of the ancient time, bewitched by evil spells); and on the water swim

great flocks of wild
duck, tame, because no
shot may be fired with-
in sound of the Palace,
but just now very much
preoccupied as to sum-
mer quarters, and talk-
ing noisily all day as to
the respective merits
of the Kurile Islands,
Mongolia, and Kams-
chatka. They cannot
stay much longer, for

A PINE BRANCH.

the heat is all but upon us. (Are the swallows circling
through your Roman sky? May would not be May
without them.)

As I said just now, we are at the heart of things.
For nearly three hundred years the tide of national life
has set towards what was a humble fishing village (the
name means the door of the bay), till Hideyoshi, the
great usurper, pointed it out to his marshal Iyeyasu as a
stronger and more central spot than the Castle of Odawara, which had fallen into their hands at the end of
some murderous civil war. It seems to me that Tokyo,
as I see it from my balconies, with its triple ring of
shallow moats spanned by scores of solid bridges, with
its vast area, and many miles of meandering streets and
gardens, would be easier to take than to defend. Here
and there, indeed, is some piece of gigantic wall, built
with uncemented blocks like those in the *ager of*

Servius Tullius in our old villa at home; but it generally frames in a wide gate, through which the armies of the world could ride with comfort. I should think it would take all the soldiers whom Napoleon slew to keep a fairly persistent invader out of Tokyo to-day. But I have not often seen a fairer city. Hill and valley, wood and water, wild-rose hedge and bamboo grove, stately pleasure-house and small brown cottage, palms and pines and waving willows —there the hills, leading up to the mountain of mountains, and there the sea, a silver line that speaks of home,—it all goes to make a picture so splendid in its breadth, and so alluring in its details, that I feel it is already growing into my mind as a necessary background to certain trains of thought. I am glad that we have come to stay for years, instead of having to rush away in a few weeks, as so many travellers do.

WISTARIA BLOOMS.

Our audience is fixed for the 17th; and as our social existence only really begins after H—— has presented his credentials, I am taking advantage of the intervening time to see all the flower shows and sights of the month. Beyond the 17th, life seems one long perspective of dinner and garden parties, of which I will tell you when they come—meanwhile I am enjoying myself! Our own gardens are quite lovely just now, with arbours of wistaria, and azaleas bursting out in masses of white and pink and orange blooms, while the great bed of lilies-of-the-valley outside the dining-room windows makes the whole air sweet round that side of the house. The lilies were a surprise to me. They do not grow in this part of Japan, but were brought down from Hakodate, where they are very plentiful, and have flourished and multiplied in the shady corner near the house. That is the corner presided over by poor Sir Harry Parkes' enormous watch-tower, which he built as a fitting place from which to fly the British Flag. (Out here we always write it with a capital F.) The emblem of empire would, it seems, have been flying some inches higher than the Imperial roofs, so that project had to be abandoned, and the Flagstaff was planted on a mound at the other end of the grounds, where it looks very dignified and businesslike, and is known by the name of Haman's Gallows. But the tower remains, and serves as a reservoir for water, and as a constant reminder of the precariousness of life in these earthquake regions. It has been cracked rather seriously in the many shocks, and is bound and clamped with iron in every direction. They say it is safe enough ; but in some slight shocks which we have already felt, it seems to set all that side of the house dancing and trembling ominously.

I am not new to earthquakes, and we have had no very alarming ones here as yet ; but the Japanese papers are unkindly promising us a severe visitation shortly. It seems that the shocks are felt very strongly in Tokyo, as they are in all places where there is a large area of soft alluvial soil ; and (consoling rider !) our house stands, so I am told, exactly where they all pass, no matter whence the current comes or whither it tends. It may be a distinction to live over a kind of Seismic Junction ; but it is bad for the nerves—and the china !

I have not yet made the acquaintance of any of the Japanese ladies. The Ministers' wives all called at about nine o'clock on the morning of the 2nd ; but I was not prepared for such an *aubaine*, and they were probably rather shocked to hear that I was not yet dressed. I hope to see something of them, if we can only manage to understand one another. It is terrible to me to be dumb in a new country. I have not experienced such a sensation since we landed at Tientsin many years ago. Our local authorities on the language look at me with indulgent pity when I announce that I mean to learn it. The Japanese Secretary (that is to say, the Englishman who superintends the Japanese side of the Chancery) shakes his head, and tells me that, though he has been working at it for seventeen years,

though he has translated three dictionaries and is now
publishing one of his own, though he is examiner-in-chief
for the Consular Service, he feels that he is but at the
beginning still, and that many lifetimes would not put
him absolutely in possession of the whole language
as it is used by the learned Japanese to-day.

May 12th.

I already feel quite like an old resident here; but
that does not prevent me from having a hundred
surprises a day. We have been driving about a good
deal, and I begin to know a few landmarks in the town.
Our first drive, indeed, was quite a sensational affair.
We had arranged to try some very pretty and only
half-broken ponies, and for a little while it seemed
doubtful whether we or they should really be broken
first; then I found constant excitement in watching our
groom racing along in front of the horses, lifting fat
babies out of the middle of the road where they sat
confidingly, leading deaf old women politely to one
side, and apparently saving a life once in every ten
yards. What legs and lungs the man must have, to
come in, as he did, fresh and undistressed after miles
of this sort of thing!

I am trying to learn my servants' names, but have
as yet only managed a part of two. Rinzo is a kind
of head boy, who says, "Okusama, yes!" to every
question, command, or reproach; and O'Matsu, his
wife, is trying to teach my new English maid to wait
on me. The Japanese woman already knows all my

ways, and finds enough to do to fill up the tasks neglected by the other girl, who has but one real taste in life—her own amusement.

I have had a list made of the other servants' names, and keep it at hand for reference; but I think it is wasted trouble. I have only to cry "Boy!" or "Amah!" after the old barbarian fashion, and immediately I am surrounded by obedient genii, much nicer than those who waited on Aladdin, for mine smile and bow gratefully every time they are spoken to. The speech may be quite unintelligible, but they would rather die than confess it; at once they fly off, and do something or other just to show their goodwill. The *amah* brings tea or a shawl whenever the bell is rung; so I conclude that her last mistress was an invalid. One of the "boys," who has lived with a bachelor, always answers the summons with a brandy-and-soda *au grand galop*—let us not ask the name of that bachelor!

We are late for the cherry blossoms, and must wait till next year to see them in their glory; but, when the wind blows, the petals are stirred from where they have been lying in rosy heaps at the trees' feet, and go whirling down the paths like belated snowflakes. It is really wistaria-time, and I have been out to the Kameido Temple to look at the famous arbours there. It is a lovely and amazing sight. The Temple grounds consist chiefly of flagged paths running round great tanks of water, shaded from end to end by a thick roof of drooping flowers. The pale-purple clusters grow

14

so thick that no glimpse of sky is visible between them, and their odorous fringes hang four and five feet deep in many places. Little breezes lift them here and there, and sway the blooms about, so as to show the soft shadings from pale lilac to dark purple; and the flowers

THE KAMEIDO TEMPLE.

as they move shed drift after drift of loose petals down on the water, where the fat red goldfish come up, expecting to be fed with lard cakes and rice balls. Low seats and tables covered with scarlet cloths are set by the edges of the tanks, and here people can refresh themselves with tea and *saké* (rice beer) as they sit to admire the flowers.

We found at one corner an arbour entirely over-grown with the white wistaria, which delighted me by its ethereal purity. Why is it that flowers which are usually deep in colour, such as wistaria or violets or pomegranates, are so astonishingly white, when the fancy takes them to leave their proper colour behind ? White violets, white wistaria seem whiter than any-thing has a right to be in a sinful world, and new fallen snow would look almost dark beside a young white pomegranate !

This Kameido Temple seems poor and dusty, and is dedicated to more than one misty divinity ; but the memory of a great scholar shares the chief honours with a marble tortoise and two stone ponies. There is a very high bridge over the central waterway, a bridge which describes exactly half a circle, with only slight bars cut in the stone by which to mount and descend. When we approached it, every head was turned towards us. My companion was Mrs. N——, a tall and handsome woman, who affects in her dress a good deal of brilliant colour such as is not worn by grown-up persons here ; so there was perhaps some excuse for the staring. She and I wished to reach the other side of the grounds, and, like brave women, made for the most direct path towards it, followed by the interpreter and our *betto* (groom), both looking surprised and pleased. We scrambled up with some little difficulty, remarking to each other that one must be prepared for everything in these strange places ; but when we reached the top, and looked down on the other side, our hearts misgave us. It was very dusty and very steep, we were both wearing nice little high-heeled shoes and fluffy silk skirts, and—a delighted crowd had assembled to watch us descend. The situation was a little strained. We did get down without a tumble, for which we were properly grateful; but I am afraid

THE HOLY BRIDGE.

it was not a dignified proceeding, and after it was accomplished we learnt that there was another way round, and that the crossing of this dreadful little bridge was never undertaken except as an act of special devotion to the misty divinities of the Temple. Our attendants' surprise and pleasure were explained; but Mrs. N—— and I came home rather soberly.

I must tell you of a strange and touching ceremony which took place in Yokohama the other day. This was a requiem service in a Buddhist temple, for the repose of the souls of a number of officers and men who were drowned when the U.S. warship *Oneida* was sunk, by a collision with a P. & O. steamer, just in the mouth of the bay nineteen years ago. Lately the wreck was bought by some Japanese gentlemen, who discovered the bones of many poor fellows who had gone down in her. These they brought to shore, and buried beside the bodies of their comrades which had been recovered after the misfortune. Having laid the bones to rest, they thought that it would be kind to do something for the sailors' souls, and organised at their own expense a magnificent requiem service called *Segaki*, or the Feast for Hungry Spirits. They invited all the foreigners and the American admiral with his officers and men. Admiral Belknap was anxious to take some share of the heavy expense, but the five merchants would not hear of that at all. It seemed to me a kind and holy thought, this unasked benevolence shown to a handful of long-forgotten strangers. A local English newspaper describes the promoters of this charitable function as a "Japanese Firm of Wreckers"!

I was just going to begin talking about Treaty Revision, which is for us the question of the day ; but the mail is going out, so that infliction must stand over till next week! Mail day seems to be the only inexorable fact in this land of leisure. A poor Englishman who was drowned in Yokohama Bay a few days ago had to be buried in haste, and without any peroration over his grave, the clergyman explaining that it was impossible to break into mail day with what Jeames (was it not?) called " Igstranious subjicks ! "

CHAPTER II.

CHAPTER II.

May 18th, 1889.

THE Emperor was away when we first arrived, so we could not have our audiences until yesterday. I was rather envious when H—— was carried off by a chamberlain in a Court carriage to present his credentials to the Emperor, whom I shall not see just now. But our visit to the Empress was most interesting. The weather was lovely, and the Imperial gardens were all bloom and sunshine, as we drove up to the Palace, a long low building standing on high ground, and rearing a beautiful outline against the sky. It is quite new, and the sovereigns only took possession of it last winter, just before the proclamation of the Constitution, the old house which stood on this spot having been completely destroyed by fire. The new Palace is a wonderful achievement, of which its architects may be proud. The old Japanese lines have been everywhere adhered to in its construction, but so modified as to meet the requirements of the Court life of to-day. The whole building is of wood, a light fawn-coloured wood, giving out the most delicate aroma, a perfume which seems to be the essence of yet unembodied marvels of carving and lacquer. This rises into floreated gables, and sinks in richly painted eaves, where the blues and greens are

23

strong and pure as those on a peacock's breast. One or two of these lovely creatures were watching us curiously from their perch on the wall of an inner garden, as we mounted the steps leading to the entrance hall of the Palace, a square room with two carved black-wood tables, on which lie the books, ornamented with gold chrysanthemums, where visitors may write their names for the Emperor and Empress. Here we were met by Marquis Nabeshima, the Grand Master of Ceremonies, and Mr. Sannomiya, his second in command, a man so kind, so dignified, and liberal-minded, that it is impossible not to be drawn to him and the class he represents at once. I have only known him two weeks, and feel as if he were an old friend already.

These gentlemen took us for what seemed a long walk through broad corridors, lined, dado fashion, with shining orange and cedar woods, golden coloured, and scented; above them, an embossed leather paper, in flowing patterns of ivory, gold, and fawn, covers the walls to the lofty ceiling, with its carved beams and rich decorations. At distances of a few feet all along the wall the flowers seem to have taken separate life, and to have burst out in graceful bells and golden leaves inhabited by vital sparks of the electric light. As one goes farther into the Palace, these beautiful galleries lead off in every direction, through doors which are marvels of lacquer and painting. A favourite design is a rabbit in gold lacquer, on a ground of such indescribable polish that the eye seems to sink through its depths as through still waters, seeking in vain for

H.I.M. THE EMPEROR OF JAPAN.

a solid bottom. The gold bunnies, being creatures of earth, are on the lower panels of the doors, sitting up and gazing with ears erect, or playing with blown leaves and grasses; while the upper panels contain more airy designs of birds and flowers. In the heart of the Palace the rooms have glass slides instead of the

APPROACH TO THE PALACE.

usual Japanese paper ones, and get all their light and air from the wide surrounding corridors, which in their turn open on enclosed courts full of fruit blossoms and palm trees and the play of fountains in the sun.

At last we were ushered into a very large drawing-room with hangings and furniture of Kyoto silk in soft shades of grey and rose. In the middle of the room rises a kind of flower temple, in rich deep-coloured wood, almost like a circular chancel screen, whose every niche is made to hold a wonderful arrangement of flowers, the orchids and roses and lilies of the West mingling happily with the fruit blossoms and bamboos of the East. Divans and easy-chairs surround the flower temple ; and against the walls are cabinets of old gold lacquer, subdued yet splendid as a sunset cloud. The ceiling of this great hall is divided by cross-beams into a hundred squares, each one painted with a different flower ; and the doors are lacquered in colours also, blues and greens and crimsons that make one catch one's breath with surprise and pleasure. All this sounds, perhaps, too brilliant and varied for true beauty : but the great space and height of the hall, with the wide outlook all down one side to the flowery court, give so much atmosphere and perspective, that the vibrations of colour float slowly before the eyes, and never clash or jar on the sunny air.

Here we found five or six of the Empress's ladies, all in European dresses, pale blue and mauve and grey satins, made with the very long trains which are not worn in Europe now. I believe this is a part of Palace etiquette, recalling the immensely long robes of royal and noble women of Japan in times past. The little ladies were most kind and cheery, the two who spoke English translating for the others where I sat with them near the flowers, while the men in their brilliant uniforms stood together waiting for the summons to the Empress's apartments. At last

H.I.M. THE EMPRESS OF JAPAN.

the doors were thrown open, and we all started on
another long walk through more glass corridors, till
a hush fell on our companions, and we paused suddenly
on a step, which ran all across the foot of a small square
room, full of flowers, and draped with blue damask.
After the three regulation curtseys, I found myself
standing before a pale, calm, little lady, who held out
to me the very smallest hand I have ever touched, while
her dark eyes, full of life and intelligence, rested ques-
tioningly on my face. Her hair was dressed close to her
head, and her gown of rosy mauve brocade had only one
ornament—a superb single sapphire worn as a brooch.

In a voice so low that even in that hushed atmosphere I could hardly catch its tones, she said many
kind things, which were translated to me in the same
key by the lady-in-waiting, who acted as interpreter.
First the Empress asked after the Queen's health ; and
then, when she had welcomed me to Japan, said she had
been told that I had two sons whom I had been obliged
to leave in England, and added that she thought that
must have been a great grief to me. Her eyes lighted
up, and then took on rather a wistful expression as she
spoke of my children. The heir to the throne is not
her son, for she has never had children of her own, and
has, I believe, felt the deprivation keenly : but perhaps
the nation has gained by her loss, since all of her life
which is not given up to public duties is devoted to the
sick and suffering, for whom her love and pity seem to
be boundless.

When at last the little hand was held out in farewell,

I went away with one of my pet theories crystallised into a conviction; namely, that it is a religion in itself to be a good woman, and that a sovereign who, surrounded by every temptation to selfishness and luxury, never turns a deaf ear to the cry of the poor, and constantly denies herself, as the Empress does, to help them, comes near being a saint.

MR. SANNOMIYA.[1]

When we found ourselves in the corridors again, Mr. Sannomiya asked if we would care to see the rest of the Palace, and we were led from one beautiful room to another till I was rather bewildered. The glass walls give an appearance of unreality to these splendid apartments, but they add greatly to the light and brilliant appearance of the whole. In all the Palace there is nothing which is not purely Japanese in workmanship, although the general design of the draperies and furniture are after European models. The silks are most artistic, many soft fabrics from the looms of Kyoto, in colours either of dazzling strength and purity, or of such tender cloud shades as one hardly expects to find imprisoned in the warp and

[1] Now Baron Sannomiya.—1898.

woof of earthly tissues. Of ornaments, apart from the studied decoration of walls and floor and ceiling, there are few—a piece of lacquer, a bronze vase, or a fine carving here and there, just serve to break the long vistas ; but everywhere there are flowers and flowers and flowers, so profuse, so artistically arranged, that it almost seems as if the Palace had been built for them.

May 25th.

Our visit to the Empress was followed by several dinners at the houses of the Ministers. One does not learn much of Japanese life at these feasts, which are, as far as their appointments go, for all the world like official dinner parties in Rome or Paris or Vienna ; but it is startling to find oneself between the host and some other big official neither of whom will admit that he can speak a word of any European language. I believe they understand a great deal more than they like to confess for fear of being called upon to speak. There is generally an interpreter within hail, and three or four times in the course of the dinner my neighbour solemnly leans forward and instructs him to address a polite remark about the weather or the flowers to me, and I answer in the same three-cornered fashion, and then subside into silence once more. But the silence does not bore me. The new faces, the old historical names, the remembered biography of some hero who perhaps sits opposite to me in gold-laced uniform calmly enjoying the *foies-gras* and champagne as if there were never a blood-stained page in his country's

A BIT OF BRONZE.

history—all this appeals strongly to one's dramatic appreciations.

The women are really attractive with their pretty shy ways and their broken confidences about the terror of getting into European clothes. Some of them look wonderfully pretty even in these uncongenial garments. There is Countess Kuroda, for instance, the wife of the Prime Minister, who has lovely diamonds, and always appears in white satin with snowy plumes set in her dark hair. She can talk a little English, and is intensely polite about everything European, as all the little ladies are ; but I fancy in their hearts they put us down as big clumsy creatures with loud voices and no manners. The very smart people here affect the most impassive countenance and a low voice in speaking; and all the change of tone and play of expression which we consider so attractive is condemned in Japan as only fit for the lower classes, who, by the way, are the most picturesque and amusing lower classes that Heaven has yet created. My daily drives in Tokyo are as full of fun and interest as was my first jinriksha ride in Nagasaki. The distances are enormous, and it often happens that I make a journey of three or four miles between one visit and another; but every step of the way brings me to some new picture or new question, reveals some un-imagined poetry or bit of fresh fun in daily life. There are parties of little acrobats, children in charge of an older boy, who come tumbling after the carriage in contortions which would be terrible to see did one not feel

LITTLE ACROBATS.

convinced that Japanese limbs are made of india-rubber. Then there are the pedlars; the old clothes-sellers; the pipe-menders, who solemnly clean a pipe for one rin as they sit on the doorstep; the umbrella-makers, who fill a whole street with enormous yellow parasols drying in the sun. Here a juggler is swallowing a sword, to the delight and amazement of a group of children ; there the seller of *tofu*, or bean-curd, cuts great slabs of the cheesy substance, and wraps it in green leaves for his customers to carry away. I love watching the life of the streets, its fulness and variety, its inconvenient candour and its inexplicable reticences. I am always sorry to come in, even to our lovely home with its green lawns and gardens in flower. It is like leaving a theatre before the piece is over, and one wonders if one will ever see it again.

I went to a garden party the other day, given by Count Ito on the occasion of his daughter's marriage with a rising politician, Mr. Kenchio Suyematsu. The wedding had, however, taken place some days before. The Count's villa at Takanawa is close to the sea, or as much of the sea as comes into the almost land-locked Tokyo Bay. The house stands on high ground, which overlooks Shinagawa and the Hama Rikyu Palace, the Empress's summer house, built half in the sea like poor Maximilian's villa at Miramar near Trieste. Count Ito's garden slopes down to the sea-level, clothed in a dark-green mantle of lordly pines with red-gold branches, lighted here and there by a cloud of rosy fruit blossom, ethereal as mist shone through by the sun. The views over sea and land are lovely, and we had plenty of time to wander from one point to another, taking it all in. There were crowds of people in brightly tinted dresses ; but I saw hardly any Japanese costumes, even Countess Ito's youngest daughter being in European dress. No one seems to talk much at these gatherings ; there is a tremendous feast, where we are all placed strictly according

36

to precedence, and are expected to eat and drink as if
it were eight o'clock in the evening instead of four in
the afternoon! Count Ito has the cleverest face I have
ever seen ; it is not noble or elevated in any way, which
is not strange, perhaps, since he did not originally belong
to the higher class of Japanese, but for sheer intelligence
and power I have seen few to beat it. Countess Ito
is a very attractive woman, with a fine delicate face,
and of course charming manners.

I am slowly learning to know one person from
another in this big new circle. I heard a Japanese say
that all foreigners looked alike to him, and I confess
that for the first two weeks of my stay here I felt
like a colley with a new flock of sheep. Now that
the personalities are revealing themselves to me, I find
my way about among them fairly well.

The great artist Kyōsai is dead. His life forms
a perfect example of God-given genius, served and
cherished with complete and simple conscientiousness.
Everything true was beautiful in his eyes, whether
it appealed to the crowd or not. As a child of three
he made friends with a frog on a long *kago* (or litter)
journey, and drew its portrait as soon as his mother
set him down at the journey's end. At seven he drew
every aspect of the human figure as he could see it
in the brawls and wrestling-bouts of the lowest quarters
of the city, which he haunted patiently, sketch-book in
hand, for weeks and months. At nine he captured
the severed head of a drowned man from a swollen
river, and brought it home to study in secret as any

other child would treasure a toy or a sweetmeat. The horror was discovered by his family, and he was ordered  to take the grisly thing back to the stream and throw it in. Reluctantly the little boy trudged back to the river-bank, the poor head in his arms; but before he threw it away, he spent long hours, sitting on the ground, copying every line of the awful countenance. The ordinary hopes and fears of humanity seem to have been spared him, and nothing daunted him where his imagination was roused by food for a picture. A wonderful story is told of how a fire broke out one winter night of 1846—a fire which threatened to destroy an immense number of rare birds kept for sale at a shop in the Hongo district. They had been carried out into a square where property was already deposited in quantities; but sparks fell on the cages, and they began to burn, so the owner opened

DRAWING BY KYŌSAI.[1]

them all, and let the birds loose to save themselves if they could. The whole flock rose up into the sky with wild screams and whirring of wings, and instead of seeking safety flew straight towards the flames which

[1] The drawings by Kyōsai reproduced in this and a later chapter have been kindly given by Mrs. T. S. James, for whom the artist executed them. They are now published for the first time.

were filling the night with tongues of fire and clouds of red light. Kyōsai was then fifteen, and seems to have been carried completely away by the sight of the gorgeous many-coloured wings turning and wheeling in the glare of the flames. Regardless of everything else, he sat down in the street and sketched with passionate eagerness, till he was bitterly reproached by his family for not lending his help to save their goods from the conflagration. Very humbly he begged to be forgiven his negligence, saying as an excuse that he believed no one had ever had a chance of drawing such a splendid spectacle before.

He got into terrible trouble once, as a young man, for following some ladies in a Daimyo's house, where he was employed in decorating a room. The girls fled from him, and he ran after them, down long galleries and across gardens, till they were terrified, thinking he had gone mad. Then he suddenly stopped, and returned quietly to his work. When reproved for his temerity, he produced his sketch-book, and showed a careful outline of a rare and antique pattern in the sash, or *obi*, worn by one of the girls, which he had caught sight of as she passed, and had sketched as he chased her.

A countryman and intimate friend of Kyōsai tells me that he possesses several of the great painter's drawings, obtained by an amusing stratagem. Kyōsai always refused, if asked outright for a sketch ; so his friend began the negotiation by offering the artist an excellent dinner. When Kyōsai had drunk deeply (he pleaded to a love of wine as an aid to inspiration) and seemed in a mellow humour, his host would call for drawing materials, saying that he felt an artistic fancy taking possession of him. No one was surprised, as Japanese gentlemen often amuse themselves in this way after a feast. The ser-vant then brought an enormous sheet of white paper, and spread it on the floor, with the brushes and Indian ink beside it. The crafty host, without looking at his guest, sank on his knees and began to draw, ap-parently ab-sorbed in his occupa-tion, but in-tentionally producing a few weak and incor-rect lines. Kyōsai watched the feeble effort in silence and grow-ing irrita-tion, and at last jumped

DRAWING BY KYŌSAI.

up, dashed the tyro aside, and tore the brush out of his hand, exclaiming, "Out of the way, you wretched bungler! _I_ will teach you how to draw!" And the result was a priceless sketch, which remained in the possession of his wily entertainer. Again and again did the great artist fall into this snare, his generous soul unable to stand by and see his art wronged.

Once this same friend was travelling with Kyōsai in a region where the painter had not been before. After dinner Kyōsai had an attack of artistic frenzy, and in a short time had covered all the walls of the inn room with wonderful outlines, and filled in the low ceiling with a picture of an enormous black cat, fierce and lifelike to an alarming degree. More fierce and life-like, however, was the wrath of the landlady, when she found her spotless paper walls and ceiling covered with strange shapes. The room was ruined, she cried; she would have justice; the miscreant must pay for new paper! Then the artist's friend whispered the name of Kyōsai in her ear. Her counte-

DRAWING BY KYŌSAI.

nance changed, her curses turned into cries of delighted gratitude, and her reproaches became entreaties that the great painter would forgive her, and would have more dinners in more rooms of her favoured house.

He was a tender-hearted man, and made the fortune of one destitute old cripple by painting a picture for him, which the beggar showed for money, earning enough to buy a house, where he lived in comfort ever after. The subject was a strange one: on one side the poverty of the demons in hell, who were represented as starving to death, and sawing off their own horns to sell for bone-carving ; on the other, the angels in heaven welcoming poor and humble penitents to eternal feasts.

He died, as he had lived, a great man with one thought. Three days before his death, when he was already so wasted that he could hardly stand, he sketched the shadow of his own figure, pitifully bent and emaciated, on the white paper wall beside his bed, but only as far down as the knees ; below were a few ruthless lines in the shape of a coffin. After he had bade farewell to his wife and family in broken, gasping words, he gave a great cry, and called on the name of his picture-mounter, to whom he gave clear directions about one of his last drawings, and then died. Happy Kyōsai, happy mortal, who from life's dawn to its midnight, with single intention and undoubting faith, filled your place and justified your vocation !

DRAWING BY KYOSAI.

Japan should make many artists. I went to a night fair two or three evenings ago, a humble show where little more than cakes and sweetmeats and straw sandals were sold; but there was one stall full of winged lights, tiny stars of green fire clustering all over it. I bought about a hundred Princess Splendours in a black horsehair cage, and brought them home with me. Do you know the story of Princess Splendour? She was, it seems, a tiny moon-child, so like a firefly that the old woodman (of fairy tales all the world over) picked her off a bamboo branch in the moonlight, and brought her home to his wife. She grew lovelier and brighter for twenty sweet years, till all the brown cottage shone with her beauty at night, and basked in it by day. Every one loved her, but most of all the Emperor, whom she loved too. But she could not marry him, because all her life was only to be twenty years, and the time was nearly up. And he hoped to keep her; but at last the day came when she had to go, and Princess Splendour travelled home on a moonbeam, crying silver tears all the way, till Mother Moon took her in her arms and folded her to her warm white heart, quite away from the Emperor's eyes for ever. And all her tears took wings, and go flying about the woods on warm nights looking for the Emperor still, though he died an old, old man hundreds of years ago. But the keeper of the strange stall at the fair (and I could hardly see it for the darkness) had captured scores of the winged lights, and sold them by ones and twos in a dainty cage two inches long, with a green leaf for provisions, for two rin, a sum so small that we have no equivalent for it. I stood for a minute before the firefly stall, and then told the interpreter to say that I must have *all* the fireflies in *all* the cages. People gathered round in crowds, and one curious face after another pushed itself forward into the dim circle of light, staring at the reckless foreign woman who spent money in this mad way! But the foreign woman knew exactly what she wanted. Princess Splendour's lovely successors were not to be sold away one by one in cages on this warm spring night. I carried them all home in the horsehair box; and when everybody had gone to bed, I crept out into the balmy darkness of my garden, opened the box, and set all the lovely creatures free. This way and that they flew, their radiant lamps glowing and paling like jewels seen through water, some clinging to my hair and my hands as if afraid to plunge into the garden's unknown ways. I felt like a white witch who had called the stars down to play with her. Some of our people thought the same, I fancy; for I suddenly became aware of a string of dark figures hurrying across the shadowed lawns in a terrified rush for the servants' quarters, and I noticed the next day that I was approached with awe amounting to panic.

In connection with fairs, of which there are so many at this time of year, I must tell you a strange thing that happened at a fair in Hakodate two or three weeks ago. The whole population was out of doors, celebrating the "Hill Holiday" by camping and feasting and wandering on the hills which surround the town. The weather was gorgeous, and the sun hot and dazzling. An old man had set out his wares in a little stall on

FIREFLY-CATCHING.

a hillside, toys and sweets, and, alas! crackers—all laid out in bright and tempting rows. He was tired with the heat and the climb, and sat down to rest while waiting for customers. One cannot doze comfortably in spectacles, so he took his off (great round horn-rimmed things), and laid them down on a box of crackers, and fell asleep. Terrible was his awakening by an explosion of great noise and violence. The spectacles had acted as burning-glasses in the hot sun, and had exploded the crackers, which in turn set fire to the whole stall. When the flames died down, nothing was left except a quite ruined old pedlar and some terrified children who had been thinking of inspecting his cakes when the catastrophe occurred.

A new treaty has been signed, really signed. Not ours, of course; an event of such import would not have been treated of in a postscript at the end of my letter. The new treaty between Japan and Mexico is a most splendid and advantageous one for everybody concerned, and promises that, in return for Mexico's politeness in treating Japan as a grown-up nation capable of attending to its own affairs and administering its own laws, Mexicans may go where they like, trade where they like, and own any land they can pay for in Japan. The magnificence of these arrangements appears a little dwarfed on both sides, when we learn that the number of Mexican residents in this country is—one. Diplomacy seems an expensive luxury in such circumstances; but, there, the principle is everything, is it not?

One of the Japanese papers has been proposing that diplomacy should be utilised in a new direction. Why, says the *Yomiuri Shimbun*, not draft off to distant embassies those statesmen who are too popular to be disregarded, and yet who give some trouble at home? What more honourable employment for a chief of the wrong party than "plenipotenching on a dollar a day and his board," as the American politician neatly expressed it? The local paper even goes into details, and suggests that Count Okuma, the present Minister for Foreign Affairs, shall be sent to England, in virtue of his splendid fighting powers; that Count Inouye, a good talker, shall take Washington under his care; and that the mission of Peking (on account, I suppose, of the high standard of morals invariably maintained by the ten mendacious gentlemen who form one Minister for Foreign Affairs in the Tsungli Yamên) had better be confided to a man of purity and courage like Count Itagaki. Purity and courage must be very alarming qualities, for Count Itagaki's return to a place in the Government after his long retirement seems to fill his countrymen with one desire—that he should depart from their coasts. The distinguished Liberal must at any rate be a generous man, for he has just procured the release from prison of a wretched fanatic who seriously attempted his life on political grounds some years ago. The pardoned fanatic insisted upon thanking his liberator, and a great deal of pernicious nonsense is being talked in the newspapers about purity of motive and true greatness, etc., etc. The national press does not yet stand high in Japan. I do not wish to be sweeping in condemnation, for one or two journals rank higher than the rest and show sound opinions on many subjects ; but reckless misstatement, misdirected gush, and extreme gullibility make some of the daily papers anything but useful or elevating. All this enthusiasm about a forgiving victim and a high-minded assassin is rather nauseating when one remembers the terrible death of poor Arinori Mori (a friend of ours in Peking days), murdered for the same thin pretext on the 11th of February last when the whole country was rejoicing at the promulgation of the Constitution. Popular representation will point out many more victims to such high-minded assassins as Aibara or Buntaro ; and it seems to me that the first work of the Legislative Assembly when it meets next year will necessarily be the protection of its members from the rancours of hidden fanaticism.

A fanatic of another kind attempted to blow up a newly erected temple in Kobe the other day. A great inaugural ceremony was to be held, and an unknown person sent five hundred candles as a gift in honour of the event. When the first one was lighted, a violent explosion took place, and the temple narrowly escaped being burnt down. The remaining candles were examined, and it was found that they were all stuffed with dynamite.

CHAPTER III.

Summer Rains in Tokyo.—The Fall of the Tokugawa Shoguns and the End of Feudalism.— Sir Harry Parkes and Count Goto.—Origin of Consular Jurisdiction.—The Samurai of yesterday and the Soshi of to-day. — The Empress's Charities. —A "Society for the Correction of Morals."

CHAPTER III.

IT is a rainy day; everything is dripping in the grounds and steaming in the house. The maids creep from room to room with little square boxes of red embers, which they slip inside cupboards and wardrobes to keep the mildew from clinging where the damp has passed. It has rained so long that we have forgotten to count the days any more. There were twenty-seven wet days in April before we arrived, and I should think there must have been forty already in June! It is a mistake to pretend that a month can never go beyond thirty or thirty-one. Each day should count double when it pours like this. The streets, as I see them from these upper balconies, look like intersecting streams, paddled in by a few drenched creatures carrying huge oil-paper umbrellas, flat and large, like monstrous toadstools. Under the umbrella is more yellow-paper waterproofing, down to a few inches below the waist perhaps; and then come recklessly tucked-up skirts and bare legs. All the houses have their screens tightly closed, and nowhere is there a glimpse into the queer little homes, which are laid invitingly open to view on a fine morning.

I feel profoundly discouraged, for I have been reading in the *Japan Mail* an indignant protest against the crass ignorance displayed in English accounts of

53

Japan and its history. A venerable firm, which we have been taught to regard as a kind of national educator, has just published a class-book of geography, in which Japan seems to have fared so badly as to rouse the just indignation of the English editor of the *Mail*, an exceptionally intelligent man, who has lived for many years in Japan. The English newspapers seem to be as bad as the venerable educating firm; for they are handing round an idiotic story of how the Emperor (they call him the Mikado, a term which is never used here) keeps a beautiful jewelled sword, which he sends to turbulent Ministers when he wishes to have them commit *hara-kiri*, and take themselves out of his way. The story goes on to say that the last gentleman to whom this compliment was paid did not carry out the Emperor's wishes, but "ran off to Paris with the sword, and sold it for six thousand pounds."

It is of course very sad and bad that otherwise rational beings should believe all this nonsense; but—but Japanese history is nearly as complicated as Japanese customs, and both so foreign to European ways of thought that we must be forgiven a few mistakes. Being somewhat new to things as yet, I shall probably fall into some of these errors in trying to give you an idea of what Treaty Revision means. And yet no one in Europe will teach you anything, so perhaps you will be glad to learn what I have learnt, the bare outlines of our political ground of being in this half-way house of the world.

Do you remember. many years ago, when I was a

AN EMPRESS OF THE EAST.

child, that charming old Mr. Townsend Harris, whom we young ones hailed so noisily on account of his enchanting stories of a world beyond our ken? I still feel the thrill which used to go through me when he described his hard-won audience with the "Tycoon." I have lived to see many idols shattered, and the unapproachable Tycoon has gone with the rest. As a matter of fact there never was such a person; but that does not in the least reflect upon dear Mr. Harris's veracity, because he firmly believed there was, having taken the Japanese expression *Daigun*, the Great Regent, for a title in itself. The personage who received him with such tremendous ceremony that his square of standing place on the matting had to be marked out beforehand was the Shogun, not, as he imagined, the secular ruler in opposition to a Mikado who bore sacred sovereignty in Kyoto, but the hereditary Regent, the chief administrator, in whose hands all the real power most certainly lay, but who was quite as much a subject of the Emperor as the obsequious nobles who formed his Court. The last dynasty of Shoguns, the House of Tokugawa, were ancestrally of lower rank than many of the Daimyos, or the *Kuge*, or Court nobles, who, poor but proudly loyal, shared the Emperor's seclusion in Kyoto. The Emperors, for over seven centuries past, had, as you know, been as sacred and as useless as the sleeping Buddha at Ta Pei Ssŭ; but the searching airs of the nineteenth century seem to have found their way to these distant fastnesses of tradition. The Southern Daimyos woke up one morning to the

57

remembrance of their past glories, to the consciousness that they were as good men any day as Shogun Yoshinobu —and better! They met and confided these bold reflections to each other, and even said that, if they must be

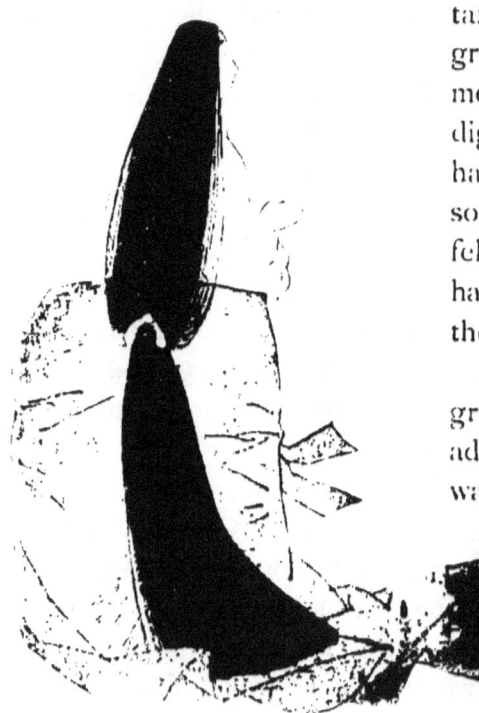

taxed and bullied and ground down, such treatment would injure their dignity less at the hands of their beloved sovereign than from a fellow-subject, as they had just remembered that the Shogun really was.

At that time the great question of the admission of foreigners was practically settled, both by the return of Japanese, who had at last been permitted to visit other countries, and who came back delighted

A LADY OF THE COURT IN KYOTO.

with all they had seen and learnt, and also because it was found impossible to keep the strangers out. Attacks on them produced such incidents as the bombarding of Shimonoseki (a political outrage, but a useful lesson), and long bills for indemnities, which it was no satisfaction to pay. The division of opinion as to admitting

58

foreigners was very great among the powerful clans, some leaders embracing one view and some another; and this state of things added to the many motives of the civil war which broke out and ended in the fall of the Shogunate, though it can hardly be said to have caused it. The last Shogun, Yoshinobu, Keiki (or Hitotsubashi, as he was called after his adopted father), accepted the office with great reluctance, and resigned it apparently with equal reluctance a year later, when the present Emperor, Mutsuhito, came to the throne. The last Emperor, Komei, had done all that he could to concentrate the executive power in his own family once more, and to escape from the bonds in which he was kept by these Tokugawa Shoguns, who had ruled the empire for two hundred and fifty years. Komei himself was strongly opposed to the admission of foreigners into the country, but had found it impossible to hold out against them. His ratification of the treaties with foreign powers, unwilling as it was, opened the way for a more independent and spirited policy on the part of his son.

The present Emperor was only sixteen (by Japanese counting) when he came to the throne; and he had of course grown up in the complete and demoralising inactivity which the Shoguns enforced in the education of the heir to the throne. It is said that the Emperor was carried from room to room, that he never stood on his feet, or even fed himself until the age of sixteen; but the moment that he was free to do so, he stood up, morally as well as physically, and, aided by the strong dislike to the Shogunate among his immediate following, made it very clear that he intended to govern in reality as well as rule in name. The Shogun was advised to retire; and in the letter which brought that advice, the Daimyo of Tosa expressed the opinion of most of his class when he pointed out that the constant troubles in Japan were doubtless due to the division of power between the two rulers, resulting in feuds, jealousies, and national weakness. Count Goto, as the representative of this great Daimyo, brought the letter to the Shogun, and earnestly begged him to follow the counsels it contained. The Shogun, after some deliberation, outwardly accepted the advice, and resigned his office in November, 1867; but much strife followed. The Ex-Shogun headed something like a rebellion, which was quelled in 1868; and on February 8th of the same year the Emperor announced to the foreign powers that henceforth there was but one Government to treat with, namely, his own. His position was greatly, albeit gradually, strengthened by the amazing fact that many of the Daimyos who had always been little sovereigns, like our feudal barons, gave up their privileges of their own accord, and laid their lands and revenues and their armies of retainers at the Emperor's feet. This portent has never been quite accounted for, but was certainly the greatest factor in the modernisation and unification of Japan. When the Satsuma rebellion broke out, some nine years later, all the resources of the country were at the Emperor's disposal, and his strength not too heavily taxed in putting it down.

The removal of the Imperial Court in 1869 from Kyoto to Yedo (or, as it was now called, Tokyo, the eastern capital) showed that the Emperor and his advisers meant to break definitively with all the effeminate conditions of the old life; but this had to be accomplished with extreme caution. The Empress remained in Kyoto for some months after the Emperor had left, and the city was given the name of Saikyo, or western capital, to place it on an equal footing with the new centre of power. It was shortly after this change that the Emperor took the oath by which he promised to grant a Parliament and rule constitutionally.

COUNT GOTO.

The Constitution took nearly ten years to elaborate on working lines, and was promulgated in February last, as I think I told you.

Before the change of capital was accomplished, the Emperor had consented to grant audiences to the Foreign Representatives; and the country learnt, in deep dismay, that the sacred countenance of the Emperor, hidden as a rule from his own subjects, was to be gazed upon by the alien barbarian. Poor Sir

Harry Parkes very nearly lost his life on his way to enjoy that honour. He was attacked by two wild fanatics, who cut down nine men of his escort before they were captured; and it was said that, but for the valour and loyalty of Count Goto, who had been appointed to accompany him, the great Britisher's work would have been cut short for ever that day. The Queen sent Count Goto a most beautiful sword in recognition of his services; and when I dined with him a few days ago, he showed me the sword with sober pride. He is a very handsome man, with keen dark eyes and snow-white hair; and his wife is one of the two Japanese women who have something like a political salon and count as an influence in public matters.

But I must finish my story, so that you may know why Treaty Revision is always coming to the front in our affairs. Sir Harry Parkes and the other foreigners who made the existing treaties with Japan could, to a great extent, count on the goodwill of the Government, but had daily reasons for distrusting the fanatical populace and the disappointed Daimyos of the north, who had lost power when the Shogunate fell. It was only natural that the foreigners who lived and traded in the newly opened treaty ports should require constant protection, so they were put under the authority of their own Consuls, who were constituted judges, and who tried all cases where foreigners or their interests were concerned. This arrangement, a learned friend[1] tells me, is of respectable antiquity,

[1] Mr. Montague Kirkwood.

having been granted by an Egyptian king to a Greek colony long before the Christian era; and it was constantly in use during the Middle Ages for Christians resident in non-Christian countries. The Arabs, he says, insisted upon the privilege for their traders in China, who in the ninth century obtained permission from the Emperor of China to be solely under the jurisdiction of a Mussulman magistrate in Canton. On this principle foreigners were, and are, practically independent of Japanese jurisdiction, and can only be arrested or tried by their own countrymen; and this constitutes extra-territoriality. The concession or settlement in the treaty port is a piece of land handed over to the foreigners, where they do their own law-giving, maintain their own police, and pay no taxes. Of course the English residents outnumber all those of the other nationalities put together, and each settlement is practically a bit of England planted where English people happen to want it.

All this seems very ideal, and perhaps was so twenty years ago, when a few enterprising merchants made large fortunes here and in China. But the accompanying restrictions which forbid foreigners to travel in the country outside the settlement, except with passports which can only be issued for a limited time (three months is the longest granted, except to officials)— restrictions which forbid them to own land or to trade outside settlement limits, — these are putting foreign trade under such disabilities, that our commerce absolutely requires their abolition at the first possible moment.

The Japanese on their side say that they have reached a point on the road of civilisation when they can no longer allow foreigners to administer the laws on Japanese ground ; and they demand that the old settlements, conceded while Japan was still emerging from her political swaddling clothes, shall be ceded to the Government ; that foreigners, as, in other countries, shall be tried by the laws of the land, now being framed on the most enlightened Western models (chiefly the Code Napoléon) ; and that extra-territoriality shall become a thing of the past. If we concede this, they in their turn promise to open up the country, and give every facility for the expansion of foreign trade.

The arguments on both sides appear quite reasonable, but unfortunately Japan is nothing like ready to be taken at her word ; and as for us—well, a whole settlement of British merchants in every port, and a Chamber of Commerce just across the water, all absolutely contented with things as they are, and furiously opposed to any change which might enrich their country but impoverish individuals,—this constitutes a quantity which is not to be neglected at such close quarters ; and the other great contracting party has still better reasons for not hurrying itself over the practical part of revision, although political decency requires that all sorts of polite things should be said about it. The truth is that very large and important classes of the population are as violently opposed to the inroads of the foreigner as they ever were, and a cautious Government finds it not easy to keep the retrograde party within bounds. It has its adherents in every class, and carries with it that tremendous factor in Japanese thought, veneration for the past and the horror of any sacrilegious rupture with national memories. Joined to this comes, among the more practical men, intense apprehension lest the all-devouring foreigner, once let loose in the country, should absorb all trade into his own hands; lest foreign money and foreign extravagance should destroy the valuable simplicity of Japanese customs; and behind these legitimate objectors is a vast body of newly made radicals, the outcome of the great

A SAMURAI WARRIOR.

army of *samurai* who were disbanded when the Daimyos gave up their power and the feudal system was abolished.

These men, trained through the traditions of a hundred generations to consider fighting the only possible occupation for a gentleman, scorned all humbler employments, and for many years flocked round their old chiefs

clamouring for leave to use their weapons. Some lost
their chief; many were younger sons of *samurai*, and
as such were not provided for in the retinue of the
local Daimyos; and all these went wandering about
under the title of *rônins*, or chiefless men, always ready
for a little bloodshed, and nursing imaginary wrongs
to keep up the fierce spirit of their class. Such were
the men who attacked our Legation at Takanawa in
1861 and 1862, and fought so ferociously that, as
an eye-witness told me, the house ran with blood
and looked as if two armies had been engaged there.
Little by little the *samurai* have been drawn into the
administration, into the police, into anything which
does not lower their dignity in their own eyes; but
the younger generation is a thorn in the side of the
Government, and promises some serious obstruction to
the progress of the country. They have received a
modern education, believe in very little, and hate
the foreigner with the inherited hatred of centuries.
These boys (for they are little more) talk the wildest
nonsense about "Japan for the Japanese." While
affecting to discard any higher beliefs than those they
have educed from Darwin, that unwilling heresiarch,
or the rather sawdusty ethics of Herbert Spencer, they
still claim profound veneration for the sacred institutions
of old Japan, and declare that there will be no peace
or prosperity for the country until foreigners are expelled
and the old regulations put in force again. They are
mostly very poor, and, as they only aspire to what
they consider occupations of honour, present sometimes

a pitifully forlorn appearance. They are so much in earnest that one cannot help being intensely sorry for them ; but they are, as far as Japan is concerned, a potent cause of drawback and delay in the revision of the treaties, and, inasmuch as they do not confine themselves to words for the enforcement of their arguments, constitute a daily danger to the public peace. Swordsticks are their favourite weapons, probably because they seem to bear some relation to the two swords of which they have been permanently deprived.

The *soshi* is a constant trouble and embarrassment in life. The other day, one, a boy of eighteen at the outside, got himself admitted into the Legation grounds on some pretext, walked into the Chancery, and demanded, rather imperiously, an interview with the Minister. The Japanese Secretary told him he could not see the Minister, and asked what he wanted, thinking from his poor clothes and wasted appearance that he might be seeking work. The boy got quite excited, and said that he must see the Minister, who, he considered, was doing a great wrong in pressing Treaty Revision on the Government. He wished to explain his views to the British Representative, and to tell him that he was only one of many who would save Japan from foreign usurpation at all costs. Mr. G——, I am sorry to say, got extremely angry with him, told him he was a mere child, and had better finish growing up before he asked to talk with men, and sent him away, poor boy, desperately unhappy. But many others come to the gate asking to speak to H—— ; and seeing their utter recklessness and their fondness for swordsticks, I am rather glad they do not get in.

The *soshi* are banded in clubs all over the country, and the Government seems to us a little weak in not dealing more summarily with them and their seditious speeches. They profess great veneration for the sacred person of the Emperor, but declare that he is surrounded by traitors, so their devotion does not make for peace and harmony.

I fancy we shall see some curious scenes when the first Parliament is opened next spring. As I have said, there are opponents of the new order here and there in all classes of society; but the visionary *soshi* are the only people who believe in the possibility of putting the world's clock back by thirty or forty years. The more educated reactionists have accepted foreign intercourse as an inevitable necessity, and are none the less polite to us individually because collectively they would like to see us sail away from their shores never to return. The law students, for instance, are protesting furiously against the codification of the laws, for which they declare the country is still unripe; but it is much suspected that their dislike to the new code is grounded on the fact that it is a task which can only be carried out by foreigners.

One of the Tokyo newspapers, the *Nichi Nichi Shimbun* (the day-by-day journal), has been giving a very just appreciation of the relative positions of Japan and China. It interests me from our having been so long in China before coming here. Though only five days distant, China has never been able to get a clear idea of modern Japan, and cannot lay aside a certain amount of swagger in her manner to the younger nation, which was once her eager pupil, but never her tributary, as has so often been asserted. The journalist dwells on the great need of caution in dealing with China, who, half jealous, half contemptuous of Japan, is always ready to pick a quarrel, which would be profoundly disadvantageous to both countries. On the other hand, Japan has the proud consciousness of never having been worsted by China in fair fight, joined to the uncomfortable conviction of her neighbour's unmerited contempt. Quarrels seem imminent; but the writer wisely reminds his countrymen that they would bring no good to either party, and would only give European powers a chance to seize territory and extend their influence under the pretext of restoring harmony. The Chinese seem to have very little in common with modern Japanese; and when we meet the Celestial diplomatists at official dinners, they give me the impression of people who are living among enemies under a flag of truce, and do not quite like the situation.

No one has been much surprised to hear that Count Itagaki's would-be assassin has found a follower in a gentleman who proposed to murder Count Goto for entering a Ministry which he condemned in public speeches last year. After all, that seems to be more Count Goto's affair than that of an obscure policeman; but the policemen evidently do a good deal of political thinking in this part of the world. A letter was seized in which the policeman confided his views to a brother, and he was arrested on his way to commit the crime. It must take some personal courage to be a Cabinet Minister in Japan.

But courage is certainly a national virtue. The other day two thieves armed with knives broke into a house where a woman was quite alone, and threatened her with death if she did not give up her property. She pretended to consent, apparently shivering with terror; and they took no more notice of her, and stuck their knives in the mats while they collected her few valuables. She waited until they were quite absorbed in their work, and then seized both knives, and attacked the robbers so valiantly that they fled, leaving their spoils on the ground.

The thieves here choose the most unmanageable kind of loot, it seems to me. Five ground pines, valued at over three thousand dollars, were carried off from a nursery garden last week! As soon as the rain will let me, I am going to some of the tree fairs, where you see everything growing the wrong way round, as it were.

I was very much amused, just after we came, to see the gardeners taking the pine trees out of their winter caging, built up to protect the delicate, shapely twigs from all danger of being broken by a heavy snow. This is done by planting a mast as a supplementary trunk beside the living one, and training a network like tent-cords down from its top to catch the larger branches and sustain their weight. From these, smaller cords drop and interlace, till every twig hangs on a string, and could carry a heavy weight of snow without injury. These supports were only removed in May, when all danger of a serious snowfall was past; and at the same time the bananas and sago palms were divested of their

THE CHARITY COMMITTEE.

straw wrappings, and shook out pale-green shoots, which had been pushing up in the darkness; they soon lost their paleness in the hot sun and drenching rain which have visited us alternately for the last few weeks.

I was speaking in my last letter of the Empress's great interest in charitable work. Rather a touching little statement has been published of the way in which she has provided extra help for an institution of her own founding, the Tokyo Charity Hospital. The Hospital had outgrown its accommodation, and new buildings had become an absolute necessity ; so the Empress started the subscription by cutting down everything that could be cut down in her private expenses (always heavily burdened with benevolent work), and as a result has sent to the Hospital the respectable sum of 8,446 dollars and 8 rin. Ten rin go to one sen, of which a hundred go to a dollar, worth about two shillings ; so you see with what loving conscientiousness the economy has been carried out. One of the Empress's ladies told me that for the last year her Majesty had hardly bought " a glove or a pocket-handkerchief," and that the thought of sick people being denied the help they needed was a source of profound pain to her. She constantly visits the hospitals, and on those occasions stops beside every bed in every ward to say a kind word to the patients. The process begins at about nine o'clock in the morning, continues till one, when a light lunch is served, is immediately renewed, and goes on till about five, when even the Empress admits that she is tired, and her ladies say they " do not know where their feet are."

She has done as much for women's education as she has for the hospitals ; and the " Peeress's School," taught in great part by English and American ladies, was founded by her. The Japanese girls fall quickly in love with the higher education, and work enthusiastically to obtain their diplomas. One curious outcome of this advance is a " Society for the Correction of Morals," composed of Japanese women, many of them Christians. They hold meetings, and get distinguished men to give lectures for them, and just now are preparing to petition the Government for a change of the laws relating to marriage, asking that unfaithfulness in a husband shall be punished as severely as the same crime in a wife, for which the penalties here are very heavy. It is not stated how they propose to deal with the legalised concubinage which, although diminishing, is still customary here, and which the pagan wife hardly resents, since it is not allowed to interfere in any way with her rights or dignity. To the Christian woman there is, of course, another side to the case. But I would like to say one thing on these subjects to my Japanese sisters—namely, that they are not the only women who have asked that men's morals should be put in petticoats and regulated by law ; and that there is but one answer possible to the demand, whether it come from women of the East or women of the West, and it is this : the only law which can enforce a pure life must be a divine one ; but the best policeman for your husband's heart is yourself. If you have not the sweetness and the wit to make him love you and you alone, you will appeal in vain to the magistrates to help you.

I am afraid this has been a very sombre day's writing ! Please put it down to the rain, which makes one feel old and serious. If only the sun will dry things a little, you shall have something brighter next time.

CHAPTER IV.

CHAPTER IV.

A JAPANESE friend has been telling me stories about the Island Temple of Miyajima, which I saw at a distance when we were passing through the Inland Sea. It has more than one name, but this one means " Temple Island "; and the divinities, seeing how beautiful it was, evidently disagreed about it, for it seems to belong to two or three in part and to none entirely. The Shinto rites are practised there, and originally they were directed to the worship of the spirits of the mountain; but these have had to give way before the alluring sovereignty of a lovely goddess, the Princess Sayori, who seems to have sprung from the wave, even as our Aphrodite did in Cyprus, and whom the sailor lads call the goddess of the sea, their especial friend and protectress. In honour of her sweetness, beautiful deer wander all over the island, and come and put their noses into visitors' hands, asking to be fed, tame and gentle as the deer in Eden, because no one is ever allowed to molest them; and it is forbidden to introduce dogs into the island. Neither may deaths or births take place there; the dying are ferried to the mainland, that the happy soil may never be tainted by grief or

77

AT MIYAJIMA.

polluted by corruption; and no child may begin life's solemn pilgrimage on Sayori's Island.

According to national tradition, the first shrine was built on Miyajima in the seventh century of our era; but its present grandeur dates from the time of Taira Kiyomori, who won here a great victory for the disputed succession to the throne of Go Shirakawa, who in consequence became Emperor in 1156. Kiyomori was raised to a very pinnacle of power, and showed his thankfulness by beautifying the spot where he had obtained his triumph. Three lovely temples are spread almost on the bosom of the water, on tiny islands connected by raised galleries one with another. These galleries, supported on piles, are roofed and latticed with

78

carved woods painted a vivid scarlet. At high tide the
footway is all under water, only its delicate pillars and
roofing showing like coral branches between sea and
sky. On festival nights, and more especially during
the Feast of the Dead, when for three days in the
heart of the summer countless pilgrims crowd to
the shrine, these galleries are hung with thousands
of lanterns, making long chains of light across the
water ; and the pines stretch their dark arms down
over the waves, as if to welcome the homesick spirits
winging unseen to shore.

There is no country in the whole world which has
been so drenched in bloodshed as Japan—it seems as
if the very sap of the trees must be red ; and yet
nowhere does the spirit of peace brood visibly and
everlastingly over sea and land, town and temple, as
it does here.

One hears of terrific volcanic explosions, of earthquakes, and of disastrous floods, such as those which
are now laying waste the villages of the south, where
the rivers are gone mad, intoxicated by too much
rain. But these things do not seem to break
through the primeval calms of Japan. The ruined
peasant does not indulge in lamentations, but smil-
ingly rebuilds his hut the moment the soil can carry
it. After whole streets of shops have been destroyed
by the frightful fires which so constantly break out
in Tokyo, one drives down to look at the ruin, and
one sees business going on again cheerily in booths
and sheds run up anyhow on the yet hot ashes of

yesterday's disaster. The inevitable need not be the irretrievable; and this knowledge must make for peace, since only the irretrievable need cause despair. But there are deeper reasons for this manifest peace, and I fancy they must lie in some yet undiscovered harmonies and submissions of the national character, which has through so many centuries of isolation had time to fill out every corner and interstice of Nature's inexorable mould. It would seem that, for the perfection of a type, internecine wars and disturbances tend to develope rather than to modify its distinguishing characteristics. The vicissitudes result in the survival of the fittest, those in whom the national character finds its strongest examples. Among Western peoples we notice that the more highly educated and developed a class becomes, the more it resembles the corresponding class of any other country : aristocrats are first cousins everywhere in Europe, and original racial differences are often only shown in the peasant and the plebeian. But in Japan the case is reversed. The peasant might find his first cousin in the Chinese, the Cossack, the Corean, or even, as some have suggested, in the Tooltec Indian of Central America ; but the Japanese aristocrat is as unmistakable as the thorough-bred. It would be more possible to confuse racers with dray-horses than to take him for anything but what he is, a fine gentleman, the outcome of a dozen centuries of pride, courage, and self-control. And this goes to support another of my theories (you know my weakness for generalisation), that the success of education, whether for school-children or nationalities, depends far more on continuity than on quality.

Such continuity has had full play here : that which is now thought good, or great, or beautiful has been thought so since the dawn of history ; crimes and virtues have the same names that they bore in the days of Jimmu Tenno, the first Emperor ; there has been no real change in the values of the important affairs of life ; and those things which have been brought in, such as Buddhism and Chinese literature, have become incorporated among Japan's properties without introducing any marked resemblance to the nation from whom she borrowed them. I think it must be this eclectic quality in the Japanese which causes them to be so severely criticised by Europeans, who see them take up new ideas with enthusiasm, and drop them again as easily. But the truth is that the "taking up," this "let us see what it is made of" system, is the only practical method of selection ; and close observers will note that, although, for instance, German waltzing and French frocks are less popular than they were five years ago, the army is on a very much more German footing, an Imperial Prince, Kotohito Kanin, has just taken his certificate of proficiency in a French naval school, and the Empress sent the matrons of her Charity Hospital to get their training in London. All this is significant enough as to the true attitude of the more enlightened Japanese ; but the education of Prince Haru, the heir to the throne, is the most notable tribute to European ideas yet paid by this country.

The little Prince is ten years old, and is, I fancy, rather delicate. I saw him driving with his governor and two boy friends the other day. He has a fine pale face, and piercing dark eyes. Perhaps the paleness has misled me as to his health (I cannot but remember the rosy cheeks of our schoolboys at home),

THE PRINCE IMPERIAL AT TEN YEARS
OF AGE.

for his own people say that he is strong and healthy, fond of outdoor exercise, and already well-trained in fencing and single-stick. He is the first heir to the throne of Japan who has mingled with his future subjects at school and play. He goes every day to the Nobles' School, a splendid building not far from us; and there he learns his lessons and plays his games just as the other children do. The innate reverence for the Imperial family doubtless prevents the games from becoming too rough, but I believe the lessons are very impartially dealt with. The Prince takes cold baths, eats meat, and will have no women to wait on him, an extremely legitimate prejudice, which recalls to my mind a family tradition of a certain Master John, one or two generations ago, who at the age of five refused to walk down the same side of the street as his nurse, saying that "men didn't care to have a lot of women hanging after them." The little Prince does not walk in the street, but is fond of a good romp on the seashore, and already delights in beautiful scenery. They say that he is kind and thoughtful to those around him and to his school friends. The whole description of the little character reminds one of the Prince of Naples at the same age. Prince Haru is fond of horses, and is sometimes taken to the mild races which are occasionally run here. The Emperor has just shown his interest in the subject by sending a thousand dollars for the new grand stand which is being built on the racecourse at Negishi, near Yokohama.

The papers tell us that the last Shogun, Yoshinobu or Keiki, who so unwillingly abdicated in 1868, has arrived in Tokyo, and is staying with his relation, Prince Tokugawa Iesato. It must be rather sad for him to return as a private gentleman to this seat of the past glories of his line. Did not Keble say :

> " But we, like vexed unquiet sprites,
>   Will still be hovering o'er the tomb
>   Where buried lie our vain delights " ?

If I had my way, I would make a little supplementary world for such splendid ghosts as Tokugawa Shoguns, and Danieli Doges, and old moons. It would make an admirable reformatory for new-broom radicals, and one might spend a few solemn days there oneself when one felt the novelty fever too strong upon one. By the

way, a Japanese acquaintance told me that the title of
Prince is never used by them except for a member of
the Imperial family. The highest title ever given to
a subject is that of Koshaku, which means Duke
or Marquis, according to the character in which it is
written. I protested, having seen this word Prince
on more than one visiting card, and in the Court
official lists.

"Why do you translate it Prince, if it is not Prince?"
I asked rather indignantly.

"Well, you see" (my friend rubbed his chin, and
looked at me with a twinkle in his eye), "we were
translating—to the Germans!"

A most amusing book has just been published here,
purporting to give the Japanese student a correct expression of his commercial aspirations and necessities
in English. Why does our unfortunate language lend
itself so easily to these absurdities? "English as she
is spoke" was hardly a greater joy than this bold
manual, and I cannot resist enclosing to you some
extracts from the witty review in the *Japan Mail*. As
I am beginning to collect curios, I shall at once send
out to buy "sea-mouse," "dqe," "chanqhor," and
"scrippers"! The writer states that the book is "for
the gentlemen who regard on commercial and an
official."

"Two dunning letters are given, and in both instances
they are plainly intended to betray the natural irrita-
tion consequent upon long-deferred settlement of a
debt:

" Page 16 :

'I beg to draw your
attention to the enclosed account, and to state that ip it
is not settled for next week
I shall be compelled to ploce it
for atternegs hond.'

The one on the following page evinces still greater
irritation at the very outset :

'Having applied to you Repeatedly but. ineffectually for a settlement, I have now to intimate . . . . that I shall ploce it in my
solicitois hands for Recovery.'

Note also the following :

'Gentlemen,
we have this day forwarde
to your care, per Orientoel slea-
mer & co., 25 packages qer " yamasiromoru "
consigned to Mr. Yamaugchi
& co., of that port. Bill of
landing, and statement of shi-
pping charges, please transmit.
At foot particulars of the shipp-
ment We are,
Jentlemen,
your edient,
particulars of shipment,
M 15 cases 1500' pice chintr.'

" Somewhat less lucid still is the following announcement of a change in the style of a firm :

'we beg leave to infonu you
that we this day admited mr
fujimura as partnor in our business here. In futu-
re the otyll of our frim will
be Yoshimwra & Co.'

The 'juniority' of the new partner in this case is admirably expressed by the want of capital letters in his name. Yoshimwra is evidently Welsh for Yoshimura, though why the author should prefer this language is not apparent. 'Otyll' we take to mean 'style'; but this, of course, must remain a mere hypothesis.

"Insinuating is the style of another letter (page 47), in which the writer requests a friend to 'glad me' with a loan, if it does not intrench on the friend's 'oawn conwenien ce'; he mournfully states that he is being 'put to exceedingey persecution,' and is in 'painfule difficulty.'

"Still another writer is incoherently indignant about the state of certain goods forwarded him. He says:

> 'of the pared of sewed mu-
> lins I have had to reject fif
> ty piels as being un saleable;
> twenty pieces are tosn in siveral places
> and the others are without headivgs.'

"This must have been a fearful blow to the shippers, for their reply is indicative of great mental pressure, if not of incipient mania:

> 'Dear Sir,
> The contents of your favo-
> ur of yesterday's date sur prised
> considerably, us our warcho-
> usemen have explicit
> instru ctioni to supply our cus
> tomers with perfect goods only,
> and return the unsound to the
> manu foctuar. It is ebidient, ho-
> weves, thot they packed your
> goods without examininy them.

We regvt excee dinglyect. . . .
Trusting that you have not been
seriously inconve nien-
ced through the monifest remiss-
ess of ovr ewpoyes.'

"At the end of the book is a list of commercial terms and names of exports, which repays perusal. 'Promissionary notes' has rather a religious than a commercial sound. 'Bankroptny' and 'bankruqty' are evidently so spelled with an eye to lessen the attendant disgrace. 'Gross waigh' is an unknown quantity. Among exports, 'soop,' 'scrippers,' 'sea-mouse,' 'quoin,' 'mouseline of lines,' 'dqe,' 'gold-wotch,' 'chamqhor,' 'ass,' 'jam,' and 'frorid water,' are of interest to the student."

These strange products of the far East are almost equalled by some for which I was called upon to pay the other day. Ogita speaks English much better than he writes it. Imagine my surprise on receiving the following bill :

" Blue Showl	2.	35.
7 7/10 yards Whitish brown ? Race	2.	31.
4 „ „ ·, ··	1.	32.
10 4 10 yards mud colour Race	1.	66 4 10."

The arithmetic got very mixed in the addition, which, with some other items, amounted to 6. 644. some-things—currency unstated. The English of the sign-boards in the streets is equally graphic : " Highly perfumed waters " turn out to be tins of kerosene : " Deal beer," " Wine and other," require reflection.

but such advertisements as this one, of new foot-balls, explain themselves!

Any walk that one tries to take just now might well be described as a mud-coloured race, for the rain still comes pattering down at intervals, though not so persistently as it did in June. Meanwhile the country

AN ADVERTISEMENT.

is very green and beautiful to look at, and the view from my upstairs verandah most alluring. I can see, I think, every house in "Kojimachi," as this quarter of the town is called; but between the houses are so many trees that one can hardly believe one is in the heart of a great city. My windows look to the west, and Fuji, the queen of mountains, bounds my world. In the dawn (and in these long warm days I am glad to come out for a cool breath in the early hours) Fuji looks cold and dimly white till the sun creeps up over the bay, and then she takes the most lovely rosy flush against the morning sky. The mountain comes to dominate outer life in a curious way, and I do not wonder that folk-lore has crowned it as a sacred and powerful personality. On the days when clouds hang between us and it, I am dissatisfied, and homesick as for the face of a friend.

But the near landscape gives me enough to watch through many an amused hour. The houses nestle close among the trees, with strange gables and latticed upper windows, from which, perhaps, looks out some dainty little lady, with a pale face and dark eyes and marvellously dressed head. She pulls a flower or two from her tiny hanging garden, and goes in again to bring out a gorgeous silk quilt, which she hangs over the balcony to air. Sounds of strange music come floating up to my window from a house in the valley below our garden. My maid tells me that a teacher of music lives there, and the place is never silent. The twang of the *koto* is strong and pathetic, and very melodious in skilled hands ; then there is the humming note of the *samisen*, which accompanies every festival or holiday-making in the humbler houses. Drums rattle farther off; the *masseur*, the blind *amma*, pipes thin sweet airs on his bunch of reeds ; the medicine-seller or the newspaper-man, as he goes on his rounds, rings a little bell continuously, a tinkle as light and musical as a falling brook ; far away a gang of coolies pushing some heavy load are marking time with a long cry and a short one ; a beautiful phrase, worthy to be the theme of a fugue, comes up to me in a clear childish voice, moving quickly along the sunken street.

I sent out to ask who it was, as it is repeated every evening at this hour; and O'Matsu, my *amah*, has just come in to say that it is a young girl selling millet cakes. And above all the rest, from the distant temple on the hill, rolls out the deep note of a great bronze bell, strong and low, and vibrating steadily on the warm air, while the lesser noises run to and fro and spend themselves below it.

As the evening shadows fall, and the rain ceases, all our servants' children come out to play in the more remote parts of the grounds, and I hear little shrieks of happiness, and see a kite tossing madly above the trees. Then one, two, three little heads will cautiously peep through the shrubs to see if any gardener is near. No, the lawn is empty, and Kokichi and his assistants have withdrawn to their quarters for the night—even the Dachs family are all engaged in digging for the toad who lives under the flagstaff; so three little people decide to commit a terrible breach of discipline, and come close to the house, first to try and have another look at the English " Okusama," who is always a most interesting object, and then to see if she is inclined to bestow any more wonderful pink cakes such as they got last Sunday! To Okusama, who is watching them as they hesitate, it looks as if the trees had suddenly bloomed into flowers; for the little maidens' garments are of the brightest colours, and in their small dark heads are set pins of silver roses and coral beads. Hand tightly held in hand, they patter across the soft grass, too fast for the smallest one, who soon drops a sandal, and

has to be comforted and shod again by the motherly
mite in charge of her. By the time they have reached
the rose garden under my window, I am ready to meet
them, with three pink cakes in three bits of paper, and
one more for a baby brother at home. The quick
Eastern night is already shedding its hush over the
quiet gardens, so I tell the mites to run along to their
mother, who lives in the gatehouse; and they nod
wisely, and look round a little frightened at the distance
to be traversed. When asked what they are afraid of,
the eldest replies that there are tigers in the gardens,
it is well known, and—nobody likes tigers! When
reasoned with, she declares that she has often heard
them roaring at night, and there is nothing for it but to
send them back under the escort of O'Matsu, who is
supposed to be quite capable of overcoming the casual
tiger. O'Matsu convoys them away smiling (nobody
can be cross with Japanese children), and when she
returns tells me that the pink cakes were considered too
fine to eat, and have been put in state on the table in
the niche of honour, beside those which I gave them
last week !

I have fallen deeply in love with a gentleman of
uncertain age (two at the outside, I should think), whom
the nuns at the Tsukiji Orphanage have induced me to
accept as a godson. He is so fat and round that he
never remembers where to find his feet, and is always
rolling over the mats in search of them. His mother,
a widow, cooks the rice for three hundred people every
day, and is very anxious about her son's manners. She

says he is three years old ; but Japanese counting is not
to be trusted in that way, since a baby born on the last
day of December is called two years old on January 1st,
because he has existed during a part of two succeeding
years. This small child is told to prostrate himself,
o'jigi, when I appear, and then the little bullet head
goes down on his fat hands on the mat with great
readiness ; but it is a terrible business to get it up again.
If one gives him something, and he is told to say " thank
you," he at once makes the sign of the cross ; it is the
only prayer he knows as yet, and the expression of his
highest feelings. I was very much overcome, when he
was baptised, by seeing the good missionary father
pour the holy water over his head out of a nice little
china teapot, kept by the nuns for the purpose.

The work these dear women do is most interesting,
and I sometimes go and spend hours in the Convent,
looking at the girls' sewing, or sitting in the quiet
chapel. They are called here the Black Nuns, to distin-
guish them from the Sisters of Charity with their white
cornettes, who have a school at the other end of the
town. The establishment is divided into two sections :
one a resident school for pupils, who pay from three
to four dollars a month for board and teaching ; while
the other—which is, of course, kept quite separate—
is the Orphanage proper, where just now there are about
one hundred and eighty children of all ages, maintained
and educated by the Sisters, who are occasionally in
very low water, and much put to it to find money for the
daily food of such a family. The Convent stands near

the Catholic church in Tsukiji, which is the foreign settlement of Tokyo, and full of Europeans and Americans. It is close to the sea, and is cooler in these hot days than our own house farther inland. When I drive down there, it always delights me to watch the junks, with their huge sails, white or saffron, moving along the wide canal on the incoming tide, to watch the woodmen piling timber in the yards along the banks, to see the crowded ferry-boats carrying the people from shore to shore. In the courtyards of the Convent it is a sea breeze that comes to play with the willow and wistaria trails, and

PILING TIMBER.

that sometimes finds its way to the chapel, which is always full of sweet flowers.

When one turns in from the road, the big gate gives admittance to a square garden. Opposite is the

two-storied wooden building which contains the chapel
and the Sisters' apartments. To the right are the
boarders' quarters—large classrooms downstairs, and
airy dormitories opening on a long balcony above.
To the left a single-storied wing holds the work and
study-rooms of the orphans,
whose sleeping apartments
open into another courtyard
behind.

A few European girls
attend as day scholars
among the boarders, and
one or two who are the
daughters of mixed mar-
riages, extremely pretty,
graceful girls. The Sisters
always beg me to talk with
them and show some in-
terest in their work; so I

THE CHILD OF A MIXED MARRIAGE.

listen to recitations and
admire embroideries and drawings with a good conscience, for some of the pupils are really clever. Two
or three of the girls are, alas! children who have been
abandoned by European fathers when they found it
convenient to leave Japan; and although no one pays
for them, the Sisters give them the same education as
the boarders receive, and keep them nicely dressed in
European costume—a considerable expense here.

But it is the other side of the house which draws
me most. There the big orphans help the little ones,

and the sweet-faced Japanese lay Sisters teach the babies their prayers, and carry about the tiniest ones; and the whole place is desperately poor, but so sweet and clean that one forgets the poverty of it.

"Don't go there!" my conductress cries, as I step heedlessly on the boarded gallery which runs round the inner court; "it is so rotten that it will only carry *les toutes petites*." And I come down again, having put my foot through a board, which gave like pie-crust. A great crowd of the children follows me about, for I want to go everywhere; and the lay Sister suddenly marshals them in the sunshine, and says in Japanese, "Sing for the lady—one, two, three!"

"Les voilà parties!" exclaims the good nun at my side, as all the little voices break out together, with a clapping of hands and nodding of dark heads, in a hymn whose strains must be heard by the junks in the canal yonder.

The children are left below while I inspect the poor dormitories, sadly in want of new mats and wadded quilts, but still, so *much* better than nothing, as the cheery Sister remarks; and when we come down again, we go to the long barnlike room, where the children are having their evening meal. Ten and five are their hours for solid feeding, with Japanese tea and bread for early breakfast. I found them seated in endless rows of benches at little narrow tables in a kind of "weight for age" arrangement. Each child had at its place a cup of water and a little wooden saucer with a scrap of fish and some pickles and sauce. This was intended as a relish to the huge bowl of rice, which made the staple of the meal. The rice is brought in in large wooden tubs, and served out by the elder girls, two of whom carry a tub between them up and down the long rows of benches, filling the bowls as the children hold them out. The rule is that as long as a bowl is held out it must be filled ; and when the tub stops its walk, all the little mouths are absolutely satisfied. A whole *koku* (just under five bushels) of rice is cooked daily, and rice just now costs ten yen the *koku*. When no more bowls are held out, the order is given to stand up and say grace, which is done very heartily ; and then the Sister in charge says, looking at me, " Allons, un bon Pater pour les Bienfaiteurs ! " And an " Our Father " goes up to heaven with such intense goodwill, that one feels it was cheaply purchased by a small contribution to the rice-tub !

The religious question seldom creates any difficulty among the children, though occasionally a paying pupil will take offence at some word said, and stop coming for a few days. The Sisters are very uncompromising about certain things. When the girls first come, they and their parents are told that they will be required to attend the religious services in the chapel and to be present at the catechism lessons. Otherwise the subject of religion is not mentioned to them by the Sisters until they come, as they often do, to ask to be baptised. But some of the girls themselves are eager little apostles, and do all they can to persuade their pagan companions of the beauty and truth of Christianity. Sometimes the parents will not consent, for the old prejudices are still strong; and then there is long waiting and much prayer before O'Hana or O'Yone can receive the Christian equivalent of her name and wear a white veil in church, a privilege reserved only for Christians.

As for the orphans, most of them are taken in as babies, and

A RICH PENSIONNAIRE.

are baptised at once. Where the child is older, she must receive instruction and really desire baptism before it can be administered; but there is no opposition of parents to retard conversion, and there much less prejudice against Christianity among the extreme poor than among the richer classes. Besides, the child's young heart is softened and warmed with gratitude for material benefits, which the nuns rightly teach her to consider as much less precious than spiritual ones ; so there are many more white veils on the side of the church where the orphans sit than on the other, which is occupied by their richer sisters.

It is a very pretty sight on these summer mornings to see the long processions of children coming down the road from the Convent gates to the church. All the heads, gentle and simple, have been carefully dressed for the Sunday Mass, the girls performing the kind office one for another ; and from the rich *pensionnaire* of seventeen, with her beautiful gold or tortoiseshell ornaments crowning her elaborate rolls, down to the tiniest orphan toddler, whose hair is combed in a deep fringe over her forehead and tied in a knob at the back, every head shines like burnished ebony in the sun. The best robes and sashes are always kept for Sundays, and happy is the child who can display a scarlet sash or inner collar to her dress, red being here the colour of youth and joy. In church the reverent devotional bearing is most impressive, and the many white-veiled heads bowed in prayer make a lovely sight.

But not only youth comes here, marshalled by the black-robed Sisters, but bowed old people, men and women, forlorn paupers, whom their charity will not turn from their doors, and who have invaded the two or three matted rooms which were meant as workshops and porter's lodge just inside the gate. The old women are the cheeriest creatures, the deaf helping the blind, and both supporting the cripples. I entered one of these rooms by mistake one day, and found seven or eight of the dear old souls, quite past work, sitting on the floor making their tea. They were very glad to see me, and said all manner of pleasant things, finishing up with what rather distressed me, the ceremonious salutation, knocking their venerable heads on the mats at my feet. In the men's room were one or two sick men, patient and very ill, with only one dread, that they might be sent away. The Sisters have many scruples about keeping any sick people so near the children, and as soon as possible propose to take a little house outside, to be used as an infirmary. Meanwhile the poor folk must stay here; for, in spite of all that has been done in that way, there are not yet nearly enough hospitals in Tokyo for the sick among its one million of inhabitants, and the very poor suffer greatly from the overcrowding of their tiny rooms.

The sight of one of these all-embracing Convent Homes, God's Casual Wards, always puts me out of conceit with the leisure and the luxury of modern life. The great cool rooms and the wide lawns and deep shrubberies of the Legation filled me with something uncomfortably like shame after my visit to the Convent School at Tsukiji.

CHAPTER V.

On the Way to Atami.—Forgotten Passports. From the Windows of the Higuchi Hotel. —The Geyser and its Habits.—Lilies and Sea falcons.

CHAPTER V.

ATAMI, *August 1st, 1889.*

THE constant rain of the early summer gave me so much rheumatism that at last Doctor Baelz ordered me down here to boil it away in a course of hot baths. The heat in Tokyo has been rather wearing; and although we had decided not to make any solemn *villeggiatura* this year, I was delighted to get away and to see something of the country. As it was my first journey inland, everything was pleasantly fresh and interesting. As far as Yokohama there was nothing new in the railway journey, except the wonderful beauty of the lotuses, which are in full flower for miles in the ditches on either side of the line. They do not reach the enormous size of the leaves and blooms in our old haunts in China; but it may be because these are wild, and those had been cultivated for centuries in the temple tanks and the ponds of the Summer Palace. Here they are called the flowers of death, and are only used for funerals. Another death-flower is blowing too, in every bank and hillock through the country-side, a vivid scarlet lily, growing in a full round cluster on one strong wine-coloured stem. It is quite a splendid sight, when the wind tosses these thousands of blood-red tassels all one way, in the sun.

The train put us down at Kodzu, a little town close to the seashore ; and while our belongings were being piled into a tramcar which runs a few miles farther on the road, we had tea in a pretty inn room, whose windows command a beautiful wide view of the bay. Indeed the room was all window, as these Japanese rooms generally are in summer. The sight of a long white beach with splendid rollers breaking on its edge was too alluring to be withstood, for

LOTUS FLOWERS IN THE RAIN.

there never were such friends as I and the sea: so I found my way down through a tiny garden and a bit of road, till I stood under one of the great pine trees on the shore. There was a world of sea and sky, a picture all painted in three colours—deep sapphire blue in the rolling main and the arching heavens, white to blind you in the sunlit foam and dazzling shore, and black green in the huge old pines that stood like blind prophets on the dune, listening to the booming surge that said they could go no farther.

I went back to the inn in a dream, and did not wake up till the rattling tram set us down in Odawara, a strange sad place that always seems to be mourning its departed grandeur. It was the stronghold of the Hojo clan, and the last place which held out against the efforts of Hideyoshi to subdue the refractory chieftains and restore order in the country. When at last it fell, he gave all this country into the hands of Iyeyasu, as I think I said before, advising him to make Yedo the seat of his government. Odawara shows little of its old greatness, except in the splendid avenue of pines which leads to it from Kodzu. They say that it was fairly flourishing as an industrial town until a fearful visitation of cholera depopulated it. It lies low, and smells horribly.

When the train left us in the market-place of Odawara, our good Ogita (friend, servant, interpreter, and *samurai*) had to charter a little army of jinrikshas to carry the party over the eighteen miles which still lay between us and Atami. An inspector of police in spotless white uniform came to pay his respects and give his assistance. He also intimated that, although he was entirely at our disposal, and took the honourable interpreter's word for it that this was the British Koshi

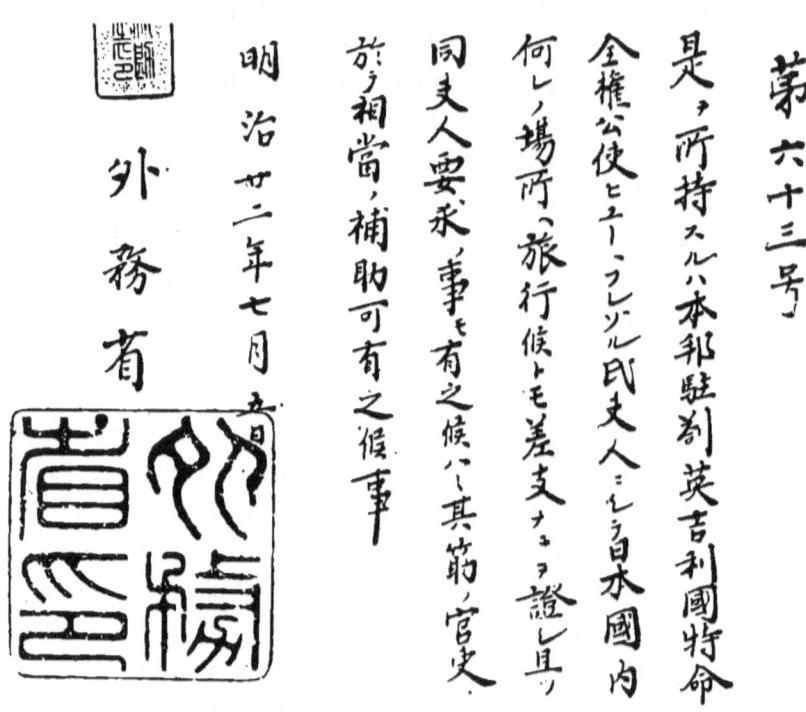

OUR PASSPORT.

Sama and his family, it would give him great satisfaction to see our passports. H—— began to feel in his pockets for a document over which we had laughed a good deal in the shelter of the Legation, for it did seem so absurd that he should have to grant himself solemn permission to travel about ; but, alas ! the despised

paper had been forgotten, and the inspector really had
to take our word for it that it existed somewhere. The
good Ogita, who is of imposing presence and warlike
deportment, talked the official quite dumb, and then
sent violent telegrams off to Tokyo about the missing
document. Meanwhile the servants had got the luggage
started, and I was comfortably packed into my Hong
Kong chair and trotted off by a team of four coolies,
who ran splendidly, but would not keep step. I find
jinrikshas frightfully tiring, so I carry the chair and
its poles about with me, and delight in being elevated
on the men's shoulders, since I thus get such splendid
views over the country.

The road from Odawara to Atami runs for a great
part of the way by the sea, and reminds me in many
places of the Cornice. There are endless orange groves,
still carrying late blossoms here and there, and pines
in their wonderful variety of shape, the most interesting
trees in the world. These are of the kind which the
Japanese call *hama-matsu*, coast fir, and they seem to
have no dread of salt water or sea breezes, for they
grow as close to the water as they can, and in some
places actually dip into it.

The day was nearly done when we at last reached
the strange little village by the sea. It lies in a bay
of its own, which sweeps inwards to the land in a lovely
curve. The beach is narrow, for the houses climb down
in terraces almost to the water's edge, and every street
seems to lead but that one way. A plain of green
rice-fields runs back from the town, rising gradually

towards a horseshoe of hills, which close in the horizon
on every side save one, and run high spurs into the
sea on either hand, so that one is fairly cut off from
the rest of creation. But from the beach outwards a
great stretch of water rests the eye ; there is a splendid
roar of breakers on the shore ; and far away, on the
sun-touched edge of the world, a misty island floats
in the haze, and sends up a constant jet of thin smoke
from its volcanic mouth.

We were housed in a *dépendance* of the hotel, a
Japanese house, standing by itself in the garden away
from the larger building, which looked uninvitingly
European. Our rooms had soft mats and international
furniture, of which the Japanese part pleased me best.
I was especially delighted with an enormous clothes-
screen in black lacquer, with wrought gilt clamps at all
corners, built in the beautiful *torii* shape, and intended
for hanging *kimonos* on, well spread out, so that they
should get no creases. The walls were decorated with
specimens of curious fern-stem work, very dainty and
graceful, and having the deep colour of a ripe pine-cone.
It is a speciality of this queer little place. My front
windows looked right out to sea ; but the side ones
commanded a sweeping view of all the Japanese part
of the inn, and in the course of the next few days I
had watched many an amusing sight in the wide-open
rooms, where life was conducted with no more regard
to privacy than that which troubled the sparrows who
came to roost in noisy thousands in an enormous oak
which grew near our house. Our fellow-lodgers seemed

A STUDENT.

to regret that our life was not as open-airy as theirs, and cast many curious glances at me when I sate at my window, which, as the house was solid on that side, *was* a window, and not a paper screen pushing back from a balcony.

I was so tired with the long journey that I was glad to go to bed early on that first evening, and fell asleep to the long roll of the breakers booming solemnly on the shore. Never was I in a place where the sea sang its old songs so loud. All through the night my dreams were set to its solemn measures, and they filled the first moments of my waking consciousness in the morning, when O'Matsu crept into my room and set the windows open to the blessed freshness of the seaside dawn. She amused me by recounting how the wife of our predecessor came down here with children and servants, intending to stay three weeks, but fled back to Tokyo the morning after her arrival, saying that she should go mad if she had to listen to that booming sea for another day. To me the sea is such an old friend that I do not care what it says or how loud it says it, so long as it will talk at all.

The sparrows left their quarters in the evergreen oak with the first flush of dawn, and my neighbours across the garden were not much behind them in beginning the business of the day. I could hardly attend to my own affairs at all for the intense interest with which I watched them. I could see into eight or nine rooms, each of which seemed to show a typical side of Japanese existence. The weather was so warm that all the paper slides had been removed, and people were carrying on life quite as much in the narrow verandah balconies as in the rooms themselves. In one of these, however, a student was trying to escape distractions, and kept his eyes resolutely fixed on his work. He was a young man, with close-cropped head and a broad heavy face, redeemed by keen dark eyes and a very earnest expression. He sat on a thin cushion before a small table, which stood, perhaps, a foot from the floor—surely the most uncomfortable form of writing-desk ever invented. A bamboo cup held his writing-brushes, and a tiny bronze teapot and stone slab seemed to account for the Indian ink. Piles of pink newspapers were on the ground at his side, and two or three open books fluttered in the breeze, and turned over their mystic characters too fast for him apparently, for he frowned, and turned them back with evident irritation. He was dressed in a single blue robe, the cotton *yucata*, which certainly cannot count as heavy clothing ; but the heat was intense, and the student had turned his sleeves up to the shoulder and bared his chest in the desire for coolness. To him, towards midday, entered one of the hotel servants, a dear little maid in striped *kimono* and red sash, bringing some light food, which she pushed towards him on a tray as she knelt a few feet from him on the mats. She was pretty and smiling, poor little thing, and only meant to be kind ; but he frowned at her and motioned her away, as if he could not bear to be interrupted in his work. After she had withdrawn, silent and chagrined, the student suddenly discovered that he had an appetite, and did full justice to the *musumé's* provisions. The cold rice and pickles did not look very tempting to me, though the bowls and cups were charming, red lacquer and white china shining in the sun.

The apartment above that of the ambitious student was occupied by a father and two daughters, people of the merchant class I should think, come here to bathe in the hot spring or inhale the fumes of the great geyser, of which I must tell you more anon. The father looks consumptive, and his daughters wait upon him devoutly. They are blooming lasses, and take tremendous interest in their head-dresses. The whole of my first morning in Atami they spent under the hands of the hair-dresser, an elderly woman, who, unlike her kind, did her work in silence. It took just four hours for the two. First one girl sat on the cushion in the verandah, and last week's coiffure was taken down (O'Matsu says that once in four or five days is considered often enough to repeat the ceremony), and the long black hair was washed with something very like egg, and spread out in the sun to dry. Tea and conversation beguiled this interval, and then the great business of the dressing began. Oh, the twisting and tying, the moulding and oiling of those black rolls! Shaped wires were inserted to hold out the hair in two long wings over the back of the neck, a twist of scarlet crape was knotted in at the summit, and one or two brilliant flower-pins, or *kanza-shis*, planted precisely in the right spot; and the hand-glass was presented to the young lady so that she might gravely examine the effect. As the girl looked down into the mirror, moving it this way and that, in the sunshine. I saw that its reflection was cast up on the white ceiling in an oval of light, with a Chinese character which means happiness standing out clearly in the centre.

When the turn of the second sister came, the whole ceremony was minutely repeated ; and then what looked like a very small sum in coppers changed hands, the Kami San bowed herself out, and the two girls ran off to gossip with O'Detsu, the daughter of Mr. Higuchi, our landlord.

Meanwhile a middle-aged man on the upper floor was suffering terribly from the heat, and his little wife seemed greatly distressed about him. All the screens had been opened ; but it was a breathless day, and no breeze came to ring the little glass bells on the hanging fern-wreath in the verandah. The man had laid aside almost all his garments, and sat with his head in his hands groaning ; while madame, kneeling on the mats behind him, fanned his back, and from time to time rubbed him down with a blue towel, an expression of the deepest respect and sympathy on her face. When he seemed a little better, she busied herself with preparing tea, which he drank eagerly, and of course made himself frightfully hot again, when she went back patiently to her fanning and rubbing.

By this time the ambitious student in the first room had given himself a fearful headache by poring over those maddening Chinese characters in the heat of the

August day, and so an *amma* or *masseur* was called in
to rub it away. The *masseur*, man or woman, is always
blind, the old law having forbidden any person not thus
afflicted to practise the trade so eminently suited for
people whose eyes must be in their fingers. The man
who came to the distressed student was young, with a
serene countenance deeply marked with small-pox, the
most usual cause of blindness here. He was led in
with extreme politeness by the little maid of the red
sash ; the patient bowed to him quite as ceremoniously
as if he had been a duke—with two eyes ; and then the
student sat down on his heels, the *amma* stood over him,
and literally punched his head with violence and precision for something like a quarter of an hour. How
the student bore it I do not know. It looked as if the
process must hurt him more than the worst headache
ever evolved from over-work. But when it was over,
he jumped up with a beaming face, evidently convinced
that he felt perfectly well ; the *amma* received his fee
wrapped up in a corner of paper, and tucked it inside
his girdle ; the little maid, who had been watching
the process, gravely came and led him away ; and the
indomitable student went back to his books.

A little later in the day, when it could be supposed
that we had recovered from the fatigue of the journey,
Mr. and Mrs. Higuchi came to welcome us solemnly
to Atami. They were accompanied by O'Detsu, their
daughter, who told me that she had been educated in
an American school in Yokohama, and could speak
some English, which came in very usefully in translating

for her parents. All the party were beautifully dressed,
and expressed their delighted readiness to place themselves, their hotel, and all their belongings at our
disposal, and apologised profusely for a thousand short-
comings which did not exist. O'Detsu seemed very
happy when I told her that I like American cookery,
and afterwards strained her invention to the utmost to
feed us properly during the three weeks of our stay.
The *menus*, it is true, were sometimes puzzlingly worded,
and such items as the following are hardly reassuring:

> " Currots Soup.
> Fish fineherbs. (Seaweed ?)
> Beef Tea Pudding.
> Dournat. (Doughnut ?)
> Boiled Sponge.
> Praised oeufs devil Sauce.
> Eclairs ala Oujam.
> Fish Squeak
> Dam Pudding ! "

You see I have written this last small on account of
the bad language.

But you will not thank me for detailing all these
minor experiences, and I must tell you something of the
great wonder of Atami, the admirable geyser, which has
made the prosperity of the place. Do not laugh at
the adjective, which is really the right one. This spring
bursts up in the middle of the village, only a few
hundred yards from the shore, with an outbreak of
boiling water, and such a thunderous roar of steam that
it can be heard far away, while its thick, white smoke-
cloud hangs over the place long after the spring has

sunk back to the heart of the earth. I have been standing close to it, and felt the earth quiver under my feet even before the voice of its coming had reached the surface. Its mouth is arched over for a little way, in order to direct the outburst toward the canals which

THE GEYSER, ATAMI.

lead off to the different bathing establishments, and to the tank where it is collected to form an inhaling-room for those who are suffering from chest and throat troubles. Before this roof was laid over it, I believe it rose two or three yards in the air, and of course much was wasted. As it is, the scalding flood which rushes out from the low tunnel is a terrific phenomenon, filling the world for the moment with fearful noises and choking sulphurous steam. It comes with perfect regularity every four hours, continues for a few minutes (not for an hour and a half, as Rein erroneously supposed), and in that time pours out a volume of water sufficient for all the needs of the bathers, and so hot that it was never possible for me to plunge into it at any time without letting it cool in the bath, although it might have been standing for hours in the bathhouse reservoir since the last outbreak.

The people of Atami count upon their geyser with the easy certainty of familiarity ; but it has its caprices, though they are few and far between. Terrible is the consternation when the geyser strikes work, and stays away for ten or twelve days together. There are no hot baths, visitors leave in disgust, and the inhabitants are left to await its stormy homecoming in deep anxiety. When at last the spring returns, it bursts out with a frightful roar and clouds of sulphurous smoke, which hang over the place for a whole day, while the geyser does its many hours of neglected work in one long spell, keeps all its forgotten appointments in a visit which lasts several hours without intermission, and threatens to drown the place in *O yu*, the honourable hot water.

During my first days in Atami, the geyser attracted my attention with a start every time it broke out ; then it came only to mark the time ; then I ceased to notice it altogether, as I had ceased to notice the booming of the surf, unless some excursion took us far inland out

of reach of its voice, and then there seemed to come a
deadness on the air, an emptiness which the bird-songs
or the wind-songs could not fill.

Atami is a seaside nest lying in the arms of two
green hills, that slope down on either side of it (fragrant
with lilies just now) to the gentle sea, that breaks in one
long roll day and night on the smooth sands. Just
where the hills meet the sea on either side is an attempt
at a rock and a precipice; but even these are all gay with
ferns, and lilies orange and white, so there is no effect
of ruggedness. The lilies are a revelation, hothouse
flowers showered down on the land by an indulgent
Providence as a reward for its humble, faithful love of
nature. The great white lily, with leaves like carved
marble gemmed with crimson blood-drops—a thing as
royal and remote as a maiden empress—here it raises
its lovely head on every hillock, reaches gracious
greetings out to me from all the hedges, and sends
waves of perfume out to bless the workaday air.
Down nearer to the sea it is a scarlet lily which spreads
its bell to the sun and the salt wind. The other day
we took a fishing-boat, and made the lean brown men
row us in and out of the rocks and caves and little bays
within the bay. It was a perfect summer afternoon,
with the fulness of the August sunshine lying on the
water; and as we floated in and out among the rocks,
which rise, abrupt and inaccessible, from the sea, it was
beautiful to find every one glorified by these scarlet
lilies, each on a single stem, waving happy and undaunted in the breeze. Close to the rocks the water

lapped and tossed in sudden foam ; one heavy wave went racing through a long arched waterway of the caves ; and out flew two lovely sea-falcons, with brown wings strained wide, startled by the sea's caprice. The men sang at their oars weird cold songs, like reminders of death in the golden glow of life, and one laughed, while the others shook their heads at the sight of the birds as if at some evil omen.

This is a long letter already, I fear, so you must have the rest about Atami next time.

ON THE ATAMI SANDS.

CHAPTER VI.

Atami's Temple and its Grove. The Great Camphor Tree. The Legend of the Boiling Spring. A Night Festival, a Dancer, and a Raid.

CHAPTER VI.

THE rooms are so full of flowers that I can hardly
move. I come in from our expeditions with
both hands full, and one of our servants (rather an
idle boy) spends three or four hours every day out on
the hillsides, and brings me little forests of hydrangea,
white and blue and lilac, with beautiful bright foliage,
and lilies in hundreds, bursting from their stem like
white fireworks, the blossoms nearly a foot in diameter,
and growing high above my head. The blue hydrangea throws long branches of bloom down the clefts
of the rocks, where they look like waterfalls reflecting
the sky. The white one reaches farther, but separates
the clusters more; and they lie like forgotten snowballs
dropped in the little angels' play, for to-day is the
Feast of our Lady of the Snows, Sancta Maria ad Nives,
and I am reminded of the old picture in Siena where
all the court of heaven are standing round her throne
with snowballs in their hands. How glad we should
be to see a little cool whiteness here! The heat is
overpowering, and I have been seeking refreshment
in the green wood of the old temple behind the town.
It stands between the hills and the plain, with the
most lovely grove of trees around it that I have ever

125

seen. They have long-pointed shining leaves of the most brilliant green, and I think are entered on the civic lists of the forest as *Quercus acuta* ; but who cares about the name ? You may be sure it is not the one they call themselves by in those long whispered conversations that they carry on among the green arches far overhead. Their venerable feet are sunk in a carpet of moss, and ferns, and translucent creepers with leaves like green stars and tendrils soft as a baby's fingers. That brooding peace that I spoke of the other day is in all the wood, and seems to have promised that the ruined temple shall not fall, but crumble dreamily in the sunshine, unconscious of its own decay. Quite near it stands a colossal camphor tree (*Cinnamomum camphora*), so old that it has fallen apart with its own weight, and is like two trees in one, the two divisions measuring altogether over sixty feet round. In the odorous brown shadow inside is set a little shrine ; but above, all is life and vigour. Every branch is smothered in fresh green foliage, the small pointed leaves shining like newly cut jade, and giving out a fine aroma on the warm air. It is supposed to be the largest in Japan ; and I think Sydney Lanier away in Baltimore must have seen its waving palace of verdure in his dreams when he wrote—

> " Ye lispers, whisperers, singers in storms,
> Ye consciences murmuring faiths under forms,
> Ye ministers meet for each passion that grieves,
> Friendly, sisterly, sweetheart leaves,
> Oh, rain me down from your darks that contain me
> Wisdoms ye winnow from winds that pain me,—

Sift down tremors of sweet-within-sweet
That advise me of more than they bring, repeat
Me the woods-smell that swiftly but now brought breath
From the heaven-side bank of the river of death,—
    Teach me the terms of silence, preach me
    The passion of patience,--sift me, impeach me,
        And there, oh! there,
As ye hang with your myriad palms in the air,
      Pray me a myriad prayer."

As I sat under the trees in the grove, Ogita told
me the story of Atami and the temple and the boiling
spring. I cannot write down for you the song of
the wind in the leaves, or the long low roll of the sea
on the distant beaches; I cannot paint the sunshine
flecking now one spot and now another in the green
carpet at my feet, or the grey and gold decay of the
old shrine. Truly the eye is not satisfied with seeing
nor the ear with hearing, when the story has to be
written and sent away with all its magic left behind.
But such as it may be, here it is:

Long, long ago, in the times of the elders and the
wise men, there lived in Atami a very holy man, a
priest. He was poor, as was all the population; for
they lived only on what their fishing could bring, and
when the winter storms swept over the sea, or the
earthquakes frightened all the fish out into the ocean,
then life was hard in the little town, and the grown-
up people looked very thin. The children were never
thin, because their fathers and mothers gave them almost
all there was to eat. The priest lived in a small temple
on the hill behind the town; and in the temple garden

was a camphor tree, very strong and beautiful, with leaves like green jade. The priest used to sit under the tree and pray for the people when the fish would not come to the nets, and his heart was sore for them.

One day, as he sat under the tree, praying hard that the fish would return to be caught, the trunk beside him opened, and a beautiful goddess in a purple robe came out and touched him on the shoulder, and her eyes gleamed angrily at the old man. " Thou foolish one ! " she said, in a terrible voice ; " why dost thou sit and pray here, far from the sea and the fish that are in it ? The fish are on the shore even now ; go down and behold them ! " And then she disappeared ; and the priest, trembling mightily, tottered down to the shore as she had bid him, and beheld a sight which filled him with sorrow and anger.

The fish were on the shore as the lady had said, and they were being thrown up in banks all along the beaches, big fish and little ones, and strange creatures that had never been caught in any net. Yes, they were all there ; but every fish was scalded as with boiling water, and was already crumbling to pieces, and a smell as of the Greater Hell[1] was upon every one. And the stench was so terrible that the priest had to cover his nose with his sleeve, while copious tears ran from his eyes, and his heart was bursting with grief at the sad plight of the poor fish and the loss to his townsfolk.

Then he climbed step by step to the hut on the promontory, where the watchman sits to look out for

[1] Ojigoku, near Miyanoshita.

the good fish coming to shore. But the watchman was weary, and had fallen asleep; and the priest stood and looked out to sea by his side, for he thought, " I shall surely see what demon is killing the poor fish." And his eyes were opened, because of his great love for the people ; and he saw far away, many fathoms below the surface, a huge boiling spring, which the demons had let loose, bursting up through the bed of the sea, and it was scalding all the fish to death. So then he roughly woke the watchman, and cried, " Thou that art young, run to the temple, and bring me a bough of my camphor tree to the shore— and stop for none !" And the watchman ran and broke off a branch of the holy tree, which is more powerful than

KWAN-ON.

all the demons ; and the priest went down to the beach, and began to pray in a loud voice that Kwan-on, the goddess of mercy, would have pity on the fish and the people. And when the watchman brought the branch, the old priest cast it on the water

with a great cry, commanding the spring to cease
poisoning the ocean. And so earnestly did he pray that
he did not hear a great rumbling on the land behind him.
But all the people ran in a crowd to the spot whence
it seemed to come; and soon they saw the earth's crust
rising in a cone, and they fled in terror to the hill behind
the town. And then the cone burst, and the boiling
water shot up into the air; and the people came and
dug round it, and made canals to take it to their houses,
and it became a great source of riches for Atami, because
the sick came from far to bathe in it. And the old priest
was glad for the fish, and for his people; and they built
a fine temple on this spot for him, and were very
punctual in their offerings because he had saved the
town. And now, as we see, his temple is very old, and
the camphor tree is as big as a cottage; and I have
stood inside it many a time, but never did the beautiful
goddess come out to show herself to me.

Have you had too much of Atami? I must tell
you of one more scene which made a great impression
on my mind. I noticed yesterday that the village
seemed more animated than usual, and the people were
hanging red and white lanterns on long strings from
high poles down to the ground, and the houses in the
chief street were all outlined with them, blowing about
violently in a tearing breeze from the bay. Strange-
looking groups formed at the street corners, and immense
excitement prevailed in and around a kind of barn,
whose doors, thrown wide, showed a high car being
decorated with wreaths and lanterns. An enormous

A CLOTH SHOP

drum stood in one corner, and was being doctored by a specialist, who kept banging the end with a bit of bamboo to see if it sounded loud enough. Little boys were jumping about, screaming and playing, and getting in their elders' way with the complete security of children who are never scolded.

Booths had been set up in the street, and all the shops were displaying their most tempting wares. At lunch, Ogita brought a message from our landlord to say that he was afraid his " rough and ignorant countrymen " would make a great deal of noise in the evening ; but he had informed the police that they must on no account let it go on too late, for fear of spoiling our honourable rest. This civility quite overcame me ; but to tell the truth, Atami was almost too quiet for me, and I thought, what I was ashamed to say, that a little excitement would make a pleasant change.

As we must soon go back to Tokyo, I spent the afternoon in collecting some of the curiosities of the place—lovely camphor-wood boxes and fernwork ; and of course was followed to the counter of every shop by a crowd of the natives, very anxious to find out what my clothes were made of, for those nearest to me kept feeling my dress, and asked Ogita so many questions that he got quite angry. But it was only good-natured curiosity, and I did not mind it at all. The one drawback to so much cheerful society is that, as all the shopping is done from the outside, with the wares spread on a low board or counter sloping out from the seller in the house to the buyer in the street, the assistants get between the purchaser and his object, and have to be removed by force before he can see what he will have.

As I have said, the little town was crowded with holiday-makers in bright dresses. Among others I noticed an Englishman, a tall smart-looking man, sitting in the native cotton dress on the step of the tea-house, laughing and chattering in fluent Japanese with a swarm of Atami girls, who all seemed very glad to see him. He looked at us, as we passed, with an amused smile, and his face seemed a familiar one, though I could not put a name to him. His dress was poor and common in the extreme. He was probably one of the harmless maniacs who travel everywhere without passports, and try to see the country from the Japanese side of life. He must have seen a good deal of it, to judge by the ease with which he was speaking the language; and he looked like such a pleasing maniac that I longed to talk to him. Of course I did not—does one really ever do the pleasant thing? But, whoever you are, my brother, your clear brown eyes and strong happy face will always make a part of my recollections of Atami.

When night fell, and a splendid moon was riding in the sky, we went out to have a look at the *Matsuri*, or festival procession. The street leading down to the sea was closely packed with people, and the air was full of the sound of drums and the songs of girls, who, sitting high in the great cars, played on brass cymbals and triangles as the men pulled them up the street. All the lanterns were lighted and swung in the breeze; their rays fell

on the dark faces and bare brown limbs of the men,
who, naked, and wild with saké, strained fiercely at
the ropes, while the huge erection, its three tiers decked
with flowers and packed with laughing girls in brilliant
robes, went tottering and swaying up the sandy street.
The moon and the lanterns showed that the wheels

DANCERS.

were wet : and the men shook the sea water from their
limbs as they pulled, for they had taken the sacred
cars out into the sea, to bless the fishes, as Ogita
explained to me, and were now returning towards the
geyser, perhaps meaning to bless that too.

As they moved very slowly in the deep ruts half
choked with sand, we went on to wait for them at the
other end of the street. We found no difficulty in

getting through the crowd, which everywhere gave
way kindly and cheerily to the two smart policemen
who had us in charge : and soon we found ourselves
standing on the step of a shop, whose owner had begged
us to come in and watch a pretty sight which was going
forward on the opposite side of the street.

On a scaffolding some ten feet high and heavily
draped in black and white, a little dancing-girl was
holding the enraptured attention of the crowd. She
was so small and slight, and so brilliantly dressed, that
as she turned and wheeled and set her great flowered
sleeves flying on the wind, she put me in mind of
some dainty humming-bird with fairy crest and gem-
like plumage. Her little head was sparkling with
ornaments, which threw out gold and silver fringes
as she turned ; and her dark eyes shone strangely in
her small impassive face, which looked dead white, un-
relieved by the usual dash of rouge on cheeks and lips.
The child danced beautifully, her feet marking the
time sharply through their soft white covering, her
movements making precise yet constantly changing
volutes of her skirts and sleeves, bewildering, manifold,
and parti-coloured as the petals of a tiger-lily shaken
by a storm. The cars were coming nearer up the
street ; the red glare of the lanterns seemed to have
passed into her robes, the white shining of the moonlight into her face, when some electric thrill ran through
the dense crowd, hoarse shouts broke forth which
drowned the clang of the drums and cymbals, and a
score of young men, wildly intoxicated and yelling

like demons, broke from the car, leapt over the cord
which had been drawn round the scaffolding, and began
to swarm up it by its hanging ropes and draperies. The
thing swayed to this side and that; a number of policemen threw themselves on the rioters, who fought
frantically; the little dancer turned a shade whiter, but
went on dancing her weird measure, though her *samisen*-
players had fled; our own policemen pulled us farther
into the shop, hurriedly told the owner to look after
us, and dashed across the way to the aid of their
comrades, who were far outnumbered by the naked
assailants of the stage. But their interference and the
delay it caused saved the little dancer, if any harm
was meant to her; for now her master, a middle-aged
man with a terrified countenance, appeared behind her,
snatched her up, and dropped by some hidden steps
from the back of the scaffolding and vanished, just as
the mob, getting the better of the police, tore the
whole thing to pieces. It fell crashing to the ground,
its draperies huddled among broken boards and bits
of theatrical properties which were stowed beneath it.
Then (for I had again come out on the step, to the
despair of the responsible shopkeeper) I turned my
head, attracted by a flash of light in what had looked
like a dark house on our side of the street. I saw
a woman holding open a side door, through which the
little dancer was borne on the back of her master, who
flew with her up a long flight of wooden stairs. Her
arms were clasped round his neck, her sleeves spread
from his shoulders like scarlet wings, and as she

turned her head at the top I saw that she was smiling. Then the door slid into place, and I never saw the little dancer again, nor, in spite of my intense curiosity, could I find out what it was all about. Ogita had abandoned us when the policemen went, and now returned rather shamefacedly to my side. He would only say when questioned that "Atami people very rough much, very common much; very sorry Okusama see tipsy people not proper!" The inspector of police apologised in much the same manner; and since there was nothing more to see (for the rioters had become instantaneously sober after they had wrecked the staging), I went back to the hotel, amused and puzzled, and very sorry not to have the key to the queer story.

A LANDING-PLACE.

CHAPTER VII.

*Our Return to Tokyo.—A Strange Situation.
Dogs and Cats in Japan.—Comedies of the
Servants' Quarters. Doctor Baelz and his
Medical Students. Tokyo's Five Hundredth
Birthday. Ueno and Its Story.*

159

CHAPTER VII.

Tokyo, *August* 31st, 1889.

I AM glad to be writing to you from here once more, though the heat is stifling and persistent. Atami was not all poetry; there was too much hot water about for that! It is difficult to keep up pure intellectual enthusiasm, when twice a day one has to lie for an hour or two, a melting mass of limpness, buried under piles of flannel to continue the effect of twenty minutes' immersion in a bath at 120° Fahrenheit. No curl is left even in the most obedient hair, one looks too frightful to be described, and one's thoughts are mostly concerned with the next thing that can be got to drink. The cure draws all the moisture out of the body; a burning thirst is the result, and one is tempted to think that Niagara would not make such a very long drink after all. At last I had had enough of it, and began to pine for my own airy rooms, and, I am ashamed to say, for my own cook. H—— had been patience itself; so had Mr. G——, whom he had brought to help him bear the exile from civilisation; but I was greeted with applause, when I said one evening, " This family will return to Tokyo the day after to-morrow."

There was any amount of packing to do ; for the more I travel the more luggage I carry, and the bare hotel rooms are always beautified by what the old American Consul used to call " layers and peanuts," the photos and books and odds and ends, which are the little familiar gods of daily life, filling up quite a place of their own in our naturally idolatrous hearts. My maid, who had completely collapsed in the heat, pulled herself together enough to do the same by my properties. Ogita the invaluable engaged eleven jinrikshas to pull the family and four coolies to carry me the eighteen miles to Kodzu, and early one morning the whole population turned out to see us depart. Old Mr. Higuchi the landlord, his daughter O'Detsu (iron), and Také (bamboo) the maid, and many others came to the farther bounds of the town to wish us good-bye and beg us soon to return. The grave policeman in gold-laced cap and spotless white clothes came some distance farther, and on the confines of another district made an amiable little speech, and solemnly relinquished all further responsibility on our account. You cannot imagine how admirable the police are in Japan, how quiet and authoritative—and ubiquitous —always there to be appealed to in any difficulty, and amiable as, I think, only Japanese and Italians (out of office!) can be amiable. It is so amusing to find that many of them can speak English. Fancy a Sorrento *carabiniere* or a member of the Devon constabulary who could talk Japanese!

After we had said good-bye to our little guardian, our troubles began in earnest. Never that I remember have we had to travel over roads in such a hopeless condition. The mud nearly swallowed up the coolies, and spattered the occupants of the jinrikshas till they were almost unrecognisable. I had the best of it in my

A PROCESSIONAL CAR.

chair; but I expected at every moment to be dropped into some black pool of mud, as my coolies swayed and slipped and recovered their footing and struggled on again. I am not very heavy; but I felt like a criminal for making them carry me at all. The men all behaved splendidly, and not one jinriksha was upset. Near Odawara we suddenly found ourselves mixed up with a huge *Matsuri* procession, which was making its slow way along on the seashore. Our own line of march was immediately broken ; I do not know what happened to my companions, but I found myself advancing solemnly on my bearers' shoulders, between two huge cars drawn by flower-decked bullocks and full of screaming musicians, surmounted by a tottering image that swayed and shook as the car advanced. On one was the figure of a woman, life size, with a dead-white face and elaborate coiffure and long stiff robes of purple and gold. She seemed to be holding out her hands to me as she swung this way and that, far above my head. The other car had a huge phœnix, the Empress's bird, with blue and purple wings and a gold crown. It was a dark lowering day, and the sea was rolling in with a heavy roar on my right hand ; while on the land side stood crowds of spectators, who cried out with delight when they saw me apparently taking part in the procession. I remembered the sacred bridge at Kameido, and hoped there was no journalist in the applauding crowd, who would at once publish an account of my conversion to Buddhism! As I could not say a word to the coolies, I was quite helpless, until Ogita found out what was happening, and rescued me from the absurd situation.

We had left Atami at half-past seven, and reached Kodzu at two—in time for the train which brought us home at 5.30 in the very worst downpour of the whole season. It seemed cruel to bring the pretty cream-coloured ponies out in it; but I was very glad to get back to my own rooms and the warm bath and the home dinner. We used to have that feeling at the Odescalchi, you remember, when we got back in the autumn after roughing it in the hills all summer.

GHETA, OR CLOG SHOP.

The next morning the rain had ceased, and in the garden the locusts and all their noisy relations were screaming aloud to each other that the heat would not last much longer, and that people who wanted to sing had better tune up and begin. No locust or wee-wee, or scissor-grinder prima donna has a note left when the thermometer falls below 85; so in these days they are all shrieking à *tue-tête*, and very distracting it is. These

last heats are rather exhausting. My dachshund Tippoo
Tib, popularly known as the Brown Ambassador, lies
on his back between door and window, with ears all over
the place, and fat brown satin paws (just like legs of
mutton in gloves) turned up in the hope of catching a
stray breeze and showing it the way to his nose. His
nose is rather his weak point, for it has been damaged
by coming in contact with more than one *gheta*, I am
sorry to say. The *ghetas* are the wooden clogs which
the Japanese wear in the street, and shed at the doorstep
as they come in. All the servants have them for
crossing the courtyards, and there is often a little army
of the curious footgear ranged on a particular doorstep
leading towards the servants' quarters. Tip is a dog
full of original sin, and his great delight is to steal all
the *ghetas* one by one, and bury them in some solitary
place in the garden. After long search they are recovered ; and then, since mankind is also full of original
sin, I fear they are occasionally shied at Tip's offending
nose. Before me he is treated with the most tender
respect, and solemnly addressed as Tip San.

I think the Japanese servants make the theory of the
transmigration of souls account for our extreme care
of and kindness to our pets. The Russian Minister has
a decrepit old pug (she was eighteen last birthday), who
rules the family with a rod of iron. He told me that
the other day he saw Gip tottering down the corridor,
where she met one of the coolies carrying wood for
the stove. The man at once stopped, ranged himself
against the wall, and, making a deep bow as the pug

A JAPANESE LADY AND HER PET DOG.

passed, murmured respectfully, "Gip San!" "Il croit que c'est l'âme de ma grand'mère!" was our colleague's commentary on the incident.

The Japanese puzzle me in their treatment of animals. Sometimes they seem devoted to them, as kind and careful as English people are to their dogs and horses. At others they show quite a cynical callousness to their sufferings. As far as I can see, they are kind to their own creatures and indifferent to those of other people. One can take a kind of family pride in seeing one's own pampered *chin* dog wearing a frilled collar *à la* Toby, and swaggering about in the sun; but there is no satisfaction to be got out of the dog of one's neighbour's grandmother, as Ollendorff would say.

To tell the truth, the dogs of Tokyo are not attractive as dogs. There are only four kinds : the coarse wolfish house-dog, only a shade less repulsive than the pariah of Peking; a middle-sized brown mongrel, smooth-haired, thick-set, and cowardly, who is much *répandu* in the dog world; and two kinds of lap-dogs, a degenerate King Charles (the *chin* above mentioned), and a smooth, rather bald beast with spots—both kinds have prominent eyes, and their sight is weak from having been brought up in the half light of Japanese houses. They generally wear Toby collars of scarlet or purple to mark their rank, and are much petted by their own masters. Even the pet cat wears a collar; and there is a woman I often pass on the Koudan hill near our gate who takes her pussy out for an airing wrapped in the folds of her own *kimono*. This is of course a tailless cat, the ugliest thing in Japan! Like all other foreigners, I have been much puzzled by this destitution of Japanese cats. Ogita declares that they are born without tails in Dai Nippon, and adds that it is a good thing too, since it is well known that a cat with a long tail is a most dangerous creature, and always turns into a witch when it grows old.

Perhaps it does! We have two weird cats here, imported with great trouble by Lady Plunkett some years ago. They come from Siam, and are a pale biscuit colour, with black ears, paws, and tails. Such tails! Longer than their whole bodies, and lashing the ground furiously when they are waiting for a spring; then their pale-green eyes shine diabolically between the black ears above and the black nose below; and their long lean bodies fly through the air in leaps that would not disgrace a panther. The servants are horribly afraid of them; and so am I, and so is Tip. They wait for him on the branch of an over-hanging tree, and drop on his smooth brown back as he saunters along in his lordly way. Then there is a fearful battle, from which Tip returns a lacerated conqueror, with tags of biscuit-coloured fur between his teeth.

The Emperor is fond of dogs, and has one especial pet, a tiny long-haired terrier, which was a present from Madame Sannomiya. The little creature is quite a personage in the Palace, and during this hot weather has a servant who sits beside it all day to fan the flies away and put bits of ice into its mouth. No one is allowed to wake it from sleep; and I believe there was terrible trouble one day when some unlucky person trod on its tail.

I wish some kind fairy would fan me all day and put bits of ice into my mouth! The heat is still overpowering, and I rather rebel against it, because as a

THE HALL.

rule I find warm weather inspiring and invigorating. This last week has been apoplectic. By half-past six or seven in the morning the sun is blazing; and if a cloud does drift across his face in the course of the day, the air only seems the hotter for it. I wander from room to room, in the thinnest of white garments, seeking for something to breathe. Just now I have been sitting on the stairs, in the hope of catching a stray breeze ; and Tip, limp and panting, came and sat down beside me. All the doors and windows are wide open, and have fine blinds of split bamboo hanging loose in them, giving out a strong grassy smell as the sun smites them from the other side. The wide staircase is half in twilight, and so is the hall below, where the palms are hanging, without a quiver on the breathless air ; and the " Heavenly Bamboo" trained on great screens has not shaken its bright-red berries once to-day. Outside in the garden everything is simmering in the heat ; not a servant is to be seen, except the slave of the hall door, who has fallen asleep on his bench ; but a hum from the farther courtyard tells me that the rest of my household is gathered there, every one at the door of his room under the shady verandah, probably in the sketchiest of costumes, smoking the afternoon pipe and consuming the afternoon tea. My English housekeeper tells me that very funny scenes are enacted in that courtyard, where she, being a great favourite, comes and goes at will. On one doorstep my *amah*, who is a bit of a character, will sit and scold her husband, the head boy, by the hour, bewailing the day when she married such a fool as Rinzo. Rinzo takes it all quite patiently ; and when she has done, hands her his pipe to clean, and suggests tea. Opposite, the pantry-boy, who has æsthetic tastes, is arranging flowers in a vase to put on the stand under a much-prized picture in his room, and remarks that he is not sorry he left *his* wife in the hills. Next to him

" Cook San " is helping his little girl to dig up her toys from a corner where Tip buried them carefully this morning ; while Mrs. Cook, who has been washing, is ironing her clothes by spreading them very tightly on a board, where the sun will bake them dry and stiff. Cook San's aides-de-camp, two idle youths in white cotton clothes, are pretending to wash vegetables for to-night's salad, but find it tempting to splash each other with the clear water from the tap. Okusama is not supposed to enter this courtyard except at stated hours ; but cannot resist the pleasure of occasionally watching, through the closed blinds of an upper window, the many-sided, brightly coloured life of its inhabitants, of listening to the hum of chatter which rises from the human hive.

Really, servants in Japan ought to be very happy ! Each man may bring his wife and children and mother to live with him, when he enters our service. I have drawn the line at grandmothers, on account of over-crowding, and also because it is impossible to impress these very elderly people with the necessity and propriety of wearing clothes in warm weather. They scoff at modern ideas, and doubtless talk of the good old times when they were young and all these absurd decency fads had not cropped up. Who wants clothes except for warmth, or to look smart in on proper occasions ? Why be bothered with them in the house, in August ? And so it happened that, when Cook San's grandmother was met in the kitchen one warm after-noon without a shred of raiment on her old brown body, then I found that there really was not room for more than three generations in our very inadequate servants' quarters, and a lodging was found for the old lady elsewhere.

Of course we do not keep house for this army of people. If we did, my good Mrs. D—— would have her hands full and her larder empty all the time. The servants' wages cover their food expenses (the wages are low on the whole), and we provide a cooking-house and fuel; each man is given one, or, at the most, two little rooms, and then he does as he pleases about filling them. Some kind of supervision has to be exercised, and this is done by D——, our good head man, who has made himself much respected by the Japanese servants; and I occasionally make a tour of inspection, accompanied by him and his wife, when I express great approbation of the tidy pretty rooms, and look unutterable things at less well-kept ones. Now there is quite an ambition about it, and the going round brings me a little more into contact with the wives and children, who amuse me greatly. Little presents to the babies also go a long way towards establishing confidence between us, and some of the tiny ones get themselves brought upstairs occasionally to see me or bring me flowers.

On one point I have trouble, and that is their dislike to foreign doctoring, and their obstinate clinging to their own queer medicine-men, who are constantly smuggled in through the stable-yard to attend them, while the illness is carefully hidden from me in its first

A FORTUNE-TELLER.

stages. When the local quack, half herbalist, half fortune-teller, has failed to help them, then I am told that So-and-so has just been taken ill, and may they send for " Baelz Doctor San "? Doctor Baelz arrives, looks into the case, and comes, full of righteous rage, to report to me that the patient has been ill for a week, and has been poisoning himself with the prescription of the Japanese medicine-man. Scolding is of no use. All one can do is to give good nursing and proper remedies a chance of overcoming the mischief that has been done —and that will be done again at the first opportunity.

Of course I am not now referring to the Japanese doctors properly speaking. They are a body of serious and learned men, educated either in Europe or here under Doctor Baelz, who is the medical professor at the University, and whose name is familiar to scientific men all over the world. In surgery the Japanese do wonderful work, their calm nerves and delicate hands fitting them to undertake the most difficult operations. They are as far removed from the strangely clad practitioner of my back yard as our great physicians and surgeons are from the quack who sells medicines from a cart at a country fair.

Doctor Baelz tells me that, like medical students at home, the young men are occasionally turbulent and unmanageable. His predecessor had had much trouble with a class, and the first time that Doctor Baelz took it they threatened mutiny of a violent sort. So, as soon as he could make himself heard, he told them in a few pithy words that they had come to him with the worst reputation in the University, that he was not in the least afraid of them, but wished it clearly understood that if they were unruly there would be no lectures to attend, and since they had all to gain from him and he nothing to gain from them, perhaps they had better reflect on it till the next day, when he would be glad to hear what conclusion they had come to. They broke up in silence, came the next morning to his first lecture, and never gave him the slightest trouble afterwards.

I could listen to his lectures with rapt attention. He has made a study, as only a German can do, of the Japanese, their bodies and souls, their country and their customs. Our people take their learning more spasmodically, and do not give it out so well. Doctor Baelz has won a great position for himself here, and is so constantly appealed to by Japanese and Europeans that he hardly has the time to follow up the questions of research which interest him most. I am glad he is the Legation doctor. One could not fall into wiser or kinder hands.

On August 26th the three hundredth anniversary of Tokyo's existence as a capital was celebrated, very noisily and dustily, but with much enthusiasm. A kind of popular festival was inaugurated at Uyeno Park, where there is a racecourse, and a temple dedicated to Iyeyasu, the hero of the day. I think I told you in an earlier letter of how Tokyo came by its name and fame—how the fishing village, with its lonely castle surrounded by many miles of swamp, came to be the

centre of power in Japan. It is said that the greatest
surprise was expressed by the warriors of Iyeyasu, when
his intention of occupying and fortifying this place was
made known to them. Iyeyasu had just been made
ruler of the eight rich provinces governed till then
(1590) by the Hojo family, who had succeeded in
becoming Regents and guardians of the Shoguns, even
as the Shoguns were the nominal Regents and keepers
of the Imperial family. The Hojo power was completely broken when Odawara, their chief stronghold,
fell before the attack of Hideyoshi, who gave their
lands and titles to his great general Iyeyasu, and
Yedo, our Tokyo, suddenly sprang into triumphant
life under the conqueror's sway. People flocked to
it; great houses were built by the Daimyos who
followed Iyeyasu, or who, living far away, were obliged
by his successors to spend a part of their time at the
centre of affairs. The district called Kojimachi (where
our Legation now stands) was one of the first to
be colonised; but everywhere the huge *yashikis*, or
Daimyos' houses, surrounded by enormous buildings
for receiving their retainers, covered the ground for
miles, and became those hotbeds of turbulence which
had to be swept away when the Emperor made
Tokyo his capital and the Daimyos were persuaded
to lay down their power.

Uyeno, the park where the tercentenary festival
took place, was one of these *yashikis*, the residence
of the Daimyo of Todo, who gave it up to the
Shogun Iyemitsu (the grandson of Iyeyasu) for the

erection of some magnificent Buddhist temples, which were intended to remove the prevalent superstition that the north-eastern quarter of a town must always be the most unlucky one. But there was another motive for the erection of these great buildings. The second Shogun, to protect himself against any possible intrigues on the part of the Emperor in Kyoto, invested an Imperial Prince (the son of his own daughter, who was the reigning Empress) with the dignity of chief priest of the Uyeno Temples. From that time the office was always filled by an Imperial Prince, who was looked upon as a hostage for the good behaviour of the Emperor. Iyemitsu did much to make Yedo both splendid and important, one of his regulations being to the effect that every Daimyo should maintain a house in Yedo and pass a portion of the year there. It was under the rule of Iyemitsu and the other Tokugawa Shoguns that the arts of Japan reached their highest perfection; and the Tokyo of to-day still shows many traces of beauty, which neither the harrow of war nor the blizzard of modernisation has been able to efface. Some of Iyemitsu's temples at Uyeno survived a fierce battle which was fought in their sacred groves in July, 1868, between the Emperor's troops and the adherents of the last Shogun, who, more persistent than their master, continued to fight after he had consented to resign. In this battle the chief temple was destroyed by—an Armstrong gun! Its site serves for the Uyeno Museum, a place where I should like to loot undisturbed for days; but the true glory of Uyeno in Japanese eyes is not in its temples or its museum, or even its historical associations, but in the cherry

THE TOSHOGU SHRINE, UYENO PARK.

trees which glorify it in the spring, and which I hope to see—next year, " Roses, if I live and do well."

I did not go to the noisy festival, which promised nothing so distinctly picturesque or sympathetic as Uyeno in its quiet weekday garb. The races and fireworks and feasting of last Monday would have

PEASANTS RETURNING FROM THE WOODS.

seemed to me vulgar and profane; for the Uyeno woods are my temples of peace, where I go and spend long hours listening to the talk of the wise old trees which know so much—so much, that we can never be quiet enough to learn. I think I must have come of the tree folk originally. Oak and palm and pine—they are individual and dear as human kin to me, and I felt at home directly in Japan, the land of trees. It is only since I came here that their hierarchy has been revealed to me. The palm is a holy pontiff; the oak a king, a ruler of men; the pine a seer, sad and faithful; the bay-laurel is a poet whose heart is warm gold; the cypress a penitent soul that will never know its own greatness; the ilex, my Roman ilex, is a pagan still, and believes only in sunshine above and warm cliffs and blue sea below. The rest, elm and ash and willow—well, they are the common folk, sweet and useful, but not royal, not indispensable, like those others.

It makes one rather selfish to be so intimate with the trees, and I grudge the deep glades at Uyeno to the screaming crowd. Also that which they call a race-course is a grassy road, running wide and low round the lotus lake, called *Shinobazu*, where just now myriads of flowers are holding white and rosy cups open to the sun or stars, while their green velvet leaves, a yard wide, lie on the water playing games with round diamond drops that run up and down on the fine veins trying to find their way back to the cool flood below. And all around the lake fly swarms of gorgeous dragon-flies, their burnished bodies and filmy rainbow wings making them seem living jewels as they dart swiftly through the sunshine. The little children, as bright and gay as they, come in bands to the green path round the lake, and fish for the dragon-flies with long fine threads fastened to tall rods of bamboo. These they fling through the air with a sharp whirl, and the long thread winds itself round the dragon-fly, and he is slipped into a fairy cage, and taken home to be fed and petted ; but all his free flying is done for ever.

So—you see why I did not go to the Uyeno festival!

CHAPTER VIII.

Miyanoshita.—A Chair Journey through the Woods.—A Resting-place in the Forest.—Hot Springs and Wood-carvers' Shops. — Family Life.—A Pretty Picture.—The Sulphur Valley. —Time to go Home, and the Autumn Typhoon.

CHAPTER VIII.

Fujiya Hotel, Miyanoshita, *September*, 1889.

IT is only a fortnight since I returned from Atami to Tokyo, and now I am in Miyanoshita among the hills. You will think that I spend my time in flying from one Japanese watering-place to another; but the truth is that Tokyo, just now, is a spot to get away from—on foot, if it could not be done otherwise! The heat gives one no rest, no air, nothing to breathe or live on. Heavy black skies like prison blankets hang over the town, full of hot rain and stored thunder. When they break, we are half drowned; and when the sun comes out after the deluges, the heat is worse than ever—steady, blazing, steaming heat, more trying than I can describe. The dampness is in everything; shoes and gloves, if left one day shut up, go green with mould, and smell unspeakable things about vaults and tombs. The maids have been spending their time in laying my whole wardrobe out on sheets in the sun (whenever the sun shone) in the upstairs verandahs; but my poor frocks have suffered terribly already. I quite refused to have all my evening gowns and pretty things soldered down in tin at the end of May, as the other women here do; having only just come, with a lot of smart new clothes, it seemed rather hard to put them all away, and wear only pongee and Japan crape for three or four months : but, alas! my pink frock has turned yellow, my blue a sickly green, my beloved black Chantilly has eruptions of grey spots all over it, and so on!

Poor H—— is terribly busy, for all the hard work comes, as a rule, at the hottest time, and Treaty Revision ranges in the Legation upstairs and downstairs and in my lady's chamber. My lady's chamber is empty just now, its mistress having abandoned her post and taken refuge in cowardly flight to the hills, accompanied by one or two friends, the faithful Ogita, and several of the servants, brought, not to wait on me, but because the poor things were badly in need of a little fresh air. Mr. G——, who is H——'s right hand in all the work, is up here too, but will probably be wired for before he has quite done unpacking his things.

The journey to Miyanoshita is the same as that to Atami as far as Kodzu, where one takes a tram, which runs for five or six miles farther, and stops at Yumoto, a pretty place, with a beautiful Japanese hotel, at the foot of the hills. From there the journey has to be continued in jinrikshas, up a steep and lovely road to Miyanoshita itself. We were fortunate in our weather, for the day was one of shifting showers and sudden sunshine, with faint ethereal mists spreading, rolling, melting away, and gathering again ; making exquisite effects of distance when fold after fold of mountain was visible, each clothed in a clinging veil of filmy gauze that seemed to catch and tear on the pine tops. The full and rushing stream of the Hayagawa was beside us for a great part of the way, making pools of light that doubled the sun and the mist, while the grey boulders tossed along its bed broke the water up in airy diamonds. The sense of rest and fresh-

THE ROAD TO MIYANOSHITA.

ness was wonderful, coming as I did from the choking atmosphere of the town.

I travelled, as usual, in my chair, on coolies' shoulders; and towards the end of the journey we left the road, and took short cuts up through splendid woods, dark and cool and full of the sound of waterfalls. I am never so happy as on such expeditions, when I generally leave the rest of the party far behind, and can have a long *zusammen schweigen* with my friends the trees. The men carried me rapidly and easily, only stopping twice to breathe in the whole long climb. Though I am not very heavy, they were rather spent from the extreme steepness of the path, and I made them stop and have some tea at a tiny brown *chaya*, which leant against the pine trunks like a bundle of brushwood. The little place was poor as a hermit's cell; but it was all sweet with the scent of pine needles, and at the door a tiny runnel of clear water trickled from a bamboo pipe into a hollowed trunk which serves as a water barrel. On its edge was growing a yellow wild flower, which quivered and vibrated with the movement of the water; while a sunbeam crept down through the branches, and danced on the clear sand at the bottom and on the bare back of my head coolie, who suddenly pulled off his blue cotton shirt and plunged it into the water. In a moment he withdrew it, wrung it out, scattering bright drops in the air, and then put it on again with a sigh of satisfaction.

"Why?" I inquired uneasily; for the proceeding looked like a recipe for pneumonia—a cold wet garment laid on a steaming human body!

"Cold wet hot wet being-is-not," was the reply, meaning, I suppose, that a garment wrung out in clear water is more comfortable than one saturated with perspiration.

The Fujiya Hotel is almost entirely arranged for Europeans, the only Japanese rooms being some low buildings in the garden, which are called the Bachelors' Quarters. Mr. G——, his dogs and boys, shook down there; and I and Mrs. N—— had some pretty rooms on the second floor, with wide views down the valley, and not too great a distance of shiny corridors to be pattered over in slippers before we got to the baths; for the baths are Miyanoshita's reason for existing, and are so delightfully pleasant that it seems a pity ever to come out of the warm reviving water. The villages here have grown up round warm springs, and there are no less than six of them in the gorges of our noisy Hayagawa; while one, the hottest of all, is used for baths at Ashinoyu, farther off in the hills, and nearer the source of the river itself in the Hakone Lake. The waters of Ashinoyu are strong in sulphur, and fairly hot, having a temperature of from 90 to 100 Centigrade; as they descend from the heights, they become cooler, and, losing their sulphurous character, take on a little more iron. At Miyanoshita the water is tepid (45–59°), and has no sulphur smell; but it has a delightfully alive feeling as if charged with electricity, and a dip in it takes all the fatigue out of weary limbs after the longest walk.

The baths are comfortably arranged; indeed one is always sure of finding an inviting bathroom in any hotel in Japan. At Miyanoshita the woods of which they are built give out in the warm atmosphere a sweet aromatic smell quite peculiar to the place. Nothing but wood is used for walls or floor or ceiling; and the deep tank where the water flows is of wood too, polished and scented, and smooth as velvet to the touch. The only drawback is that every sound pierces the thin wooden partitions, and people are tempted to make remarks or discuss family affairs with some member of their own party in the next bathroom, forgetting that probably all the others are occupied as well. This applies to the bedrooms too ; and I was kept long awake by a cheerful lady on the verandah, who sat there telling impossible stories to a circle of friends till late into the night.

I was up fairly early the next morning, and wandered out in search of some shady corner where I could make friends with a tree and read a little ; and I found what I wanted not far from the Bachelors' Quarters, where, as I afterwards learned, my appearance in the garden, fully dressed, at ten o'clock in the morning, caused profound consternation among the inhabitants. The men take it very easy in the mornings in summer, and the cool pyjamas, or *yucata*, are not exchanged for clothes proper till various drinks and newspapers have been discussed on long chairs in the verandahs and the gossip of the day fairly threshed out. When the holiday-makers saw me approaching, Mr. G—— says they all fled indoors and began to shave, thinking I was bent on inspecting their domain. He himself, buried in the new dictionary (which just now consists of several thousand little squares of loose paper), could not abandon the treasure to be the sport of the elements, and was rewarded for his valour by seeing me subside into a seat with my back to him and his bachelor friends.

THE VILLAGE OF RIGA.

I had been perfectly unconscious of their presence, and was taken up with wondering how—and if I could reach the highest point of the surrounding hills, which, in spite of their beauty, troubled me by closing us in all round. That is why I never care for hills so much as for the sea ; there is more space to think in, when the horizon is blue and very far away. I found that the hills would be beyond my strength, and went instead up the road which leads along the gorge above the river, to the little village of Kiga, where there are more warm baths and a number of Japanese hotels.

To reach it one has to pass close to a thin sheet of waterfall, which covers the road with spray for many yards, and spreads most welcome coolness on the air. Kiga itself is all built against the cliff, so that many of the houses have the rock itself for their inner wall. It is a pretty, friendly place, with glimpses of pretty tea-house gardens and girls flitting to and fro, and the sound of the Hayagawa everywhere. I sat down for a moment in one of the gardens to admire the flowers and feed the goldfish ; and then, since the sun was getting high, I returned to Miyanoshita, and plunged into some of the woodshops in the village—cool dark shops, full of lovely work, on which one could spend many dollars with great satisfaction.

The work itself is mostly wood mosaic, intermingled in a thousand lovely patterns with fretwork or solid carving. The screens are particularly pretty, having a square of delicate open lattice-work in each panel, mostly in white wood, set in many-coloured inlaid work, and

the whole panel mounted in a richly carved ebony
frame. These are purely Japanese, and so are the
boxes and cabinets; but beside them are writing-tables
of cruel ugliness, made to please the European eye.
Also one can buy screens and brackets of white wood
precisely like those one gets to paint in England.
Altogether the foreign element is very strong in the
Miyanoshita shops. On the third day of my stay it
rained, and I wanted a new book. I had read all that
the hotel contained except one—a religious novel, which
made much stir a year ago, and which, partly from
obstinacy, partly because I prefer to take my religion
and my novel separately, I have steadily refused to
read. On board ship, in railway journeys, in country
hotels, this valuable work has been recommended to
my notice—in vain; but I might have been tempted
to read it at Miyanoshita that day, had not somebody
told me that at one of the carving-shops there was
actually a lending library, where one could get books
for five sen a day. I at once put on my rain-cloak, and
flew down the street, which was quite deserted, and
noisy with the rattling rush of the rain. My poor
interpreter had to come too, much against his will.
When we reached the shop, and explained our errand
to the woman who kept it, her face brightened, and she
said yes, she had many books, twelve in all, to hire
out, and would I like this one? The volume she held
out was—the religious novel that I had been running
away from across two continents!

For me the real interest of Miyanoshita lies in the

family life of the wood-carvers. From the father down
to the tiny children everybody helps, and it is evident
that woodwork is considered the only honourable or
interesting trade in the world. I have haunted the
shops just to watch the people, and bought heaps
of things I did not want, as an excuse for lingering
among them. Many of the workers have no shop of
their own, but supply one establishment with various
details of objects, which are afterwards put together.
There was one little house where I never saw them
making anything but red gods of happiness, little bloated
creatures, who resolved themselves into boxes contain-
ing smaller editions of themselves in two and three
chapters. These were blocked out by one son of about
seventeen, turned on a lathe by another, finished by
a third, and painted by the father, whose skilful laying
on of his few colours was approvingly watched by the
family baby from over the mother's shoulder. But
in some of the big shops one sees lovely designs in
every stage of completion, every member of the family
working at them except the mother, who is always the
saleswoman, and whose bright face and cheery talk
make you willing to part with a few dollars if only
for the sake of the grave ubiquitous baby whose eyes,
from his throne on her back, watch you solemnly, and
seem to take in every detail of the bargain.

Poor Mr. G—— was wired for after two days, and
set off at 4.30 one morning to rejoin the Chief, who
is gasping over cipher telegrams and Treaty Revision
in Tokyo. It cleared off up here, and we had a day's

excursion to Ashinoyu, the sulphurous spring high on the way to Hakone. It was a long climb, through green gorges and up steep mountain-paths ; but when we reached a kind of pass behind the solfatara, I felt that I could breathe at last. There were splendid wide views over the country, and far away a deep-blue line which meant my friend the sea. Ashinoyu is a sad place, full of sick people and terribly strong sulphur fumes, and only stern necessity could induce one to remain there. It is, however, a favourite place with the Japanese, who must be less subject to melancholy than Europeans, I think. They walk about a good deal in the hills, and one comes sometimes on parties of young girls, full of fun and laughter, with flowers in their hands and flowers in their hair, springing along light as young fawns on the hillside.

I met a typical group the other day in the woods. It must have been a family party, since it included a handsome elderly man and two boys, besides two or three girls. It was one of these that I saw first, coming down towards me through the green glades, and a pretty picture she made, though one that might have startled an inexperienced traveller. Her robe of soft blue *crêpe* had been thrown off, and was only held on round the waist by a rich silk *obi*, leaving her arms, shoulders, and bosom bare and white to the daylight. Her slender limbs were incased in tightly fitting white silk gaiters buttoned up to the knee, and the skirts of her *kimono* were kilted high through her girdle. Her head was bare, and the sunbeams came down through

IN THE WOODS.

the leaves on her shining hair and dark eyes, on the sheaf of wild flowers laid in a fold of her naked arm, even on her little feet, bare too, except for light straw sandals tied on with wisps of grass. She stood still for a minute when she saw me, and laughed shyly, and laid down her flowers, and pulled up her *kimono* over her pretty shoulders ; then her brothers and sisters burst through the bushes with cries, and laughter, and flying draperies, and bare young limbs, and the whole band ran away from me through the sunny woods.

In such surroundings there seems nothing shocking or unnatural in seeing young human bodies bare to warm air. At Atami one day I was looking out of my window rather early in the morning, and noticed a pile of brightly coloured garments lying on a wood heap. Nobody was about; but I heard laughter and young voices coming from a tumbledown bath-house near by, and then, swift as light, a slender young girl came running out, the water flying in shining showers from her limbs as she sprang at one bound on the pile of wood; there she stood, naked and unashamed, her arms stretched high above her head, laughing out the joy of her heart to the rising sun, and breathing in all the freshness of the new day. I never saw a more beautiful picture of innocence and happiness.

There are lovely walks round Miyanoshita, though all but one or two involve a good deal of climbing. The view from a spur of the hill behind the Bachelors' Quarters of Fujiya's hotel is quite lovely. A sharp ascent leads to a deserted tea-shed, where one can sit and gaze out towards the sea, with the long low island of Enoshima lying like a dark hull on its bosom; while inland, Fuji's solemn outline dominates the lower hills. The weather is still so warm that I have not felt inclined to push up to Hakone, but was betrayed into visiting the smoking spot called indiscriminately "Ojigoku" (the Greater Hell), or "Owaki-dani"

THE SMOKING VALLEY, OJIGOKU.

(the Valley of the Greater Boiling). There constant clouds of sulphurous smoke break through the thin crust of earth, and come rolling down the gorge; the earth is everywhere hot to the touch ; the rocks are caked grey and yellow with sulphur ; and the fumes are overpowering. I never saw a more awful place. There is a narrow path, where one has to follow the guide very carefully ; in many places the ground on either side will give to the slightest touch, and there have been some frightful catastrophes, owing to the carelessness or incredulity of people who came to visit the sinister spot. A young English girl whom I knew stepped on this treacherous crust, and at once sank in the seething mud which it concealed. She was rescued by her

BAMBOO AND VINE.

companions, and did not lose her life, as some have done ; but she was terribly burnt, and will carry the marks of her accident on her limbs to her dying day.

There is a distinct fascination about the place. We saw it on a grey day, when the sky seemed dark with coming storm ; the air was heavy and breathless, and there was not the slightest current of wind to interfere with the volumes of sullen white smoke, which rose and rolled and curled in a thousand weird shapes in the desolate gorge, where not a blade or leaf can grow. The hill which rises directly behind the boiling valley is clothed in a garment of dense green forest, making a surprising contrast to the scorched foreground of the picture, where everything is white with ashes or crusted with deathly looking sulphur. Japan is certainly richer in hot springs than any other country in the world. They meet you at every turn, and are immensely prized and appreciated by the people.

It was a relief to come down from the horrible choking fumes and ghastly colouring of the boiling valley to friendly Miyanoshita, with its bright shops and sweet wood smells, and its miles of bamboo piping, through which the warm water of the springs is conducted to every inn, almost to every house, in the town. The universal application of bamboo to the needs of man is one of the real successes of Japanese ingenuity. It is always used for conducting water, the sections of its hollow cane fitting tightly and strongly together. Water-cans, basins, boxes, cups are made from segments of the variety which has a solid division at every knot, and which, when mature, lends itself to beautiful polish and carving. Then the building fancies, the garden decoration, the elaborate lattice-work are as charming as they are surprising; and one can hardly believe that the material for all these is supplied by one plant. A bamboo spear is, I am told, one of the most dangerous of weapons, and has been known to transfix two men at once; the leaves serve for more uses than I can mention ; and the new shoots make an excellent vegetable. I used to say that I would only live in the countries where grapes were grown ; it always made me feel forlorn and away from home to be north of the vine line : but I shall miss the bamboo quite as much, I think, when fate says " Shift!" and sends us back to brick houses and leaden pipes and tin utensils, all as costly as they are hideous.

The heat is lessening. Little breezes come up from Odawara and the sea every evening. There are sure to be heavy storms towards the end of the month, and—I think it is time to go home!

Токуо, *September.*

I was glad that I left Miyanoshita when I did ; for just after my departure a violent typhoon came whirling across the country, and did much damage there. That part of the hotel where I had my rooms suffered heavily, many houses were completely wrecked, and everybody was horribly shaken and frightened. The Nabeshimas (Marquis Nabeshima was at one time Japanese Minister in Rome) were staying in the pretty hotel at Kiga, where I had gone in to admire the flowers and the goldfish a few days before. A great part of it was blown off its rock perch, and poor Madame Nabeshima and the children had to be rescued from considerable danger in the dead of night in torrents of rain. Even here in Tokyo, where we were much farther removed from the centre of the storm, the commotion was terrible. Bricks and slates were flying in every direction, trees were uprooted and tossed about like dry leaves, jinrikshas and carriages were blown right over in the streets, and it rained—ramrods!

This is the first bad typhoon that I have seen on land; and though it is certainly less terrible than when it catches one at sea, it is a sufficiently fearful visitation. It seems to have started somewhere far to the north of Japan, and to have found its way to us along the warm current which is our gulf stream, giving us palms and camellias in the open air all through a winter which will keep North China or Jersey City ice-bound for months in the same latitude with us. Truly climate is to a country what environment is to individuals. One has to pay in some way for advantages in both directions; and Japan's gulf stream does not seem dear, even at the cost of an occasional typhoon. The storm moved here at the rate of fifty-eight miles an hour, which was nothing like the velocity at the centre, over a hundred miles away. The incessant roar of the wind and the iron rattle of the rain which always go with it make a serious typhoon intensely fatiguing to live through, and I fancy that it must be accompanied by some acute electric disturbance which tells painfully on the nerves. Sensitive people feel unreasonably depressed at the approach of a typhoon, some hours before it has declared itself; and those who have lived through many such storms tell me that they always feel that stress of personal conflict and final exhaustion which I experienced during the hurricane.

THE HEART OF THE TYPHOON.

At sea it must have been horrible ; some of the skippers
say that they never encountered more awful weather,
and they and their passengers were amazedly thankful
to find that they had really survived it. Of course
all the rivers are in flood, and there has been pitiful
loss of life in the districts where the storm was at
its worst.

CHAPTER IX.

*The Attack on Count Okuma.—Soshi Agitation.
—The Campos Incident.—A Concert and a
Charity.—The Saddest Thing in Japan.—
Father Testevuide and the Leper Hospital at
Gotemba.—Japanese Helpers.*

191

CHAPTER IX.

THE course of Treaty Revision, which was beginning to run a little more smoothly with Count
Okuma's help, has suddenly come to a standstill in a
rather tragic way. Count Okuma, who has been Minister
for Foreign Affairs for several months, is a man of much
intellectual power and resolute character. At one time, I
believe, he was strongly in opposition to the new ideas ;
but he has advanced with the times, and is now accused
by the anti-foreign politicians of yielding too readily to
our demands, and of granting too much in the proposed
treaty, especially as regards the retention of foreign
judges in Japanese courts. I must say, in passing, that
what his countrymen called his absurdly generous terms
were indignantly refused by our people on the ground
of their complete inadequacy to meet our requirements.
Of course poor Count Okuma has not got thus far on
the road of progress without making for himself many
enemies. With the *soshi* he has long been known as
a marked man, and only two months ago one of these
gentlemen, called Koyama Katsutaro, tried several times
to gain admittance to his presence, but was always
prevented from doing so. At last he climbed over the
wall into the garden of the official residence, and

suddenly appeared, as Count Okuma came out of the house to get into his carriage. Koyama asked if that gentleman were the Minister, and the coachman, suspecting evil, answered that he was not. Koyama was promptly arrested, but proved to be unarmed, and after a short time was set at liberty again.

The Cabinet Ministers are always accompanied by one or two detectives, who follow them about in jin rikshas, generally at too great a distance behind the carriage to be of much use, but near enough to mark it clearly to any one looking out for an official victim. All this escort business was annoying in the extreme to Count Okuma, a bold and self-reliant man ; and its uselessness was shown by a sadly practical demonstration a few days ago.

The Count was returning from a Cabinet Council, where there had been a rather stormy debate about Treaty Revision. As the carriage turned into the drive leading up to the house, a quiet-looking, well-dressed young man stepped forward, holding a small parcel rolled up in a violet handkerchief, such as the official employés use for wrapping papers in. Taking aim at the Count, he flung the parcel at him with all his force, and as it exploded cut his own throat and fell dead. The missile did not strike the Count full in the body, as it was meant to do, because the coachman, seeing the man raise his arm, had whipped up the horses, who plunged forward, thus causing the bomb to explode on the side of the carriage ; but the splinters struck Count Okuma's right leg, which was crossed over the left, and shattered his knee. The horses were terrified, and galloped on, but were stopped at the door of the house, and the poor gentleman was lifted out and taken upstairs. He did not lose consciousness or composure for a moment, and was found holding his knee, or what remained of it, with both hands. Some one who was there told me that the wrecked carriage and torn limb presented a terrible sight, but Count Okuma's perfect calmness and cheeriness greatly impressed every one. That the act was inspired by fanaticism was made clear by the suicide of the assassin.

That, in Japanese eyes, was as it should be. It is the correct and gentlemanlike end to such an affair. The excuse being supposed to be pure patriotism, the deed is not complete unless the doer gives his own life with that of his victim. The man who made this attempt seems for a long time past to have contemplated something of the kind; and that the deed was the result of pure fanaticism was shown by his end. When he cut his throat, he did not know whether he had succeeded or not. His name was Tsuneki Kurushima; he was twenty-seven years old, and the son of a former retainer of Count Kuroda. Poor, partially educated, an eager reader of the newspapers, and especially of those which indulge in violent anti-foreign agitation,[1] his brain seems

[1] Some time after these occurrences, I made the acquaintance of the gentleman who was at this time the editor of the *Seiron*, one of the most advanced of the anti-foreign papers. He told me that the proposal to retain foreign judges in the courts of appeal (the arrangement was to be terminable in a few years) roused a storm of feeling in Japan such as even we were unaware of. All patriots looked upon it as an insult to the country's inde-

to have been filled with vague ideas of patriotism, and he used to tell his friends that he was well qualified to die for his country, having no one dependent on him. He had been thoughtful and silent for a few days before making the attack, and evidently looked upon himself as a martyr to his country.

As generally happens in these cases, the outrage has awakened a good deal of indignation, and sent the weight of public sympathy over to the other side of the scale. But among the *soshi* and the Radicals it seems to have roused the anti-foreign feeling somewhat strongly. We are occasionally met by scowling faces in the streets. The other day, as we were driving through a rather rough suburb, a *soshi* insisted on running beside the carriage for a long time, certainly not from friendly feeling. He suddenly disappeared, when we could have handed him over to a policeman ; but, after all, the roads are free, he had committed no greater breach of the peace than my *bettos* do when they run beside the horses' heads, and it would have been absurd to take notice of the small annoyance. I am sorry to say that once or twice stones have been thrown at the carriage ; but here again the offender was some half-grown boy, and it seemed a pity to complicate our

pendence and a direct breach of the Constitution. Although a man of high education and much political acumen, he himself felt it his duty to oppose the measure by every means in his power, but was horrified to hear of the attack on Count Okuma, which was the direct outcome of the agitation.

Needless to say Great Britain had no wish to hamper Japan's independence, but only to protect her own subjects during the time when the Japanese were learning to administer their own laws.

very amicable relations with the Government people by constant small complaints; so, as it only happened when I was driving alone, I held my peace, and have not even told H—— about it. I hate to be kept inside the compound, and so go out as usual; while H—— refuses to take the slightest notice of the agitation, and walks all over the town, quite alone, rather to my terror. Mrs. N——, who was horribly alarmed, poor thing, was wailing to me that we should all be murdered, and added that it was a great grief to her that her husband was nearly the same height as the Chief, "for I am sure they will kill him instead of Mr. Fraser!"

This was such a comforting way of putting things, was it not? I was very

A SOSHI.

angry; but of course I laughed, as I always do when people expect me to look solemn. Mr. G —, who knows more of the Japanese than most people, has made me promise not to use the open carriage, or let the Chief show himself in it, as it makes such a mark for a shot or a bomb. A *soshi* would not

197

attack a tall Englishman face to face on foot, says our friend and adviser, but—we will draw the line at the victoria. So H—— takes his usual walks, and I hear occasional pebbles rattle on the roof of the brougham without undue concern.

But I am very sorry for the Okumas. They are some of the nicest of the people here, and have been so kind and friendly to us since we came. He is cheery and full of talk, and the little Countess a dainty smiling creature, exquisitely dressed, and devoted to her home, and her beautiful gardens at Waseda, which are one of the sights of Tokyo. They say she was as calm and courageous as her husband under the dreadful shock, and is nursing him devotedly. He is getting on well, but has had to lose his leg, as it was too hopelessly shattered to be saved. One has a horribly uncomfortable feeling about the whole thing, a kind of futile and unreasonable self-reproach, because the catastrophe was caused, however indirectly, by our Treaty Revision business.

We had just had a proof of the good dispositions of the Japanese Foreign Office in a tiresome little affair of our own, the settlement of which would have been impossible had they not chosen to be amiable about it—entirely out of personal feeling towards H——, as they took care to explain to me unofficially. I do not know why I was told, for as a rule I keep very clear of talking about business, and confine myself to my own domain. The complication began in the flight from justice of a man called Campos, a Spaniard by birth, but a British subject, who had escaped from Hong Kong, where he was "wanted" on a charge of forgery. The Hong Kong authorities traced him to Kobe, and, without asking H——'s permission, wired to our Consul there to arrest him, which the Consul (also without asking for instructions) managed to do outside the foreign settlement, on Japanese ground. Here was the making of an extremely pretty quarrel by "small sword light." The Japanese naturally protested against our arresting malefactors in Japanese territory; our Extradition Treaty with Japan has not yet been framed, and cannot be thought of till Revision is done with, and I think there was a moment of honest bewilderment on both sides as to what to do with Campos. The papers were noisy, and British jingoes (of whom the East is, alas, full) talked of the fine old days and Sir Harry Parkes, and a week or so went by. Then H—— suggested that a simple plan would be for us to set Campos at liberty, and for the Japanese to rearrest him and politely return him to us for extradition, which was accordingly done, everybody was satisfied, and there was no quarrel left to talk about.

No one can imagine how much trouble our own people sometimes make by their tall talk in peace and their tendency to panic in moments of excitement. Somehow the least educated and weakest are always the most disposed to aggression and interference. The higher class of British merchants less often come to the fore than the smaller men, who always seem glad of a chance to give trouble and stop the course of affairs. There are one or two inferior journals pub-lished in the Yokohama Settlement in order to air the complaints and offer the advice of this class, which reminds me of Samuel Pepys' description of the French when the Spaniards had beaten them in the fight for precedence at St. James's—"Never saw I a people more overbearing in the beginning of an undertaking, or more abject after the failure thereof." I have stopped reading these rags, which always attack us, or the Home Government, or the Emperor, when news is scarce. I can stand intelligent abuse, or good-natured ignorance; but the two nouns in unqualified conjunction make me tired, as the Americans say.

All these commotions have interfered sadly with a particular design of my own, which, being what the sporting papers call "an event," had to come off in the midst of them, and turned out a great success all the same. This was a big charity concert, given in aid of two things—our Leper Hospital at Gotemba, and a much-needed chapel to be built in the Asakusa district. You know how an undertaking of this kind shunts all one's other affairs off on the sidings of life for the moment, and how one gasps with relief when the thing is well over. This concert gave us no end of work, but has turned out a great success, and we have made more money than we expected. The great hall of the Roku-Meikwan, the Nobles' Club, was lent for it, and was beautifully decorated with palms and flowers. Everybody who could play or sing offered their help, and the hall was crowded, in spite of the fact that the concert took place on the day after the attempt on the life of Count Okuma, and that, owing to his critical condition, it was ruled that none of the Diplomatic body would attend. I was much disappointed at not being present, and was also sure that my absence would be misunderstood by my collaborators in the work. However, all went well, and we shall have the satisfaction of sending a good round sum to both our charities. My own sympathies are strongly interested in the little Leper Hospital at

BLIND BEGGARS.

Gotemba, which has already done so much good during its short existence.

The prevalence of leprosy is one of the few sad sides of Japanese life. Through a kind of false shame the authorities refuse to acknowledge the necessity of either providing special hospitals for lepers or of preventing the spread of the disease. It is generally of a very insidious character, and, except for experts, by no means easy to diagnose in its first stages. The lobes of the ears become thick, also the nostrils; there is loss of sensation in the extremities, and the nails begin to shrivel; the face takes on a dark-red colour, and then the fingers and toes gradually disappear; and in some cases the disease stops at this point, and the sufferer may live many years without growing any worse. This is one well-known form of the sickness in Japan; but there are a multitude of cases of the more virulent sort, producing terrible suffering, and an appearance too horrible to be described. The Japanese do not believe in contagion, the caprices of the malady giving a certain amount of excuse for the error. Sometimes it is contracted at the first contact with the sufferer; but in other cases people may live for years in daily intercourse with lepers, and be none the worse. Among the better class it is looked upon as a terrible disgrace, and never called by its proper name, the sufferer being hidden away in the house and tended in secret. Among the lower classes very little notice is taken of the first approach of the disease; but when the unfortunate patient becomes an object of loathing and horror, when he is most in need of care and help, he is cast out to linger on in misery and die an agonising death—alone.

Such cruelty is really foreign to the national character; nowhere is there more help and kindness shown in the family and the tribe than in Japan, and the treatment of the wretched lepers, horrible as it seems to us, can only be put down to the exceeding loathsomeness of the disease itself and the stigma of disgrace that it carries with it. The Japanese doctors regard it as, to a certain extent, curable, and have devoted much science and research to the subject. One in particular, Doctor Goto, has made some successful cures, and the boiling springs of Kusatsu are useful in the earlier stages; but such aids are for those who can pay something for the use of them, and the condition of the pauper leper in Japan remains one of the greatest misery and suffering that any human being can be called upon to endure. One of the Empresses (her name was Kōmyō Kōgo, and she was a devout Buddhist), many centuries ago, touched with pity for this wretched class of her subjects, founded a hospital for them, where, although she was the most beautiful woman of her time, she was not afraid to go every day to wash their sores and attend to their wants. But no trace of her charity remains now. Lepers are received with other sick people in a very few hospitals of the old simple sort,—I was in one not long ago where I saw leprosy, typhoid, and diphtheria in the same ward, but the hospital accommodation is still pitifully insufficient. A few very bad cases of leprosy may be put together for the convenience of tending them; but, roughly speaking, no provision is made for such sufferers, and the University Hospital, directed by Doctor Baelz, the Empress's Charity Hospital, and most of the others very rightly refuse to receive lepers at all. Doctor Baelz inclines to the opinion that the disease, as a rule, is not violently contagious here, and assures me that he would rather share the apartment of a leper than that of a consumptive patient; he also tells me that I probably meet many of the former every time I go out of the compound, so perhaps it is fortunate that I have no special dread of contagions in general, such as induces one of my friends here, a very nervous woman, to use only Apollinaris water for toilet purposes!

DR. BAELZ.

All this being so, you see how great was the need for the little Hospital which was founded, three years ago, by Father Testevuide, one of the French missionaries here. Like many great undertakings, it had a very small beginning. A poor woman, a hopeless leper, cast out by her family, was dying slowly and quite alone in a deserted shed, when Father Testevuide discovered her, naked, blind, going out from the agony of life to the darkness of death. The priest nursed and tended the poor creature, did all he could to lighten her sufferings, and made them more endurable by the hope and promise of a future life beyond the reach of pain. He tried to get her admitted to some hospital, but found it impossible; there was no place for such patients as that.

Then Father Testevuide asked and obtained the Bishop's leave to devote himself to the work of founding a hospital for lepers. A little money was sent to him for charity, and he applied it to this, hiring a small house near Gotemba, a village lying on the lower slopes of Fuji San. All sorts of difficulties had to be overcome. A course of treatment for the patients was recommended by Doctor Goto, who was most kind in letting the Father have what remedies he needed on the easiest terms; but good nourishing food was a part of the cure, and the cost of a patient's treatment could not be brought lower than three yen (about six shillings) a month, and this seemed to be beyond the limits of the income on which the founder could

FATHER TESTEVUIDE.

count. However, he started, taking only six patients, and having the pain of being obliged to refuse constant applications for admittance. Then the Gotemba people got frightened, and asked him to depart from their coasts, and take his sick people with him. It seems that Father Testevuide's landlord was heavily

ON THE ROAD TO GOTEMBA.

in debt, and the village elders threatened to make him pay up unless he turned out the priest and the lepers. But in the end this proved to be a good thing;

for a little more money coming into his hands, the Father succeeded in buying a small piece of land, about six acres in all, on which the Hospital was built. The situation is most beautiful, and the air divinely pure. The spot is so far removed from the village of Gotemba, that there is no question of danger to any of the inhabitants, and yet it is sufficiently central for patients to be easily brought there. A little money has come in from different sources, and has been spent with the exquisite care which I have always noticed in the work of holy people. Twelve hundred dollars (less than one hundred and fifty pounds) has bought the land, built and furnished the house, and provided for the requirements of the patients and employés for three years—and paid for one funeral! Some of those treated have so far recovered that all external signs of the disease have been arrested, and they are able to go out and earn their living. The Fathers say that they themselves do not yet believe in a completely permanent cure, and that all they can say to their convalescents is, " Come back again for treatment the moment you find that the symptoms are showing themselves afresh."

Of course the ground on which the Hospital stands is made to yield the larger part of the food for the inmates ; and those who are strong enough to do so take their share in the work of cultivation, and have the joy of feeling that they help to maintain themselves. The advanced cases are kept apart from the less acute ones ; and, once received, no one is sent away, unless he or she is temporarily cured. For the hopeless it is a home where, until the last minute of life, their sufferings will be alleviated as far as possible, and their hearts cheered by kindness and the hope of a better life. No questions are asked, and the obstinate pagan receives just as much care and tenderness as the born Christian or the convert; but of course the whole atmosphere is warmly Christian. The poor souls for whom faith is pointing to brightness and peace when death shall cure them for good and all—they are eager to bring new-comers in to share the hope which so greatly helps to lighten present suffering. I am sure there will never be a despairing death-bed in the Gotemba Hospital.

The Fathers say that they have found ready help among Japanese Christians for the work of tending the patients. One good man, whose name has at his own request been kept a secret, has shut himself up for life with the lepers, on condition of food being found for his family which he supported by his work. As for Father Testevuide, much has been said about his heroism and goodness, and of course he is constantly compared with Father Damien, the saint of Molokai. The world catches at the name of one good man, and extols it to the skies. We Catholics are rather surprised at the noisy enthusiasm, for we expect these things from our missionary priests. When dear Father Testevuide (whose health is very frail from all his hard work) shall be called home, there will be found many others ready and eager to step into his place.

CHAPTER X.

The Maples at last. The Maple Club. A Reception Day at the Palace. — Manners, Eastern and Western. — Artistic Confectionery. The Maid of Honour's Dolls. Chrysanthemum Gardens. — A Unique Specimen. Flower Groups. — Family Life in the Little Homes. "A Party for making Tea in Old Age."

CHAPTER X.

THE autumn has come at last, and the maples are all on fire. Since one autumn, when I wandered through the New Jersey woods as a tiny child, I have never seen such a gorgeous explosion of colour, such a storm of scarlet and gold. Since the spring brought the white of the plum blossom and the rosy glow of the cherry, the colour has been deepening on the cheek of Nature, and has flushed out strong and high in the sunset of the year. All the gardens are mantled in wide panoplies of the wonderful foliage, which grows in a lovely equable way on the branch, each star-shaped leaf coming well to the surface of the mass, so close that no space between it and its neighbour breaks the stretch of colour, but also well spread forth to the light, none crowded out of the honours of the show. I have been to one temple garden after another, and drive almost daily to Oji, the maple village, which is all alive with Japanese holiday-makers.

That which impresses me most in all these shows is the extraordinary variety of the specimens. I believe our European botanists only admit some twenty species in Japan (America boasts nine in all); but the Japanese subdivide these again and again, and a maple gardener told me that he knew three hundred and eighty separate varieties. Those which please me most are, I think, the kind which grow about ten or twelve feet high, with leaves in five or seven long points, exquisitely cut, and growing like strong fingers on a young hand. They always seem to be pointing to something, and one involuntarily looks round and about to see what it is. They are deep red in colour all the year round, and are constantly grouped with vivid greens, making splendid masses in the shrubberies.

The true autumn maples are quite glorious for these few days during which they last. There is a lovely verse describing them in Chamberlain's book, the classical poetry of the Japanese :

"The warp is hoar-frost and the woof is dew,
Too frail, alas! the warp and woof to be :
For scarce the woods their damask robes endue,
When, torn and soiled, they flutter o'er the lea."

One storm will rob the trees of their splendours till next year. This beauty is their death ecstasy, and I think the very evanescence of its loveliness must have endeared the maple to the hearts of the people. It has come to be one of the emblems of all that is happy and gay and fragile. One sees its starlike outline on festive robes, on wine-cups, in lacquer and in carving. There is a kind of club restaurant in Tokyo called the " Kwoyo Kwan," or Maple Club, where everything is marked with the maple, from the tea-cups and the carved screens to the *musumé's* dresses. Everywhere the leaves seem to have floated and fallen, and all this honour is only on account of their beauty, for they do not carry the symbolic meaning of the pine, the bamboo, and the plum blossom, which are emblematic of long life, strength, and happiness, and are constantly intertwined in decoration.

A gift is often called "a little pine needle" by the giver, and there is a saying that even a humble pine needle is precious if it is given from the heart. The distinctive name for the maple is *momiji*, but the word *kwoyo* is applied by the Japanese to all leaves which change their colour in the autumn (they are called flowers, not leaves, then); and very few other trees make any show when

MAPLES.

the maples are flaunting their gorgeous banners in the autumn sunshine, so the name is used chiefly to designate them. The maple is a thing apart from daily life, and yet constantly referred to, as it were.

A favourite subject with artists is the fall of the leaf
on running water, or down the glassy steeps of
waterfalls, where the red wings swarm and float like
thousands of drowning butterflies.

With the maples have come the chrysanthemums,
the Emperor's flowers, chosen for the crest of the
Imperial Household. Everything at Court is marked
with the round gold mark, which always looks to me
more like the sun than any flower. All the communica-
tions from the Palace come on chrysanthemum paper,
all invitation cards have it heavily embossed in gold,
the Court carriages carry it on their panels, the flunkies
on their liveries.

Thursday is the reception day at the Palace, and
last week I went to call on the *grande maîtresse* and
the Empress's other ladies, who all receive together
in a huge crimson drawing-room, reached through
labyrinths of the glass corridors which I described
to you on the occasion of our audience in May.
Relays of servants are posted along the way, and
one is handed over from one set to the other, till one
reaches a table where a secretary sits with a big book,
into which he copies the names off the cards which
are handed to him by our escort. Two or three
Palace officials stand round the door in the Household
uniform ; but there are never any Japanese gentlemen
in the drawing-room, and the element is so feminine
that European men are rather shy of it, and none
of our own staff will ever go except under my protection. The little ladies are so bright and sweet,

that I prefer these visits to many that I have to make in European houses. They manage very well, too, as to the difficult question of language, so that one need never take an interpreter. The *grande maîtresse*, Viscountess Takakura, is a gentle pale woman, always dressed in some shade of pansy or mauve. She speaks no foreign language, nor does Countess Muromachi, her next in command. This lady is a little older than the others, and is much loved and respected by both the Emperor and Empress, who are said often to take her advice on important matters. She wears soft dove-coloured satins as a rule, while the younger women affect pale blues, water-greens, and rosy greys. Black is not worn at the Palace, except during a Court mourning.

These younger ladies do the interpreting for the others. Two, Miss Kitajima and Miss Kagawa, have travelled a good deal, and speak English fluently. Another, a charming girl, with almost a European type of beauty, has been in France, and talks French well ; and yet another can speak some German. So no one need be tongue-tied on these occasions. It has sometimes happened to me to wish that the Japanese ladies understood less than I imagine they do of foreign languages ; for some of our colleagues' wives affect an almost brutal rudeness towards them, speaking of them in their presence with sublime contempt, and complaining loudly of an official visit, which perhaps has broken up a more amusing conversation. When, horror-struck, I have expostulated, the

reply has been, " Bah, elles n'y comprennent rien!"
I was paying a visit at one of the Legations, when
a Japanese great lady, Princess S——, was announced,
and immediately followed the servant who announced
her. It was my hostess's reception day, and she
should have had a competent interpreter at hand,
as we are all supposed to do on these occasions.
Therefore the Princess, although she can speak no
foreign tongue, had not brought one with her. As
she entered the room our hostess threw her arms in
the air with an expression of despair, and exclaimed
(I had better not say in what language), " Good
Heavens, what am I to do with this creature! What
an odious bore! Where is So-and-so (the interpreter)?
Somebody run and find him! Could anything be
more tiresome?" All this was said at the top of her
voice, with gestures which must have made the meaning
only too clear to the dignified woman who was thus
outrageously received. I did what very little could be
done to save the situation; and Princess S——, like the
true lady she is, pretended not to understand it for
the few minutes during which she remained. I fled
when she said what I fancy will be a long good-bye
to our hostess, and for the first time in my life I
blushed at being a European.

I met this adornment of diplomacy coming away
as I was advancing along the Palace corridor on
Thursday, and did not get past her without having
to hear some noisy criticisms on the manners of the
women she had just left, and who, by the way, have

loaded her with kindness. Manners! If they were—as in a measure they may be—the passport to heaven, the Japanese women would certainly have reserved places, and many a "smart" European would have to take a back seat. Kindness and modesty, a wakeful, real consideration for the

MAPLE LEAVES.

feelings of others—surely these make up for a little unwilling ignorance of the higher subjects which most interest us, and which, to tell the truth, are hardly better known to the "smart" European with her social preoccupations and her rattle of "chaff," than they are to the little hothouse ladies of the Palace.

But this is digression, and I wanted to tell you how amused I was to find that all the sweetmeats of these Household tea parties must represent nothing but the flowers and fruits and leaves in season. On Thursday last the cake plates were filled with every variety of maple leaf, made in sugar and variously flavoured, but so perfectly moulded and coloured that it would be difficult to detect the imitation from the real leaf. Large and small, pale pink, deep crimson, green and orange, with three leaves, or five, or seven, they were piled on the delicate china in such artistic fashion that I could not refrain from an exclamation of pleasure when they were offered to me. With them were autumn grasses and tiny wild chrysanthemums, just the handful of loot that a nature lover would bring back from a walk in the woods.

The maids of honour laughed merrily at my surprise, and told me that the Empress will only eat the most airy of these delicate sweets ; so that the Court confectioner has come to be a great artist at producing them. Then nothing would do but that I must take some home with me ; and in spite of my protest, a sheet of Palace paper (thickly crinkled, and heavy as watered silk) was fetched, and a large assortment of the bonbons was picked out by half a dozen dainty hands, wrapped up, and confided to a servant to be put in my carriage.

One day in October, after I came back from Miyanoshita, I thought I would go and see one of these ladies, although the regular reception days would not begin till after the Emperor's birthday, November 3rd. I went alone, and asked for Miss Kitajima Itoko, with whom I had made friends before we all broke up for the summer. The servant took my card, and was away a long time, while I sat in the carriage, waiting to know whether the lady was at home. At last he returned, and invited me to enter; and I followed, thinking to be received in the usual red drawing-room. But the man beckoned me past its closed doors, and I followed him on and on, through corridors and across courtyards, and finally up a long flight of rather narrow stairs, which I was surprised to see, as the Palace possesses no visible upper story. Here I was shown into a small sitting-room, papered in pale blue, inhabited by an—army of dolls! No other word will describe the collection, ranged all round the walls in glass cases which stood out quite a yard into the room, and ran up some eight or nine feet in height. A crimson carpet, a few black-wood chairs, a window shut in with paper screens like those in an ordinary Japanese house—that was all that the room contained, except the dolls; and they were so amazing that I hoped I should be left alone with them for a long time. Many of these weird creatures were life size, and so real that I felt as if I must have got into some corner of the Palace which was sleeping a charmed sleep through these times of change and trouble. There were tall Daimyos, with impassive masks, dressed in stiff white robes like cere-cloths. Their fine bluish fingers seemed to be pointing at me in scorn; their black eyes gleamed in the subdued light; and their black hair seemed to bristle under the strange conical caps, blacker even than the hair, and tied under their chins with forbidding black bands. Beside them were lovely women (I cannot help speaking as if they were living creatures), in poses light and dreamy as the swaying of the lotus stems moved by water. Their faces were pale and sweet, and there was a kind of tragic grace in the bent heads, the slender, submissive hands held out in supplication towards their lords. One or two were kneeling, one lying down, all in robes stiff with gold and brilliant in colour. Among these life-sized images were crowds of smaller ones, some gorgeously dressed, some simple old dolls such as any child would love. A few European dolls, horrible mechanical gimcracks in tarnished finery, were given places of honour among the nobles and princesses, who seemed too sad to resent the elbowing of the parvenus from over the water. The room itself was still as death, and I was all alone with the silent inhabitants, enclosed as in a glass tomb ; while outside, the ripple and murmur of life hummed through the great Palace ; voices of children at play came close to me, on which side I could not tell, and then tinkled away in the distance. A *koto* was being played in one of the near rooms ; there were outbursts of girlish laughter, as sweet and full as the songs of mounting larks, which came and went with a patter of sandals and brushing of drapery along the corridors ; and across my paper screen (which opened to some balcony flooded with sunshine) shadowy forms came and went, a young head beautifully dressed, a branch of leaves, or the outline of a delicate hand was laid for a moment on the paper. All the place seemed busy and warm as a hive of bees in the sun— all but the silent heart of it where I sat gazing at the portrait-images of long-dead men and women.

Then the slide opened, and Miss Kitajima, in a

tightly fitting European gown, came in, and the atmosphere of romance shrivelled up, and left me rather cold in the light of the *fin-de-siècle* day. I asked, of course, about the dolls; but my friend was not communicative, and seemed a little ashamed of them. "They are dolls, foolish things," she said; and at once turned the conversation to some other subject. And I came away disappointed and puzzled, as this is not the time of year for the dolls' festival, which takes place in March, "on the third day of the third month."

The Emperor has been ill, so there is to be no garden party at the Asakusa Palace, and I shall not see the Imperial chrysanthemum show this year. I am sorry; but I believe some of the public exhibitions are nearly as good, and these I have been visiting carefully. As far as the beauty of the flowers themselves is concerned, I give the palm to those which develope naturally and make masses of bloom growing in their own characteristic way, as they are allowed to do in Europe. But for masterly cultivation, for the triumph of human laws over those of nature, for results which look as if they could only have been wrought by magic, the Japanese gardeners certainly take the palm.

The chief place for chrysanthemum gardens is a village or rather a suburb of Tokyo, called Dango-Zaka. To reach it one drives through miles of quiet ways, bordered with gardens of every kind, whose low bamboo fences with their tyings of black string make a pretty hedging to the brown road, all flecked with sunshine through the overarching boughs, which are getting thin in these autumn days. In the village, and indeed long before you reach it, every gate leads into a garden, where, by paying two sen, you may

THE GOD OF LIGHTNING.

walk about and look at group after group of historical or mythological figures—all made out of chrysanthemums! Here, at the turn of a path, is a shed built in pretty white wood, open in front, and lined, sides and ceiling and floor, with a pattern resembling old damask, all worked in living flowers, which, having been put in place with their roots behind them, bloom and flourish happily for weeks in these unnatural positions, refreshed by an occasional spraying of water. On a raised bridge inside the shed is a group representing a scene in Japanese mediæval history, in which the hero Yoshitsune has a fierce duel with the strong man, Benkei. The masks and hands of the figures are in carved and painted wood, the expression of the faces is brilliant, fierce, and lifelike, and the hands are beautifully fine and true. The costumes of the warriors are all made in growing chrysanthemums, every detail of the armour being recognisable. The

railings of the bridge are also made of flowers. For
this kind of living embroidery only the small-flowering
chrysanthemum is used, its thick masses of white
or red or yellow lending themselves kindly to these
strange uses.

But the gardens are not without beautiful specimens
of single plants. One of these was trained in the shape
of an umbrella, the single stem rising straight for about
six feet from the ground, and being of the same thickness from top to bottom. At the top a number of shoots,
starting with perfect regularity from the same point, fell
downwards, forming a dome of about three feet in
diameter. It was edged by a fringe of pale-pink
chrysanthemums in full bloom, each hanging from the
end of a shoot; three inches farther up was a perfect
ring of blossoms slightly less opened, all arrested at the
same point of development; three inches farther up,
another ring of just opened buds; and close to the
stick, a small circle of green balls, buds which showed
no sign of colour. Apart from its uncanny artificiality,
the thing was beautiful, and probably represented the
patient labour of several years.

The crowd of Japanese sight-seers seemed more
inclined to stare at us than at heroes or chrysanthemum umbrellas, and followed us as we went on to the
other pictures, which Ogita explained to me in his
quaint way. Under one shed was a little pond, which
was supposed to represent a stormy ocean, out of
which a fearful bogy, with horns and tusks and red
hair hanging down to his knees, had risen with a

pitchfork to frighten some quiet travellers who were crossing the sea in the lightest of skiffs—all made of flowers, of course. The passengers represented Yoshitsune and some of his adherents trying to reach the shore, and kept back by a fearful storm roused by the

THE SHIP OF HAPPINESS.

ghost of an enemy whom he had killed in war. He had taken the precaution to bring a holy exorcist with him; and this figure, with a long white beard and venerable countenance, was standing up in the boat, regardless of balance, praying that the demon might be overcome.

In another picture a faithful wife has thrown herself between her sleeping husband and the sword of an enemy, who is stabbing him from behind a paper screen. The masks of the women are far less artistic than those of the men in these groups, denoting subtly the Japanese ideals of male and female beauty. A man should have a fierce, strong expression, and many masks overstep all the limits of art and show the most grotesque contortions of rage and hate ; but the female faces are absolutely smooth and expressionless, even when represented in the most exciting circumstances. The only sign of tragedy is the absence of the smile which a Japanese woman is supposed always to wear for her family and friends. She may cease to smile in heavy grief, but no spasm of pain or anxiety must appear on the fair face with its downcast eyes ; the countenance must be unlined by the invisible harrow of thought, unstained by tears, unthrilled by emotion. If I painted a sphynx, I should be strongly tempted to make her face that of an ideal Japanese woman. No stone mask could be more impenetrable.

But I must describe to you the finest of the show pieces which I saw at Dango-Zaka, and of which I have obtained a photograph from a friend. This was an enormous ship, the ship of happiness, as Ogita explained ; and in it were seated some of the cheeriest-looking divinities I ever saw—the six gods of riches. On the prow was Benten Sama, the beautiful benevolent goddess who has eight arms, so that she can help on sea as well as on land, and give precious gifts to men according to their capacity for receiving them. Her companions are broad-faced smiling personages, Dai-Koku of the big cars and the rice-bags, the white-bearded, peach-shaped god of old age (a very old acquaintance of mine in Peking), and others whose faces are less familiar to me. Everywhere the work is the same, a fine patient flower mosaic built into great lines and bold shapes. One, a god of lightning, I think, was really full of splendid "go" and vitality. The contrast between the violent distortions of the masks and the calm impassive faces of the people who come to gaze at them is rather curious. Of course all the little gardens are crowded with visitors, chiefly of the middle and lower classes. How people who have to earn their living can find time for all this holiday-making is a puzzling question. Perhaps one answer to it is that, with few exceptions, shop life is family life. No one is bound to work so many hours a day. The staff consists of the family, with perhaps an apprentice or two ; and if the tailoring, or fan-making, or mat-weaving tasks have not been accomplished in the day, the whole family will sit round the one lamp at night and make up for lost time.

Now that the days are drawing in, it is one of my great pleasures to drive home after night has fallen on the city. Then the little interiors are lighted up, and yet left open to the street, because the autumn days are mild still, and because the Japanese kitchen, consisting as it does of a hole in the middle of the floor, where the fire crackles and smokes gaily, makes it convenient to leave the screens open as long as possible. I am often out rather late (you know the

THE EVENING MEAL.

confidential moment at the end of a friend's reception day, when the outsiders have all gone and the intimates really begin to talk!), and as I come home there is a little bustle of preparation for the evening meal going on in almost every home. Here the family of some prosperous tradesman is getting round the *hibachi*. The old grandmother mends the fire, glad of an excuse to be so near the flame. The mother, young and smiling, waits on her husband; while the family idol, the only child probably, laughs and chatters, and insists on being served first, much to the father's amusement. The children rule everything in the little homes— and are not a bit spoilt. When they come to what is considered the age of reason (anywhere between six and ten), they abdicate their sovereignty of their own accord, and seem to grow up in a day; for they at once begin to take their share of the family work, and smile indulgently, just as their elders do, at the baby ways and make-believe tempers of their successors on the throne.

Sometimes there are no children, and one sees a pale woman resolutely turning her head from the sight of the little ones over the way. She must have lost a child, and that little plate of dainties that she is putting aside—tiny morsels of fish and *daikon* and rice—will be placed before the wooden tablet which bears the little one's dead name—the name given at birth is left here with the worn-out garments, the tiny ravelled sandals, and the broken toys; and the soul, new born to another phase of immortality, is given a new name at its passing, that by which it

came and went in this world finding its fitting grave
in the silence of the mother's heart.

Almost sadder is the glimpse of two old folk, grey
and faithful, sitting beside a fire whence all the children
have gone; the old woman nursing a cat in a solemn
frilled collar, and the old man smoking as he stares at
the flame. Or it may be that he is one who, left alone
in his old age, looked round among his friends and
acquaintances till he found and married a widow as
lonely as himself, glad to cheer his and her own declining
years by the kindly companionship which the Japanese
call, " A party for making tea in old age !" I see many
such pictures of humble married faithfulness, as I pass
in the darkness of the street—many little homes so
poor that thieves would find nothing there to steal,
and yet whose indwellers seem very rich in peace
and kindliness. Truly the best things in the world
have no market and no price.

CHAPTER XI.

*The Empress-Dowager and her Mushroom-
hunting.—Mushroom Picnics on Inari-Yama.—
The Tosa Monkeys.—The Prince Imperial and
the Ceremony called* Rittaishi.—*A Sword of
State.—Count Yamagata.—Prince and Princess
Sanjo.—The Five Regent Families.*

CHAPTER XI.

Tokyo, *November*, 1889.

I WAS much amused a little while ago to hear that the Empress-Dowager was leaving Tokyo, and taking a journey of several hours' duration, so as to enjoy some good—mushroom-hunting! The Empress-Dowager does not show herself in public, and is, I believe, an ardent adherent of the old modes of life and thought in Japan. I cannot find any foreigner who has seen more than the outside of her *norimono*, or closed palanquin; I know her Grand Master of Ceremonies, and one or two Japanese who belong to her especial Court, and they wear an habitual expression of disapproving reserve, of patient deprecation, which has the effect of a dumb protest against changes of any sort, and more especially against the admission of the *stultus vulgus*, the profane foreigner, into the sacred precincts of Japanese life. Perhaps they are chosen for their dignified offices because their peculiar views harmonise with those of the royal lady; perhaps they have imbibed them through intercourse with her, for I have often noticed that the opinions of great personages are extremely contagious. Be that as it may, a high wall of conservative precedent is built round the Empress-Dowager; and when one expresses a desire to see her, one is met by a mournful shake of the head and dead silence, as if to mark the hopeless temerity of the wish. She must be kind and benevolent; for when we had our charity concert for the Leper Hospital and the new chapel, she took thirty tickets, and a message came with the contribution to the effect that her Majesty was much interested to hear of the Leper Hospital, and wished it all success.

Having grown accustomed to the idea of an elderly lady living in absolute retirement, I was rather amused at the thought of her running about the slopes of Kanayama hunting for mushrooms; but I find, on looking into the matter, that this has always been considered as a kind of artistic sport, especially near Kyoto, where the fruit (or is it flower?) grows in great abundance. The following account of mushroom parties comes from the kind Japanese friend who has answered so many of my tiresome questions. It seems that there are many kinds of edible mushrooms in Japan: the *shi-také*, which grows on decayed oak trees; the *kikurage* (literally "wooden mollusc"), found on mulberry trees; the *sho-ro* (dew of the pine), which can only live on the sand of pine woods close to the sea. But in the hunting parties only one specimen is sought after, the *matsu-také*, which, as its name implies, grows among the splendid pine trees of the hills. The *matsu-také* has a strong pungent flavour; and the soil of some of the pine woods is so highly impregnated with the spawn, that a little of it put down in woods where no mushrooms grow will at once render the ground abundantly fruitful. Inari-Yama, the mountain of the fox-god, near Kyoto, yields wonderful harvests of *matsu-také*; and there the little foxes are the worst enemies of the dainty weed.

The time for mushroom parties is the autumn, when the summer heats are over, and what the Japanese call the *ko haru*, or lesser spring, hangs over the land for a few weeks. Then the rains have ceased, the mornings are gloriously fresh, the lengthening nights chilly; but the sun is still strong in the day, and the sky clear and blue. Then the pleasure-loving people of Kyoto say one to another, " Let us go out and behold the autumn woods, which are beautiful as ripe and healthy age. Let us walk on pine needles and quote poetry, and let us also gather and roast the *matsu-také*, for its time has come."

So a party is made up, men and women agree to leave all cares behind for a day, and in the freshness of the autumn morning they start for the pine woods of the hills. First come the men, walking all together, dressed with extreme care, for mushroom-hunting has a prescribed costume, and must be as rigorously correct as if one were going to court. A distinctive feature of the men's dress is the wearing of tight-fitting green silk leggings, or *patchi*, which are freely displayed when the upper robe is pulled high through the girdle to leave the limbs free. The women follow the men, in a group by themselves, in costumes of which every detail is carefully in accordance with the proper traditions. Their gaiters are of white silk, joining the *tabi*,

A REFLECTION.

or sock, just above the ankle; the girls wear narrow under-skirts of pure scarlet, the married women embroidered ones of white or purple silk, and these flutter like anemones when the *kimono* is kilted through the *obi* for freer movement. The little ladies' hair is elaborately dressed, but is covered now with a tiny white towel, *tenugui*, carefully folded, which keeps the dust from dimming the lustrous sur-face, or the pine boughs from catching in the coils. Behind the women come the servants, carrying *bento*, or food-boxes, and gourds, beautiful polished things, often highly carved, full of saké to refresh the seekers after their labour. Gourds and boxes are, of course, slung on the ever-present bamboo. Everybody laughs and talks, the clever ones ex-change quotations, and elaborate puns, to which the intricacies of the language readily lend themselves. On they go, through the solemn woods, till they have reached a spot, sheltered, dry, thickly carpeted with pine needles, which will answer as a dining-hall. Here the servants are left to prepare things, and the party break up and go off in many directions after the object of the day. Some go alone, some in twos (for human nature must be allowed its preferences even on Inari-Yama), and every one hopes to bring back a notable harvest to add to the general store. The dainty things grow quite hidden under the carpet of pine needles; so these have to be pushed aside in the search, and then the strong sweet odour of the brown earth comes floating up on the warm air. Little fingers get sadly stained in this digging process; but nobody cares as long as the basket is filled. It must be a pretty sight to see the bright-coloured garments waving in the breeze or catching on boughs, as the girls dart to and fro like the butterflies of which some of their own poets write—the " butterflies who come in the early summer to seek in the deep green places for the last red blooms of spring." Some of the girls do not take baskets, but string the mushrooms one by one on a brown pine needle, whose ends are joined into a ring, and slipped over their fingers till the small hands can carry no more.

Then little by little they all come back to the trysting-place, where the servants, while waiting, have gathered pine twigs and needles together to make the fire over which the mushrooms must be cooked. Saké and rice and other food is provided; and I know without being told that the dishes will be ornamented with pine twigs and needles too. The seekers come in with their spoils, and those who have gathered much are congratulated, while those who have made a poor harvest apologise in mock humility for their stupidity and awkwardness, which render them unworthy to be members of such a distinguished party. Then begins the business of roasting the mushrooms, in which everybody helps; and great enthusiasm is shown over the delicious odour they give out. " Ii nioi ! Ii nioi de gozaimasu ! " (Good smell ! Honourably good odour !) exclaim the ladies, as they deftly peel the outer skin off the toasted fruit, which is then shred into small pieces, flavoured with *shoyu* (soy) and vinegar, and eaten with *o'hashi*, the honourable chopsticks. People are hungry, for the autumn air is keen in the brown woods ; so they declare there is nothing in the world so delicious as a mushroom toasted over a pine fire. When they are satisfied, the larger part of the " take " is carefully packed away in baskets, or *furoshiki* (crape wrappers, in which every kind of thing may be carried), to take home to relations and friends.

If a storm comes on in the night preceding a mushroom party, the expedition must be put off; for the thunder (so say the Japanese) destroys the *matsu-take*, and after a thunderstorm hardly one will be found. My friend suggests laughingly that the thunder-god, Raijin, comes and picks them all for himself; but this explanation does not quite seem to cover the case.

In one province, Tosa, whole trees are cut down expressly to make a bed for the mushroom called *shi-take*, which will only grow on the bark of oak trees ;

A MUSHROOM PICNIC.

and when these are sufficiently rotten to produce the fungi, a keeper is put in charge to see that the precious things are not stolen, and that the monkeys do not carry them all away. The Tosa oak woods are full of monkeys, who feed on the *ki-no-ko* (the " child of the wood," as all fungi are called in that part of Japan) greedily and destructively. If a keeper surprises these marauders at their feast, they turn in rage, and tear to pieces all the mushrooms they can reach before they finally make their escape, chattering angrily among the pine trunks.

I am no longer surprised to hear that the Empress-Dowager has gone mushroom-hunting, and I wish I had been asked to join the party !

Prince Haru has been solemnly installed as heir-apparent, having completed his tenth year on Sep-

THE MONKEY WHO STOLE THE MUSHROOMS.

tember 6th. The *Rittaishi*, as this ceremony is called, was put off until the birthday of the Emperor, November 3rd, and was then carried out in the Palace according to the old custom. It seems that it is not enough to be born heir to the throne in Japan. The young Prince must be officially recognised by his father, and presented to the nation as such. The reason of this, I imagine, may be found in the fact that until our own times it was not a matter of course that a man's eldest son should succeed to his father's titles and property. A younger child, or an adopted son, or an uncle or brother might be designated as the heir; and Japanese history gives countless examples of the exercise of the privilege, which has given rise to many a blood feud hardly healed to-day. In such circumstances a public declaration of the heir to the throne would almost seem to be a necessity; but there is much more than that in this ceremony of the *Rittaishi*—much which is intended to impress the child himself with the fact that manhood is not far off, and that already he must prepare himself to take up its duties and responsibilities. The Empress sent the little Prince two sets of pictures, symbolic of the happiness she wished for him, and the

THE STORK.

brave heart he must have if he would succeed in attaining to it. Among the drawings illustrative of happiness, one represents the god of happiness accompanied by his attribute, a white stag; others the pine for strength, the stork for long

THE CARP.

life, the tortoise for riches, and so on. The second set deals with sterner subjects: a hawk symbolises courage; a bear in snow, endurance; a carp swimming up the waterfall is the emblem of perseverance. Although the Empress is not Prince Haru's mother, she is said to have a great affection for him, and one hears of his paying her visits pretty constantly.

The Emperor gave his son the Sword of State which he himself received on a like occasion many years ago. No great pomp accompanied the ceremony, and no Foreign Representatives were invited to be present, at what would be considered a purely religious and family affair, were not the boy a Prince and his affairs therefore the business of the nation. A salute of one hundred and one guns was fired at midday, and a paragraph in a gilt flourish appeared in the *Official Gazette* about his being confirmed in the title of

heir-apparent. At the Nobles' School, however, where the Prince has many young friends, fireworks went on all day in the beautifully decorated gardens, and there were rather extensive illuminations in the city. The little Prince is now entitled to wear the uniform of a second lieutenant in the First Life Guards (how odd it sounds over here!) and the Grand Cross of the Chrysan-

THE PRINCE IMPERIAL, AT A RECENT DATE.

themum, and his household is put on a more cere- monious and increased footing. A good deal of interest attaches to the sword given him by the Emperor. It is very beautiful, and has been handed down for so many generations in the Imperial family that the date of its forging and the origin of its strange name, Tsubo Kiri (the jar-cutter), are completely lost. The name of the maker is Amakuni, who wrote on the blade that he made it at the command of an Emperor unnamed. The Amakuni family have made all the Imperial swords since the year 701, when the Visigoths were still ruling in Spain, and the seven Saxon kingdoms had not yet been united; so that date does not give much clue to the age of the blade. It is about two feet long, double-edged, with a guard of pure gold, and a handle inlaid with mother-of-pearl, and, as is fitting, it lives in a case of gold brocade. There is to be some sword-forging soon at one of the art exhibitions, and I hope to see the Amakuni at work.

I have looked at a few Japanese swords, and can realise a little what it must be to see them flashing thirstily in the sunshine of a fight. Beautiful and terrible are the only words to apply to them. The perfection of the steel, the blue lights that shoot down its glorious surface, the weight of life and death in the blade, and the exquisite, almost tender beauty of the bird or wave or blossom worked in the gold and bronze of the guard—all make it for me the very manifestation of strength and loveliness, the word by which Matter speaks as man and woman both.

A kind of lull has fallen on the political world since the attack on Count Okuma, which, though apparently the act of an isolated fanatic, was at any rate syn-chronous with a kind of panic about the foreign owner-ship of land involved in the proposed Revision of the Treaty. It is significant that several bombs precisely like the one thrown at him have been discovered by the police in Yokohama. That they are made in the country is evident, because two of them were broken up, and were found to contain scraps of Japanese newspapers crushed in among the explosives. The bombs are now supposed to have been charged with dynamite which was recently stolen from some public works. There is a kind of revolutionary club of young Japanese in San Francisco, and people at first suggested that the missile thrown at Count Okuma had been manufactured there and brought across for this purpose, the beauty and finish of the workmanship making it appear unlikely that it could have been made by quasi-amateurs here. But the fragments of newspapers in its newly found companions seem to prove that it was a home-made article after all. Count Okuma is recovering well; but it will be some time before he can take up his work again, and I fancy he will resign as soon as any one can be found courageous enough to step into his place. We are bombarded with telegrams from home, where they want Treaty Revision done with as soon as possible (it has only been on the Chancery table for fourteen years!); but the Japanese seem afraid to touch it, and are making an excuse of Count Okuma's accident to let it lie, until, so to speak, the smoke of Kurushima's bomb has cleared away. The Acting Minister for Foreign Affairs, Viscount Aoki, will probably take Count Okuma's place if he resigns. Viscount Aoki has lived many years in Berlin, and is married to a German lady, and their house is one of the pleasantest here. He is supposed to be a great advocate of progress, and I have had one or two very interesting talks with him about his country people. He said to me one day, in regard to the anti-foreign agitation: " The whole trouble arises in the ignorance of the people (as to foreigners and their aims); until that is dispelled, the work of progress cannot be thorough. The enlightened classes are almost all on the side of progress; this is a revolution started by the Court and the aristocracy, and opposed by the lower classes. When they have learnt their lesson, we can do our work." Count Ito has resigned the post of President of the Council, Count Kuroda has ceased to be Prime Minister, and Prince Sanjo has very unwillingly taken his place as leader of the Cabinet. That must be an extremely arduous post, since the present policy of the Government is to include all well-known statesmen in the Cabinet, irrespective of opinions

VISCOUNT AOKI.

and party. I should think there might be some lively sittings. This Utopian arrangement was advised by Count Kuroda, who now retires, having found it impossible to keep that place with such a political opponent to manage as Count Yamagata, who has at last declared himself against the treaty programme as it now stands.

Count Yamagata was requested to hurry back from Europe a little while ago (he had been filling a Diplomatic post) in order to deal with Treaty Revision, *soshi*, and various minor questions. After his arrival and

entrance into the Cabinet, he maintained a strict silence
for some time, unwilling to criticise the actions of his
colleagues, who were generally in favour of a rapid
conclusion of the question. At last, however, he spoke ;
and being a man of great intellect combined with
strength of character, his dictum carried such weight
that the Ministers above-mentioned felt that they must
either work on his lines or retire from the Cabinet.
Count Kuroda retired ; Count Okuma has practically
done the same, although no public announcement has
been made of the fact ; and every one expected to see
Count Yamagata take the leadership, from which Count
Ito and Count Kuroda had retired in succession. But
that he has refused to do, foreseeing probably the
very difficulties which led to the withdrawal of his
predecessors. A Cabinet which may not be composed
of one party for fear of giving dangerous offence to
the others, but where the old clan spirit is still strongly
alive, creating a gulf between the Satsuma and the
Choshiu peers, who must be included in fair proportions ;
public opinion against the treaty programme, and the
Government to a great extent pledged to the Foreign
Representatives to carry it out,—all this Count Yamagata
found, to use a slang term, not good enough, and
remains a Privy Councillor. Poor Prince Sanjo, who
thought he had entered into peace some years ago (in
1885), has been peremptorily ordered by the Emperor
to take the command of the political battalion. He
begged in vain to be excused ; but there was no one
else to be put forward, and he finally accepted under

protest, with a rather touching entreaty that "his Majesty would quickly find some person to replace him in a position for which he had neither the strength nor the inclination."

Prince Sanjo's health is delicate, and he gives me the impression of a man who is sadly bored with politics. He falls to my lot at many of the big entertainments, and is always so kind and amiable that I like to have him for a neighbour, although he speaks no foreign tongue. We smile over bouquets and *menus*; he tells me the Japanese names for all the rare fruits and flowers; and when we have to walk in the little official processions, we try to be dignifiedly unconscious of the funny appearance we must present—I looking taller than ever in the absurd trains we are expected to wear here, and he a mass of gorgeous decorations, his head not nearly reaching to my shoulder.

Princess Sanjo is quite charming, though extremely plain. She is conscious of this, poor lady, and the other day asked a friend of mine to tell her in confidence whether there were any women in Europe as ugly as herself. She has a daughter who is extraordinarily handsome, and who speaks English well. The Princess just missed being Empress instead of the Princess Haruko Ichijo, who was finally chosen for that honour. Both ladies belonged to the Regent families of the Fujiwara clan, from whose ranks the wives of the Emperors must always be selected. There are five of these princely families (the group

is called in Japanese *Go Sekke*, Five Regent Houses),
and their respective names are Ichijo, Nijo, Kujo,
Konoye, and Takatsukasa. In the modern classification
of the nobles, they were created Dukes; but as I have
shown, they are called Princes in the official lists. The
title Prince Sanjo now bears was bestowed upon him
as a reward of merit for great services rendered at the
time of the restoration of power to the Emperor. Prince
Sanjo was then Prime Minister, and greatly endeared
himself to his sovereign by the splendid assistance he
rendered to his cause. His marriage with Princess
Haruko (her name is the same as that of the Empress)
was a mark of Imperial favour, as it constituted an
alliance with the reigning family, although not one which
can furnish heirs to the throne. If Princess Sanjo's
daughter marries one of the Imperial Princes, as she
probably will, I shall have to make *plongeons* before her,
and treat her as a royalty. Now she sits in a corner of
my drawing-room on reception days, nibbling bonbons and
talking nonsense with all the other girls. Her father is
building a beautiful European house in Azabu, and meanwhile they are living in their very simple Japanese home,
a low house surrounded by mournful yews. The rooms
are small, but have beautiful carved lattices in their
divisions; the foot sinks noiselessly into the silky
floor-mats; and there is an old-time silence and
stateliness about the place which suits the inhabitants
better than the white marble house on the hill can
ever do, I think.

CHAPTER XII.

Sir Edwin Arnold, a Baby, and the Japanese Grammar. —How Countess Kuroda's Portrait was painted.—" Very Old, over Twenty." My Second Visit to Atami.—A Vision of Fuji.— Forgotten Medals.—The Attack on the Legation in 1861.

CHAPTER XII.

DID I tell you in my last letter of the delightful surprise we had, in the way of a visit from Edwin Arnold and his daughter? These last weeks have been very full, as you will see presently; but these guests were of the sort who refresh your few leisure moments, and take care of themselves in your busy ones.

I knew how the poet would enjoy his first visit to Japan, and I wanted to see him enjoy it; so he stayed with us for some little time, and fell so much in love with Tokyo that he has taken a house for six months, where he insists on sleeping on the mats Japanese fashion, much to his daughter's horror. He was brought here, he says, by that enchanting book, Chamberlain's *Colloquial Japanese*, which came under his notice in America. After he had read a few sentences, he decided that it was absolutely necessary to visit this land of glorified politeness, where, if phrases are to be believed, a man would honourably sacrifice his own soul, his wife, and children, and all his belongings rather than be convicted of a breach of etiquette. The book which proved such a bait for the great Sanskrit scholar was carefully studied on the journey

across the Pacific, in a sheltered corner near the funnel,
whence Sir Edwin, I am told, only emerged at stated
intervals to take charge of a certain small baby, whose
weary mother thus got a few moments for rest and
food. He says that sometimes the baby was good, and
then he would walk up and down with it on one arm,
learning Japanese phrases from the book held open
with the other hand. When the baby was fretful, it
took his whole attention, and had the Japanese good-
night crooned to it, "Oyasu mi nasai!" (To receive
sleep condescend). The pair must have made an
amusing picture; and I can believe the story is true,
for our servants' children, shy with most people, have
made friends readily with the poet of the grey hair
and the kind eyes still so full of the blue fire of youth.
He made such use of the handbook, that he can
speak to the children in their own language, much to
their delight.

I called him in the other day to see Countess
Kuroda, who had come, by appointment, in a lovely
Japanese dress, to have her portrait painted by Mr.
Walter S. Landor, who is staying in the compound
at "Number Two," the N——s' house. It sounds
rather a complicated method of having one's portrait
painted, does it not? But there was no other way
to manage it. The little Countess was very anxious
to see her pretty face on canvas; Mr. Landor was
equally anxious to draw it there; but—well, Count
Kuroda is a man of an extremely jealous temperament,
and his wife clearly let us understand that he would

not care to have a foreign gentleman staring at her for hours together in her own house when his own public duties would call him away. How would it be, she shyly suggested, if she said that she was spending the day with the English Koshi Sama's Okusama?

Her husband would be sure that she was quite safe if she was with Mrs. Fraser, and—really—perhaps nothing need be said to him about the picture just now, after all! It would be such a nice surprise for him afterwards! As my conscience did not oblige me to tell the Prime Minister that his wife was having

THE COUNTESS KURODA IN COURT DRESS.

her portrait painted, the matter was arranged; Mr. Landor came, and of course picked out for his studio a gaunt north room that we never use unless the house is very full; I filled it with flowers and screens; and then the little lady arrived, dressed in the softest of

255

crapes and the most gorgeous of *obis*, her hair shining like black satin, her eyes dancing with excitement, and a round spot of brilliant rouge (or *béni*, as it is called here) on her lower lip. She was delighted to find that Sir Edwin could speak her own language a little ; but did not look at all pleased when he admired her hands, fine and small as a child's. From the Japanese point of view, such personal compliments constitute a breach of etiquette.

"Very dirty, very dirty!" she said, laughing, as she tucked them away under her long sleeves ; and I laughed too, not knowing the phrase, which is merely one of polite deprecation when anything of the speaker's is admired. I have since heard it applied to people's houses, clothes, and I think to their dinners, if one had chanced to praise a feast ; if one admires a child, it is at once said to be ugly, and anything so intimately a man's own as his wife is invariably called stupid. I remember the Chinese word is much the same ; "The stupid person of the inner chamber" being the ordinary name in Peking, if a wife has to be mentioned at all.

At last I got Countess Kuroda installed in a pose which suited her, but which caused the artist to wail in lamentation ; for she insisted upon standing, in what she called the only attitude possible for a lady, square to the painter, with both sleeves tightly pulled down to hide her ten fingers. She was a good deal scandalised, on coming round to have a look at the result, to find that Mr. Landor had drawn her hands quite outside her sleeves. She shook her head gravely, and then sighed.

"What is it?" we asked; "is there something wrong with the picture?"

"I ought not to show my hands," she said; "only peasant-women do that! And—oh dear, what a pity I am already so old!"

"Old!" I cried; "why you are just twenty-two!"

"Very old," she insisted, pointing to the picture where Mr. Landor had already got the face in, round and pure and pale. "If I were still young, I could wear paint on my cheeks, and my picture would also have rosy cheeks. But now I am old, over twenty, and I must never paint my cheeks any more!"

This defect was quickly remedied, and she forgave Mr. Landor about the hands when he threw a rosy flush over the little face in the picture. At the second and third sittings the Countess became quite enthusiastic, and seemed to enjoy the change and liberty that the visits brought. When the whole thing was finished, Mr. Landor made a present of the painting to Count Kuroda, who was so pleased that he forgot to be angry; and I have ever since been receiving gorgeous bunches of chrysanthemums or presents of eggs or bonbons in token of gratitude from his wife.

All this time we have had an invalid in the house, a poor Englishwoman, who came out as governess in a friend's family, and almost immediately had to undergo a severe operation at the hospital. Her employers have shown endless kindness and forbearance, Mrs.

H—— leaving her little children for a month, and shutting herself up in the dreary hospital room with her friend. We brought the sick woman here to recover, and also to give Mrs. H—— some rest; and I cannot say how touched I have been by Sir Edwin Arnold's kindness to this poor soul. I am so busy that I have to be away a great part of the day, leaving her in charge of her nurse and the servants, who have been very good; but the time must often have seemed long to her, and you can imagine what it has been to have such a companion as Sir Edwin for an hour or so every evening. He said nothing to me, but quietly took to dressing for dinner an hour earlier than any one else, and then going into her room, where I found him installed, reading aloud, when I came to see if all was right. I am sure that delightful hour every day has really helped the poor thing to crawl back to life and strength.

I broke down again when she was better, and since I last wrote have had a few days in Atami, the town of the geyser and the long beaches by the sounding sea. I found it much warmer than Tokyo, except on one or two days; and then I piled up sweet woods and fir cones in the little grate of my sitting-room, and took quick walks in the crisp air, and mightily enjoyed the scalding baths. My landlord's daughter, O'Detsu, was fired with ambition to learn to knit mittens for her beloved father's honourable cold wrists; so we sat together for hours, she poring over intricate stitches, and I directing her eager stiff

fingers. At last, after using all my wools, she turned
out a splendid pair, which the old gentleman at once
put on. They form an extremely comfortable addition
to the wide empty sleeve of Japanese costume. The
Japanese ladies tell me that they find their own dress
terribly cold in European houses, where they are
expected to sit on high chairs, and every stray draught
may blow up their poor unprotected limbs. The
tabi, or white sock with divided toe, stops short at
the ankle, and there is no stocking to continue the
covering. A closely wrapped woollen crape skirt,
scarlet or white, represents all the underclothing for
which there is room beneath the tightly clinging *kimonos*,
worn one over another like linings of the upper robe.
In a Japanese house, with its warm mats, everybody
kneels or sits on thin padded cushions on the floor,
and the cold cannot creep up as it does when people
have to perch on chairs. Women of the lower
class almost always sink down on their knees in
serving one, and the movement is wonderfully graceful
and easy.

I had one black wet day in Atami; but it was made
up for by one jewelled morning after another—days
when sky and sea, woods and waves and islands, were
all a vision of immortal shining loveliness; and oh,
the music of the long waves on the shore! It always
sets life to its own grave sweet cadence, and helps me
to think as I never think elsewhere. I went down
alone; but H—— came to fetch me, and brought me
home over the hills by Miyanoshita, where we stayed

a day or two, thinking to take a house there for next summer.

Our journey over the pass to Miyanoshita was a

AFTER THE SNOWSTORM.

thing I shall never forget. It was a bitterly cold morning when we set out, and a heavy snowfall had turned my world white. The dear old temple and the camphor tree, the empty rice-fields and the village street, were all uniformly dazzling; for the fall had ceased when the sun rose, and he was shining brilliantly in a sapphire sky, as if beyond some crystal dome, which showed us all his glory and forbade his touching us with his warmth. I had not brought my Hong

Kong chair this time, and decided to try the Japanese *kago*, the basket litter slung on a pole and carried on two men's shoulders. I had seen my little *amah*, O'Matsu, jump in and out of these things so easily, and look so happy as she was dandled along the road in one, that it seemed worth trying, especially as the only other method of going over the pass would be on foot, and I never was a great walker. "Wo worth the day," as the old ballads say, when I undertook to double my stiff European length into a kind of basket too short to lie down in and too low to sit up in ; for the little pent house-roof which ran along the carrying-pole knocked my head even when I had taken my hat off, and was further weighted with various bundles

A KAGO JOURNEY IN SUMMER.

261

of food and clothing, the property of the coolies who were to bear me between them. The cold seemed all the more intense for that blue sky and laughing sunshine. I was rolled in many rugs; and O'Matsu lighted two fire-boxes before we started, and put one at my feet and one inside my jacket. I think they did much to keep me alive, and perhaps my delight in the beautiful scenery did the rest. In spite of the cold and the intense fatigue caused by the cramped position and the broken trot of my coolies, I would not have missed the sights I saw for anything. It seems to me that the memory of such beauty will follow my spirit long after the bones which ached so wearily shall have been blown away in dust.

On leaving Atami, we followed a raised highroad which runs across the rice-fields to the foot of the mountains, and then scales them for a little way, ending short off in the hills, and obliging the traveller to take to a steep and narrow footpath, which mounts abruptly (far too abruptly!) up the skyey stair. I gasped as I saw my boxes going up this before me on the coolies' backs. The black basket trunks, which had seemed of so moderate size in railway trains and even on jinrikshas, absolutely grew, stood out enormous on these poor men's shoulders, and the sight of a large " Fraser " painted in white on black leather scrambling up the rocks on two staggering brown legs filled me with compunction and dismay! H——, who is an invincible walker, found it all he could do to get himself and his stick up to the top; but, at any rate, he did it at one stretch, while I and my boxes and my coolies had to stop every few minutes, and I felt like a wicked tyrant for letting myself be carried at all.

As we rose higher and higher, the most surprising

FUJI IN SNOW.

views spread out all round us. The sea seemed to be climbing the sky, there was such an outspread mantle of it, dimpling in a million diamonds in the morning sun. Peak after peak of the hills rose before us; and at last we saw three seas one beyond Atami, which we had left behind, and one in a deep bay on either side of us, thousands of feet below, but so near that one could see every detail of the houses in the little fishing villages washed up like brown shells on the shores.   We were on the highest point of the pass, where a deep-runed stone tells the traveller that from this spot his eye can wander over ten provinces of what the old writers called the Kingdom of Japonia. But we hardly cared to look down, for there before us, in midday splendour, rose Fujiyama, white, dazzling, a marble pyramid against a sapphire sky.   Mists rolled thick round its feet, as if the mountain-goddess had but just dropped her robe that we and the sun might look on her beauty ; then invisible hands seemed to be raising the airy garment higher and higher, till the veil swept over the proud white crest, and the vision was gone.

Once or twice in the course of the day it returned, but never in that perfection.   The road was long, and so heavy with snow that the men made but slow progress with my litter, which hung too near the ground for me to get much outlook on the scenery from under its wooden roof.   We stopped as little as possible, fearing that the short winter day would close in before we had sighted the friendly lights of Miyanoshita ; and this was what happened after all.   The last part of the journey, a rather steep descent, was accomplished in the dark, and the coolies tried every step with their sticks before they moved.   We knew that we were close to a torrent, because the roar went beside us for a long time ; and the cold, which was intense, became even more marked when half-frozen spray was blown in one's face out of the night's black mouth. I was so cold that it seemed impossible I should ever move my limbs enough to get out of that dreadful little litter, and I was greatly relieved at last to see a forest of red and white lanterns, bearing the well-known mark of Fujiya's hotel, come bobbing and dancing through the blackness, and our coolies' shouts were answered by those of the men who had been sent out to look for us.

It was not long before we were housed and warmed, and laughing over the day's discomforts before a blazing wood fire; but I cannot say that I had quite for-

FIGURE OF BUDDHA CARVED IN THE ROCK NEAR HAKONE.

gotten them, and some trace of stiffness remained for several days. The journey is hardly one to undertake in winter; but I am glad we did it, for it has given me an impression of Fuji which I could never have had in the warmer weather.

A Diplomatist's Wife in Japan 🐌

Many people go to Miyanoshita for Christmas, especially the foreign colony established in Yokohama. To me there is something so dreary in spending these anniversaries in hired rooms and strange scenery, that nothing would induce me to try it. As time goes on they change their meaning, indeed, and become less gay, but not less sacred. Out here I live my mind life in a curious three time, owing to the enormous distance from home. My Christmas letters had to be written and sent off on November 20th; in a few days they and the quaint collection of gifts that went with them will cause great joy in the little home circle; but I shall have no word of thanks till the end of January, or later. We get in the papers distorted telegrams about events in Europe, but long before the true account of the thing reaches us its very existence has gone out of one's mind; and so, little by little, the vivid interest in home politics dies out, and is replaced by smaller and nearer subjects. But one is not moved or excited about them as one is in Europe. There is so much time here, so much stored leisure to be discounted, that hurry drops out of life to a great extent, and nobody frets when that which should have been accomplished last week is hopefully announced to take place next year. That is the *ambiente*, the moral air of this morning land; and Europeans soon imbibe the easy philosophy.

A curious instance of this trick of willing waiting was brought to sight a little before our arrival. A safe in the Chancery, which had been unused for some years, was opened for some reason or other, and was found to contain a parcel of apparently forgotten medals sent by our Government to be distributed among the Japanese who helped to defend the British Legation against the attack of some *samurai* in 1861! When it was known that these medals would now be distributed, over twenty-seven years after the event,

THE CHANCERY HOUSE.

every one seemed inclined to deprecate the precipitation shown by our authorities in such matters. Why not wait till the few survivors of the affray had joined the majority, and then hang the medals on their tombstones all at once, and so avoid unfriendly feeling? The local papers made merry at our expense, and the tiresome people who only live to ask questions to which there can be no possible answer rose like one man, and insisted on knowing the cause of the delay. When at last the truth was told, the delay turned out not to have been of our making at all; it came from the heroes themselves, who in those early days had no desire to be distinguished as the friends and protectors of the abhorred foreigner, although their obedience to orders had made them quite ready to strike a blow in his defence.

The story of the attack is such an old one that you may have forgotten it. It was told me in graphic language by Laurence Oliphant a few years ago; and often in driving past the spot where the Legation then stood that record of bloodshed has come back to my mind. In those days our flag flew from a green knoll in Takanawa, close to the sea, which afforded opportunities of protection by a passing gun-boat. The Shogun's Government kept one hundred and fifty men to guard the compound; but for some undeclared reason they failed to stop fourteen *samurai*, desperate, conscientious fanatics, who made their way into the Minister's quarters on the night of July 4th, 1861, and succeeded in wounding Laurence Oliphant and the other Secretary, and in killing some of the guards, before they were driven back. Once roused, the guards fought well; and it was in recognition of their services that these medals were sent from England, with warm expressions of thanks for their loyalty. But nobody wished to be reminded of the affair, and the Tokugawa Government refused to supply the names of the men who had earned the British

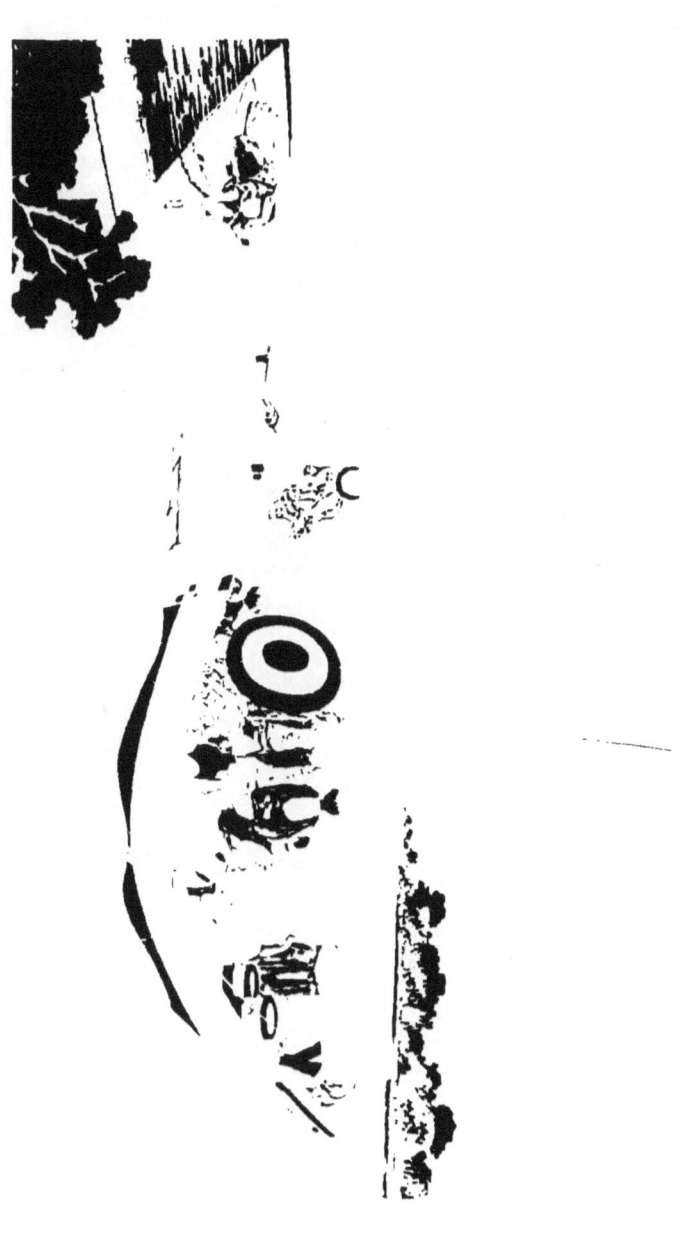

decorations, which would at that time have marked
out their wearers as traitors in the eyes of the fanatical
samurai and the country at large. So the medals were
quietly put away in a Chancery safe, which, with other
valuable objects, escaped destruction in 1863, because
the persevering *samurai* who then burnt down the new
Legation buildings did so on the very night after they
were completed, and before the British Representative
and his staff had taken possession.

For this last outrage there was something like an
excuse, since the site of the buildings had been, strictly
speaking, extorted from the Government at the point
of the bayonet. Various beautiful sites were offered
when the Takanawa Legation was condemned as being
isolated and inconvenient ; but our authorities would
have none of them, having set their hearts on what
was a favourite resort of the townspeople, a beautiful
public garden, endeared to the Japanese by the fact
that their hero Iyeyasu had held his Court there when
he first made Tokyo his seat of Government. It is
interesting to remember that Count Ito, to-day the great
advocate of progress for Japan, the chief framer of her
Constitution, was one of the *samurai* engaged in this
incendiary exploit. He laughs over it now, and says
that if medals are being given to the protectors of
the foreigner he certainly ought to have one, having
planned and lighted his bonfire when the new buildings
were empty and no lives could be lost.

But I must go back to the story of the safe. It
travelled with the rest of the official properties from

one place to another, till, eighteen years ago, it was
lodged in the present Chancery, a strong little building, well away from the gate, and placed between the
Minister's house and the quarters of the two English
constables who are all that now remain of the numerous
escort necessary in Sir Harry Parkes' days. Then the
times changed; and when the Queen sent swords to
Count Goto and Nakai Kozo for defending her Representative from the perennial fanatic in 1868, her gifts
were received with pride and gratitude. But the medals
were forgotten; the keys of the safe were lost; it was
supposed only to contain old accounts, which nobody
wished to consult; and something very like consternation filled the establishment last spring, when the
energetic head of the Chancery said he would not
have useless lumber lying about, the old chest must
be broken open, and its contents sorted or destroyed,
according to their values! Then the medals, silver and
gold, with their yellow diplomas, came to light. The
active official conscience insisted on their being given
to the men for whom they were intended, and a busy
search brought one or two of these retiring braves to
the light, and caused considerable amusement to the
foreign public at large, who, not instructed as to the
original causes of the delay, felt delightfully healthy
and virtuous in having found such a good case against
red-tapeism and official procrastinations, and in proof
of the general uselessness of public servants.

CHAPTER XIII.

New Year's Day at the Palace.—A Christmas Tree.—Japanese Children. "Come back Next Year."

CHAPTER XIII.

NEW Year's Day was marked by a reception at
the Palace far more formal than corresponding
cercles held by sovereigns in Europe. I was glad
to have another chance of walking through those
beautiful rooms in the great house across the moat.
It was a cold snowy morning, and there was not much
comfort to be found in putting on a low dress, even
with an interminable train attached to it. We drove
off, a goodly procession, preceded by Inspector Peacock,
looking very smart in full uniform on " Polly Perkins,"
an old charger, who is the *doyenne* of the stables,
having come to Japan, it is said, in Lord Elgin's time.
We have to make a long round to reach the State
entrance to the Palace ; and so many carriages were
already drawn up inside the enclosure that I began to
fear we might be late. This reception was for the
Diplomatic Corps ; but the poor Emperor and Empress
had already held two that morning—one of the Cabinet
Ministers and other members of the Government, and
one of the Peers and their wives ; and yet earlier
the Emperor had performed a religious ceremony before the tablets of his ancestors. The afternoon was
to be devoted to receiving the military officials, and

A PALACE OFFICIAL.

altogether the programme seemed one which would have taxed the strength of even the " Reise Kaiser" to carry out.

We were received by a number of the Household officials in the entrance hall, and the men waited while we women took off our cloaks in a beautiful little dressing-room full of long glasses and supplied with pins and powder in the most hospitable fashion. I did not want either, but lingered a minute to speak to the dressers who were there in attendance. There were four charmingly pretty girls, two dressed in European frocks of grey silk, and two in their own brilliant costumes, carried out in superb materials. Their smiling faces, and the fine deft fingers which removed my wraps and shook out my finery, made me feel that on the whole Japanese ladies have nothing to envy us in the way of lady's maids. To them I think the whole thing was a delightful treat, and they betrayed a good deal of curiosity as to how the white plumes and the long veil were fastened to my head.

When I came out, we started on that long walk through the corridors which I described in one of my first letters. To-day the endless glass galleries were warmed by steam, and full of bright dresses and uniforms. The great drawing-room where we all gathered presented a beautiful sight; the flower temple in the centre, a mass of orchids and roses, was surrounded by a crowd of men in all the Diplomatic uniforms of Europe, with many military ones scattered among them. The women's gorgeous trains wound in and out like serpents of velvet and gold, and the bright sunshine which had succeeded the snow danced gaily on their jewels as they moved. Outside, the courtyard that I had last seen full of cherry blossom was all a fairyland of snow, and the fountain played above it, throwing rosaries of diamonds about in the sunshine. There were no Japanese ladies to receive us, except the wife of the Minister for Foreign Affairs; and she went to take her stand by the Empress before we were summoned to the throne-room.

This is a large square room in another courtyard, and is at some distance from the drawing-room. As we approached, I

A TREE PEONY.

saw that the walls of this hall, which I had hardly noticed separately before, are all of glass, except on one side, where the two thrones are placed on a raised daïs, lined with heavy draperies of Kyoto silks. The floor of inlaid woods was so highly polished that I looked at it with some apprehension, having been a little lame with rheumatism of late. We had to wait our turn to enter (the French Minister is just now our *doyen*), and I could watch the ceremony through the glass. The Emperor and Empress stood on the top step of the daïs, a few yards apart, he having the Imperial Princes and his aides-de-camp behind him on his right, and the Empress the Princesses and her ladies on her left. The Emperor, whom I now saw close to for the first time, has a very plain but interesting face. The lower part is heavy and impassive ; but the eyes are piercingly brilliant, and the brow that of a thinker. He is of medium height, and has a good figure, which is shown to advantage, as he holds himself extremely well. The appearance of many Japanese gentlemen is spoiled in European dress by their peculiarly short arms ; but the Emperor does not suffer from this defect. He looked very dignified in his marshal's uniform, covered as it was with splendid decorations. The Empress was in white brocade, with two of the most perfect diamond rivieras round her neck that I have ever seen. I think they are finer than those of the Empress of Austria. She wore a magnificent tiara, too heavy for her small head ; and she looked, poor lady, terribly pale and

tired. Her white dress was crossed by the broad
orange ribbon of an Imperial order, which was also
worn by the Princesses. The effect of this flaming
band on a soft rose or pale-green satin gown is rather
disastrous.

When it was our turn to make our bow to the
sovereigns, I found it a very long way from the entrance
to the daïs, and the floor was even more slippery than
it looked. However, I got through all the curtseys
without accidents. The Emperor and Empress only
bowed as we passed before them : the Princesses nodded
and smiled in a row ; and then we had to back out and
down, across more miles of gleaming parquet, and
through a door, from which I could stand and watch
as the next victim underwent the same ordeal. The
whole ceremony did not last five minutes, and I heard
more than one of our colleagues grumbling violently
at the trouble and fatigue involved. Perhaps I shall
do the same next year ; but this was the first time for
me, and the spectacle pleased me. There was something rather fine about the great sombre room, with
its crimson background and glass screens, its sovereigns and their court, all silent as the dead, watching
the Representatives of the world file past them as they
stood on that daïs-step, which seemed for the moment
to be the high-water mark of the country's advance
towards friendship and equality with great unseen
Europe.

When it was all over, I flew home and tore off my
finery to throw myself into the preparations for a huge

Christmas tree, the first that had ever grown in our compound, for the children of our servants and writers and employés, who make up the number of our Legation

SOME JAPANESE CHILDREN.

population to close on two hundred, beginning with H——, and ending with the last jinriksha coolie's youngest baby. I could not have the tree on Christmas Day, owing to various engagements; so it was fixed for January 3rd, and was quite the most successful entertainment I ever gave!

When I undertook it, I confess that I had no idea how many little ones belonged to the compound. I sent our good Ogita round to invite them all solemnly to come to *Ichiban* (Number One) on the 3rd at five o'clock. Ogita threw himself into the business with delighted goodwill, having five little people of his own to include in the invitation; but all the servants were eager to help as soon as they knew we were preparing a treat for the children. That is work which would always appeal to Japanese of any age or class. No trouble is too great, if it brings pleasure to the " treasure-flowers," as the babies are called. I am still too ignorant of their special tastes to trust my own judgment in the matter of presents; so Mr. G—— left the dictionary and the Chancery for two or three afternoons, and helped me to collect an appropriate harvest for the little hands to glean. Some of them were not little, and these were more difficult to buy for; but after many cold hours passed in the different bazaars, it seemed to me that there must be something for everybody, although we had really spent very little money.

The wares were so quaint and pretty that it was a pleasure to sort and handle them. There were workboxes in beautiful polished woods, with drawers fitting so perfectly that when you closed one the compressed air at once shot out another. There were mirrors enclosed in charming embroidered cases; for where mirrors are mostly made of metal, people learn not to let them get scratched. There were dollies of every size, and dolls' houses and furniture, kitchens, farmyards, rice-pounding machines—all made in the tiniest proportions, such as it seemed no human fingers could really have handled. For the elder boys we bought books, school-boxes with every school requisite contained in a square the size of one's hand, and pen-knives and scissors, which are greatly prized as being of foreign manufacture. For decorations we had an abundant choice of materials. I got forests of willow branches decorated with artificial fruits; pink and white balls made of rice paste, which are threaded on the twigs; surprise shells of the same paste, two lightly stuck together in the form of a double scallop shell, and full of miniature toys; *kanzashi*, or ornamental hairpins for the girls, made flowers of gold and silver among my dark pine branches; and I wasted precious minutes in opening and shutting these dainty roses—buds until you press a spring, when they open suddenly into a full-blown rose. But the most beautiful things on my tree were the icicles, which hung in scores from its sombre foliage, catching rosy gleams of light from our lamps as we worked late into the night. These were—chopsticks, long glass chopsticks, which I discovered in the bazaar; and I am sure Santa Klaus himself could not have told them from icicles.

Of course every present must be labelled with the child's name, and here my troubles began. Ogita was told to make out a correct list of names and ages,

"TREASURE FLOWERS."

with some reference to the calling of the parents ; for even here rank and precedence must be observed, or terrible heart-burnings might follow. The list came at last ; and if it were not so long, I would send it to you complete, for it was a curiosity. Imagine such complicated titles as these : " Minister's second cook's girl. Umé, age 2 " ; " Minister's servant's cousin's boy. Age 11 " ; " Student interpreter's teacher's girl " ; " Vice-Consul's jinriksha-man's boy." And so it went on, till there were fifty-eight of them of all ages, from one year up to nineteen. Some of them, indeed, were less than a year old ; and I was amused on the evening of the 2nd at having the list brought back to me with this note (Ogita's English is still highly individual !) : " Marked X is declined to the invitation." On looking down the column, I found that ominous-looking cross only against one name, that of Yasu, daughter of Ito Kanejiro, Mr. G——'s cook. This recalcitrant little person turned out to be six weeks old—an early age for parties even nowadays. Miss Yasu, having been born in November, was put down in the following January as two years old, after the puzzling Japanese fashion. Then I found that they would write boys as girls, girls as boys, grown-ups as babies, and so on. Even at the last moment a doll had to be turned into a sword, a toy tea-set into a workbox, a history of Europe into a rattle ; but people who grow Christmas trees are prepared for such small contingencies, and no one knew anything about it when on Friday afternoon the great tree slowly glowed into a pyramid of light, and a long procession of little Japs was marshalled in, with great solemnity and many bows, till they stood, a delighted, wide-eyed crowd, round the beautiful shining thing, the first Christmas tree any one of them had ever seen. It was worth all the trouble, to see the gasp of surprise and delight, the evident fear that the whole thing might be unreal and suddenly fade away. One little man of two fell flat on his back with amazement, tried to rise and have another look, and in so doing rolled over on his nose, where he lay quite silent till his relatives rescued him. Behind the children stood the mothers, quite as pleased as they, and with them one very old lady with a little child on her back. She turned out to be the Vice-Consul's jinriksha-man's grandmother; the wife of that functionary was dead, and the old lady had to take her place in carrying about the poor little V.C.J.R.S.M.'s boy-baby.

The children stood, the little ones in front and the taller ones behind, in a semicircle, and the many lights showed their bright faces and gorgeous costumes, for no one would be outdone by another in smartness—I fancy the poorer women had borrowed from richer neighbours—and the result was picturesque in the extreme. The older girls had their heads beautifully dressed, with flowers and pins and rolls of scarlet crape knotted in between the coils; their dresses were pale green or blue, with bright linings and stiff silk *obis*; but the little ones were a blaze of scarlet, green, geranium pink, and orange, their long sleeves sweeping

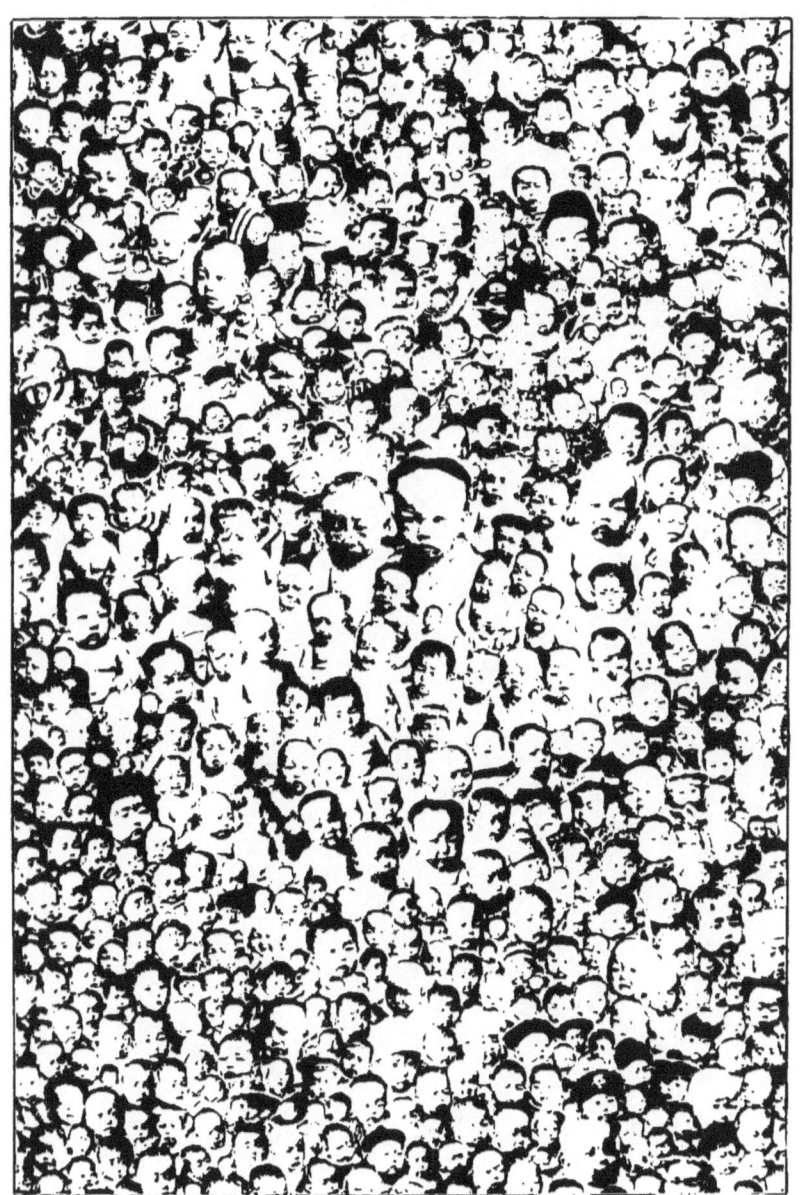

SOME JAPANESE BABIES.

the ground, and the huge flower patterns of their garments making them look like live flowers as they moved about on the dark velvet carpet. When they had gazed their fill, they were called up to me one by one, Ogita addressing them all as "San" (Miss or Mr.), even if they could only toddle, and I gave them their serious presents with their names, written in Japanese and English, tied on with red ribbon—an attention which, as I was afterwards told, they appreciated greatly. It seemed to me that they never would end; their size varied from a wee mite who could not carry its own toys to a tall handsome student of sixteen, or a gorgeous young lady in green and mauve crape and a head that must have taken the best part of a day to dress.

In one thing they were all alike: their manners were perfect. There was no pushing or grasping, no glances of envy at what other children received, no false shyness in their sweet happy way of expressing their thanks. I had for my helpers two somewhat antagonistic volunteers—Sir Edwin Arnold, basking in Buddhistic calms, and Bishop Bickersteth, intensely Anglican, severe-looking, ascetic. There had already been some polite theological encounters at our table, and I did not feel sure that the combination would prove a happy one. But each man is a wonder of kind-heartedness in his own way; and my doubts were replaced by sunshiny certainties, when I saw how they both began by beaming at the children, and ended by beaming on one another. I was puzzled by one thing about the children : although we kept giving them sweets and oranges off the tree, every time I looked round the big circle all were empty-handed again, and it really seemed as if they must have swallowed the gifts, gold paper and ribbon and all. But at last I noticed that their square hanging sleeves began to have a strange lumpy appearance, like a conjuror's waistcoat just before he produces twenty-four bowls of live goldfish from his internal economy ; and then I understood that the plunder was at once dropped into these great sleeves so as to leave hands free for anything else that Okusama might think good to bestow. One little lady, O'Haru San, aged three, got so over-loaded with goodies and toys, that they kept rolling out of her sleeves, to the great delight of the Brown Ambassador Dachshund, Tip, who pounced on them like lightning, and was also convicted of nibbling at cakes on the lower branches of the tree. The bigger children would not take second editions of presents, and answered, " Honourable thanks, I have !" if offered more than they thought their share ; but babies are babies all the world over ! When the distribution was finished at last, I got a Japanese gentleman to tell them the story of Christmas, the children's feast ; and then they came up one by one to say " Sayonara " (" Since it must be," the Japanese farewell), and " Arigato gozaimasu " (The honourable thanks).

" Come back next year," I said ; and then the last presents were given out—beautiful lanterns, red, lighted, and hung on what Ogita calls *bumboos*, to light the guests home with. One tiny maiden refused to go, and flung herself on the floor in a passion of weeping, saying that Okusama's house was too beautiful to leave, and she would stay with me always—yes, she would! Only the sight of the lighted lantern, bobbing

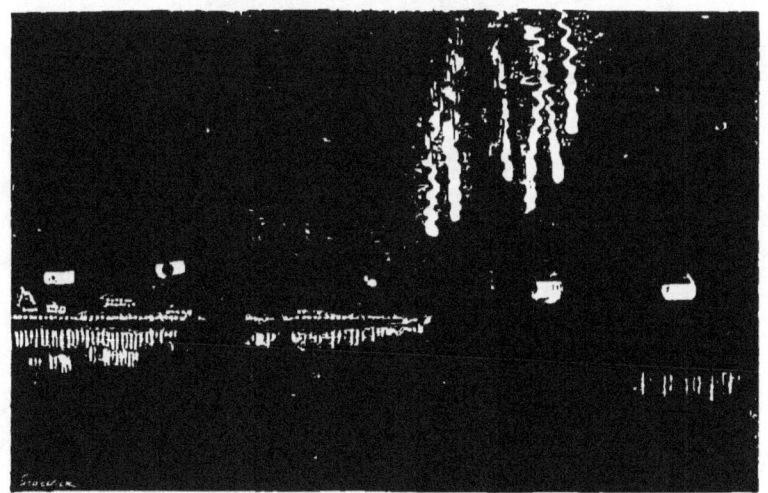

PUTTING UP THE LANTERNS.

on a stick twice as long as herself, persuaded her to return to her own home in the servants' quarters. I stood on the step, the same step where I had set the fireflies free one warm night last summer, and watched the little people scatter over the lawns, and disappear into the dark shrubberies, their round red lights dancing and shifting as they went, just as if my fireflies had come back, on red wings this time, to light my little friends to bed.

CHAPTER XIV.

CHAPTER XIV.

I WAS so taken up with our own doings when I
last wrote, that I forgot to tell you anything
of the Japanese New Year customs, which would probably have interested you more. It is the time when
the people, from highest to lowest, make holiday—
the most important moment of the whole year. For
many days beforehand preparations were on foot for
keeping the feast with due pomp. New clothes were
being made in every family—clothes as smart and
bright as the winter season and people's purses would
allow. Ogita came and represented to me that it
was customary to pay all the wages on December 30th
instead of two days later, when they would naturally
fall due ; and this because all debts and bills must
be settled before the New Year should dawn. All the
servants had new liveries, dark-blue silk robes and
black silk *haori*, or coats, with their master's crest
embroidered on the back and shoulders. At this time
every house is cleaned and put in repair ; sweet-
smelling new mats are laid down, wherever people
can afford them ; the sliding screens are covered with
fresh paper ; and every doorway, great or small, is
decorated with garlands of pine and bamboo, gemmed

THE HOME OF THE PINE TREES.

with golden oranges, which twist and swing in the sunshine, while splendid red lobsters brandish their claws among the leaves and fruit. The lobsters are symbolic — of great age; and the gift of one implies a kind' wish that you may live until you are bent double like the lobster. They are also a favourite food among the people; it sounds absurd to us to call them decorative, but the Japanese do not think so, and employ them ornamentally with excellent effect. Across the garlanded doorway, the Shinto emblem, a thick straw rope, beautifully plaited and knotted, is hung, to give a blessing to the rest, and to keep out all evil spirits ; and on either side is planted a tall bamboo, decorated with its own feathery leaves, and with branches of pine, the never-forgotten emblem of happiness and fortitude. The shops are full of such presents as are fitting for the festival. Some one sent me a ship of happiness, a junk, about two feet long, all worked in sweet clean straw. It was wreathed with twigs of pine, and loaded with tiny models of rice-bags for riches, and lobsters for long life ; the mast was a growing branch of pine, and the sails were gold and scarlet paper, bearing auspicious inscriptions. I was rather surprised at seeing the straw ships, having thought that these were only used for the *Bon Matsuri*, the Festival of the Dead, which occurs in summer ; but they evidently belong to the New Year as well, for I see many in the Japanese houses.

The streets are crowded with people all through the last night of the year ; buying and selling is going on everywhere in the open air, in spite of the sharp cold ; and it is only when the dawn has broken that the good folk go home to rest for an hour or two before beginning their round of visits among relations and friends. It is said that in very old times this was the only whole holiday taken by many of the working-classes from year's end to year's end. Be that as it may, they all enter into it with joyful eagerness now. The shops send out ornamental carts, piled high with what are called the first wares of the New Year; and these are drawn through the streets by parties of shop-boys, calling attention to the many useful articles they have to sell. On the 2nd of January, when the excitements of New Year's Day have subsided a little, the first customer in every shop receives a present, and business begins very early indeed, some buyers starting even at two o'clock in the morning to make sure of the gift. All those who can afford it get new clothes at this time; there are few so poor that they cannot spend a few sen on New Year's presents, and the booths show such piles of cheap and pretty things that one begins to think that value and beauty should be calculated here on inverse ratios. Many of the stalls, both in the street and the enclosed bazaars, are devoted to battledores of every variety of design; and probably many thousands are sold on the last night of the year, since on the 1st of January every girl in the town, from the babies up to the brides, will be playing battledore and shuttlecock through most of the daylight hours. The battledore is a bat-shaped wooden instrument, merely painted or gilt on the side meant to meet the shuttlecock; but the back is generally ornamented with reliefs in crape, skilfully combined with painting and gilding. One will bear a scene in history, the faces of the figures being painted, and their garments applied in moulded bits of crape and brocade. Or else a Japanese beauty smiles out of her window, or from the heart of a curling peony blossom;

a snow landscape, the white rabbit and the monkey who live in the moon, a fierce warrior, or a bunch of blossoms all jostle each other, and are solemnly judged and contrasted before the buyers decide which to take.

THE RABBIT AND THE MONKEY WHO LIVE IN THE MOON.

Twenty-five or thirty sen (six- or sevenpence) is a good price to give for these perfect little fancies. More lovely, however, are the real flowers, the early plum and dwarf pines, which the florists offer as the first-fruits of the year.

There is a great temple bell near us, which rang

in the New Year solemnly at midnight over the heads
of the busy, light-hearted crowd. One hundred and
eight strokes rolled slowly from the deep bronze mouth,
and hung in long vibration on the air; twelve times
nine, to ward off all evil from the city for the incoming
year. No one seemed to take much notice of the
signal, and I fancy many people even stayed out in
the streets and restaurants until the dawn, when the
more pious ones would go to the eastern heights of
the city to see the first sunrise (*hatsu-hi-no-de*)—an
event which is sure to bring good luck to the beholder.
Then comes a pilgrimage called the " Happy-direction-
going," for which a different temple is chosen every
year by the bonzes; and after this the visiting and
feasting, the real business of the day, begins.

It is very important to start the year with propitious
dreams; but as those of its first night might be un-
pleasantly affected by the conviviality of the evening,
the 2nd of January has been chosen as the night
whose dreams truly foretell some event of the coming
year. The Japanese dream doctrine is not so complicated as that of the *Libro dei Sogni*, by whose aid the
Romans translate their dreams into lottery numbers;
but it is well laid down, and goes into many quaint
details. The visions of the second night of January
are to be noted down as soon as possible; and then,
on comparing them with the dream-book, one may find
that one has, as it were, drawn a large cheque on the
bank of happiness. Happiness is foretold generally,
and on a great scale, by dreaming either of Fuji San,

or of ascending to the sky, of a falcon, or of an egg plant, or a very fine day. If you dream that you are struck by lightning, you will suddenly grow rich; but do not dream of frost, for that means bad fortune all round. A dream of eating a pear means divorce (that cloud overhanging the Japanese woman's life); but a mirror or a wine-cup means a beautiful child. A dream wind portends sickness; rain, a feast; a mulberry tree, the sickness of one's child. It is rather touching to see in these lists so many evidences of the woman's imagination, the woman's fears, the woman's circumscribed life and her intense interest in its small events. For one dream that would affect a man's career there are twenty that would go to the heart of a woman's existence; and I think the wise astrologer has had to answer many an anxious wife or mother, and has prepared his book chiefly for her. He does not say that you can buy a lucky dream from some one else; but there is a story in Japanese feudal history which seems to imply that one can.

The story goes that Masako, the wife of Yoritomo, bought an auspicious dream from her younger sister, paying her with a beautiful mirror, the day before Yoritomo sent her a love letter. Yoritomo was in exile then; but Masako persuaded her father to espouse his cause, and in the end he overthrew all his enemies, and came to great power and glory, and Masako sat by his side, all for a dream's sake.

There is a still older dream story in the chronicles of Japan. In the first years of our era, there reigned

A FEUDAL HERO.

in Japan an Emperor called Suinin, who lived, if dates be true, to a very great age. He had the misfortune to be married to a woman whose brother desired to supplant him on the throne. The Empress loved her husband, but she loved her brother more ; and when the latter gave her a dagger and bade her slay the Emperor in his sleep, she promised that so would she do. And one day the Emperor, weary with care, laid his head on her knees and slept ; and she knew that the time had come, and looked down once more on the face of her husband whom she loved, and hot tears fell on his face as she looked ; and he awoke, crying out that he had had an ominous, terrible dream. And he sat up and told her the dream : a wet rain wind in his face, and a small crimson snake round his neck—such was his dream. And he looked into her face as he told it ; and she fell down before him, and wept bitterly, and confessed her own and her brother's crime. So the Emperor was saved; and the Empress fled to her brother, and perished in his Palace, which was burnt down.

It seems as if the last trace of the old feudal life had been wiped out now; for the Emperor has just issued a stringent prohibition against duelling, imposing heavy penalties for fighting or attending a duel, and ranking the killing of an opponent as ordinary murder, to be punished to the full extent provided for by the criminal law. But I think it will be a long time before the old feudal heroes cease to be the idols of the

people, the patterns and ideals set before the boys of to-day from their earliest childhood. Every picture-book is full of their exploits; every flower show sets forth their adventures in wonderful life-like groups; and even I, a stranger of the strangers, cannot help being intensely

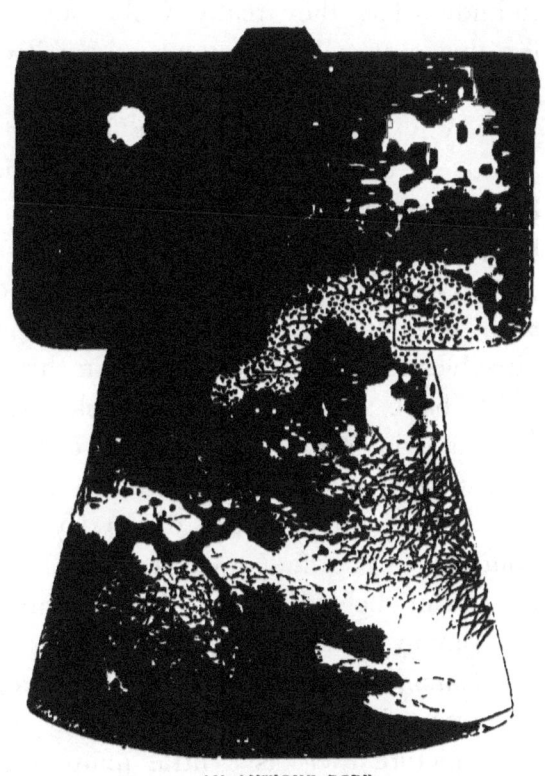

AN ANTIQUE ROBE.

attracted and interested by the atmosphere of pure romance which hangs around their names. The lower classes still have their idols ; witness the daily pilgrimages and the splendid flower offerings at the tombs of the fanatics who have tried to arrest the modernisation of their country by murdering the men who were in favour of it. "May a little of his spirit descend upon us!" cry the *soshi*, reaching out for something to satisfy their hunger for the ideals of a dead chivalry. As for the nobles, their close reserve makes it difficult to know what they really feel ; but a poignant regret for the past will sometimes show itself in a look or a word.

"Why do you not wear these lovely things?" I asked of one of the Empress's ladies, as we were looking over a pile of antique robes, embroidered in bewildering beauty of silk and colour and gold.

"There are no Daimyos' houses now," she replied, with flashing eyes ; "do you think we would show ourselves to the common people in those costumes?"

I have a little picture-book which purports to give drawings of all the warlike occupations of a great feudal chief. The variety and importance of them make the military life of to-day look common by contrast. The first picture given is the portrait of a warrior belonging to the half-mythological period of Jimmu Tenno (660 B.C.); the face is extremely handsome, and is of a strongly marked Assyrian type, in spite of the oblique eyebrows. From this to the next picture there is a little jump of eighteen hundred

years or so, when a warrior of Hideyoshi's time is
shown in full uniform, lacquered armour, foxtail sword-
sheath, helmet be-dragoned like King Arthur's, and
feet shod with bear-fur sandals. His arms are bow
and arrows, two swords, and the iron battle-fan which
one sees preserved in some of the museums—an effec-
tive weapon at close quarters, but giving a strange air
of foppishness to the man, who carries it lightly in his
right hand, while the left grasps the huge bow. He
sits on a camp-stool, over which is thrown a fur rug,
and is having a serious colloquy with a brother-chief,
who sits cross-legged on a mat, in cool undress, also
holding a fan, while his armour is thrown behind him
in a palanquin built in shelves, especially made for
carrying it in. Then in my picture-book come
journeys, where the common people gaze open-mouthed
at the proud young Daimyo travelling past in state ;
and at last he reaches his own home, where, for some
reason not explained, it becomes necessary to cut out
and make a new standard. This is a ceremony which
must have the blessing of the gods, and a sacrificial
table is placed in the middle of the floor, incense
and saké and rice are offered on stools all round it,
and in the centre is set up what looks like the Shinto
emblem, a short pole with quantities of prayer leaflets
attached to it. Near by, in rapt attention, the Daimyo
sits in full dress ; a young page squats behind him,
holding his sword ; and another personage, dressed like
a bonze, is also in attendance. The standard-makers
kneel at opposite ends of an oblong board, which is

the body of the standard, and are fitting on it a scroll,
which the younger of the two is about to cut with a
long knife. Their bows and arrows and swords lie
beside them, laid out
with geometrical pre-
cision on the floor;
and from the pro-
found solemnity of all
the faces one can
gather that standard-
making was a cere-
mony of the gravest
importance.

THE DAIMYO ACCEPTS A PRESENT.

Then comes a
scene connected with
New Year's Day,
when an enormous
rice-cake (*mochi*) was
offered to the god of
war, and afterwards
divided among the
men and boys of the
family. The god is
personified by the
Daimyo's armour, laid
in an open box in the
place of honour. On a stool before it is an offering
of pine boughs and bamboo leaves and lobsters, just
such things as are in every house in Tokyo to-day;
and the Daimyo near by, with saké and cakes before

him, and his swords on the floor by his side, sits and
watches two youths of his household, who are dividing
two huge cakes with a bow-string. "Why a bow-
string?" I asked, puzzled at the unusual detail.
"Because," said my friend, smiling gravely, "since
the cake is offered to the god of war, it would be too
personal, what we should call rude, to use a knife.
That is his own property and connected with bloodshed; so on an auspicious day like this one, and for
a feast in his honour, it could not be employed."

There are wonderful pictures of fights by sea and
land: the Daimyo (always the same smooth-faced
haughty young lord) conquers his enemies, sinks their
junks, takes them prisoners, accepts their presents
scornfully on the end of his spear, and finally has a
triumph like that of a Roman consul; then he seeks
relaxation in warlike games, such as shooting at a ring
as he flies past on his galloping steed, hunting with
falcons, and (the least warlike of games this last)
shooting blunt arrows at a poor dog, who howls as he
is driven past. My friend turned this page quickly,
murmuring an apology for the cruelties of feudalism,
and we came on a delightful scene in a corner of the
princely household, where the keeper of the falcons
sits on a step of the verandah tipping arrows with
feathers, and squinting down the arrow's length to
see if it is straight, just as the English boy squints
down the spine of his bat. The feathers are being
heated in the *hibachi* before he uses them; and opposite is the man's wife, a woman of the people, untidy

and querulous, scolding violently about something
without making the slightest impression on the man,
who is absorbed in the interest of his work. On
the front verandah (for you see right through the
dwelling) is my lord's lacquered luncheon-box, with its
silken cords; while thrown in a corner in a careless
heap is the humble outfit of the keeper. A splendid
falcon sits outside on a lacquered perch in the sunshine;
and the keeper's dog, a rough puppy, has rolled himself up in the shade of the step. Behind the man
himself, on the farther verandah, the Daimyo's horse
is enjoying a good feed, his nose in a bucket, a clean
napkin carefully tied round his neck. The very spirit
of feudalism breathes in the queer little picture—the
old idolatrous respect for the chief and his belongings,
and the self-effacement of the plebeian before the noble.

I did not realise the intense difficulty of translating
our thoughts into Japanese words till the day after
our Christmas tree, when O'Matsu came to me looking
very puzzled, and said that she would like to ask a
question: why did Imai San (the gentleman who made
the little address explaining the meaning of Christmas)
say such a dreadful thing about "Jesu Sama"? He
had said that Jesu Sama was put into a bucket, such a
thing as the ponies have their food in! That seemed
very horrible and undignified to her. I tried to
explain that in Palestine the animals did not eat out
of buckets; but I saw that I made very little impression. Imai San was a man, and a Japanese, and
evidently my Bible history carried no weight in

comparison to his. A day or two after this I sent all the maids and children down to the Convent in Tsukiji, where my friends the nuns had made a beautiful *crèche* for their children. Here, in lifelike figures, were the Mother and the Babe, Joseph and the Shepherds, and the crib with its straw, all the scene splendidly decorated with pine branches and imitation snow and gold paper stars. O'Matsu came back beaming. "I understand it all now," she told me; "eyes speak better than words. Buckets, indeed!" and she laughed triumphantly. The children, great and small, were enchanted with the nuns' grotto, and came in little parties to thank me for sending them to see it.

A STREET IN WINTER.

CHAPTER XV.

*A Cabinet Minister and a Fortified Carriage.—
A Memorial to the Throne.—Count Ito and
Treaty Revision.—The Japanese Spring.—" The
Eldest Brother of the Hundred Flowers."—
Popular Festivals.*

CHAPTER XV.

VERY little of interest has been happening in the political world. Count Okuma has recovered entirely from his wound, and has made a little testimonial to the trained nurses from the Charity Hospital who tended him during his long imprisonment. He sent them some valuable presents, as he also did to the surgeons who operated on his unhappy limb ; and now he pretends to laugh over the disaster of its loss. But he will not take office again at present, preferring to have the rank of Privy Councillor, which admits of his offering an opinion, without holding the portfolio, which would be as yet too heavy a tax on his strength.

His successor, Viscount Aoki, strikes one as a man hardly great enough yet to deal with the question of Treaty Revision, the only question of any importance before the Government just now. But he has knowledge, and patience ; also he is modest, and apparently not fired by personal ambition or party feeling, so that greatness may not be far off. I pity him sincerely. The post of Foreign Minister is so little sought after, that, since Count Okuma's accident, it seems difficult to find anybody of the right kind to fill it ; and the man who does so carries his life in his hands.

A Diplomatist's Wife in Japan

I watched Viscount Aoki drive up to our own door a day or two ago. He was seated in an open victoria with the hood raised, and inside the hood on either hand hung a revolver in a leather pocket, with a heavy chain fastening it to a ring in the carriage frame. The weapons are carefully loaded before the Minister takes his airing, and I fancy that any stranger who tried to stop the carriage or looked into it suddenly would have rather a sensational reception. Three detectives in plain clothes accompany him, as well as a policeman, who sits on the box. The effect is that of a condemned criminal, or a dangerous lunatic out with his keepers. Madame Aoki tells me that the constant watch and guard make life quite intolerable. Wherever she and her husband go, if it be only for a turn in their own garden, the policeman appears, and follows at a not too respectful distance, admiring the flowers and assiduously pretending that he does not hear a word of their conversation. She confided to me that they occasionally amuse themselves by giving their protectors the slip, stealing out like runaway children by a door which opens on a side-street, whence, plainly dressed and on foot, they can take something like a walk. I believe that the consternation is great when it is found that the Minister has really left his own grounds unprotected by the law, and the detectives generally run him to earth and come home with him again.

It all seems rather useless, for Treaty Revision is far less active than it was, and the disputes about the question of Foreign Judges threaten to break up the negotiations altogether. The public here, the mass of middle-class, fairly well-educated people, have outgrown the stage (existing honestly a few years ago) when they would tolerate the temporary employment of foreign judges sitting in Japanese law courts conjointly with the native judges, to ensure justice to any foreigner who might be brought up for trial. The arrangement was only intended to last a certain time, until the Japanese should have shown themselves capable of understanding and impartially administering their new laws, which are not yet entirely codified. Count Okuma and other members of the Government were in favour of the admission of foreign judges in cases where foreigners were concerned; but the vernacular press, the *soshi*, the people in general, have reached a stage in political development where bumptiousness takes the place of prudence; they consider that the concession would be an insult to their national integrity. But our own Government will not go back on the proposition, feeling that Japan is still too young to the ways of justice to be trusted blindly and entirely with the liberty, the property, perhaps the lives of British subjects. This is the now famous nineteenth article of the proposed treaty. It cannot be granted, and it cannot be re-nounced; hence a pause in the endless negotiations—a pause during which the Cabinet seems to be constantly unmaking itself, to be built up in a different manner with most of the same names, a process which reminds me of nothing so much as of the children's boxes of coloured bricks, where the same fragments serve as an

arch, a doorstep, a fireplace, or a pediment, according
to which of its six sides you turn uppermost. No
sooner have I learnt which peer holds which portfolio
than they all—excuse the simile—seem to toss them
into the air, and catch who catch them can in the fall.
The Sanjo Cabinet, however, has retired with some
majesty. Its farewell was a very earnest appeal, em-
bodied in a memorial to the throne, to increase the
responsibility of Ministers and to build up the power
and dignity of the Cabinet by first making it responsible in full for all measures promulgated by individual
Ministers ; secondly, by making each Minister sign the
orders for his own department, instead of having to
have them countersigned by the Minister President,
as is now the case, before they can take effect—an
arrangement which, says the memorial, throws too much
power into the hands of one man ; thirdly, that whatever
passes at Cabinet Councils be kept absolutely secret,
the obligation of silence not ceasing with the retirement
of its members. In fact, the whole memorial is a plea
for responsibility, unity, and reticence as the only
means by which the Cabinet can maintain its proper
position in the State or carry out the functions entrusted
to it. The coming elections and the opening of the
Imperial Diet are referred to as rendering the proposed
measures absolutely necessary to ensure the harmony
and efficiency of the Government.

Count Ito kept out of all this very carefully.
Watching him as I do from the place of the unlearned,
I have come to the conclusion that he has a strong

sense of dramatic effect and
of the wisdom of inactivity
when other people are doing
dangerous work or seem on
the point of making fools of
themselves. His prolonged
reluctance to take office probably comes from this acute
sense of self-preservation, combined, as I have said, with the
other sense of the value of
dramatic effect. Is the Cabinet
torn with dissensions or in de-

COUNT (NOW MARQUIS) ITO.

spair because Great Britain will not yield that one little
Article XIX., are the *soshi* rampant and the Radical
newspapers being suppressed by scores, every one
cries out, Where is Count Ito? Where is the man who
made the Constitution and brought in the foreigners?
Then Count Ito is sure to be in his beautiful villa at
Odawara, contemplating the codification of the laws, or
the growth of his rhododendrons, or something equally
impersonal and removed from the sphere of dispute.
He is entreated to return, to advise his sovereign, to
strengthen his party, to pacify and reassure the public ;
and he always comes and does it. And it seems to me
at these times that when the others have done all the
drudgery, then he reaps the glory of some popular
measure ; or it goes the other way—an unpopular thing
must be done, a bad moment passed, moral accounts
faced ; then Count Ito feels an irresistible desire for

peace and retirement, and his colleagues have to do without him, until the scene is properly set for him to step forward again. He is a very astute yet broad thinker, determined and ruthless, has absolute control of personal emotions and ambitions—all that which constitutes "the moment" with its opportunity or its danger; and any one who knows him would, I fancy, lay heavy odds on the probability of his ultimately attaining any object which he considered important enough to desire.

The regulations have been published for the coming elections, and have caused a good deal of interest. In order to vote, a Japanese subject must be twenty-five years of age, and must have been paying direct taxes to the amount of fifteen yen yearly for at least a year before the day when the electoral lists are made up, April 1st of this year. The actual election day will be July 1st, and stringent measures will be taken to keep it peaceable and orderly. We shall be away in the hills I hope in July; but I shall look forward with great interest to the opening of the Diet in November.

November seems very far away just now. The spring is here, young and weak as yet; but every day adds something to its conquests from winter. Already in January the early plum bloomed in white flakes that might have been mistaken for falling snow but for the crimson knot that held it to the grey branch. These valiant fragile blossoms are greatly endeared to the Japanese, because they come long before one has a right to expect open-air flowers at all. One warm

UMÉ SAN COMES RUNNING OUT TO GATHER THE FIRST BLOSSOMS OF HER
SISTER NAMESAKE.

midday hour, perhaps between snow and snow, will give them courage to shed their brown sheath and shake out their ethereal petals to the tepid sunshine. But they go with the snow too ; only for a few days do they rejoice us with the certain promise of a yet invisible spring, and then, yielding to wind and snowstorm, they dance on their airy way ; the tree is bare of their beauty long before a leaf has dared to show itself, but their message was given faithfully, and the later flowers will keep all the promises that the early plum had made for them. Eldest brother of the hundred flowers, as it is called here, a whole body of poetry and tradition has grown up round the shy evanescent blossom which passes so soon and leaves such a rich harvest of fruit for early summer's garnering. I think I saw the first flowers in Viscount Hijikata's garden on January 13th ; but the spot is a sheltered one, and other trees did not follow till much later. Now, in these early February days, the plum-gardens are in full bloom, and crowded with enthusiastic visitors, who, undaunted by the snow, go to admire what they call the "Silver World," a world with snow on the paths and snow on the branches, while snowy petals, with the faintest touch of glow-worm green at the heart, go whirling along on the last gust of wind from the bay. At night, when all is quiet and the second watchman has gone his rounds, an eerie cry is heard ; and if I step out on the verandah and look up, I see a string of three or four wild geese passing swiftly between me and the stars, their long necks strained in

the speed of their flight, the head cleaving the air as
a prow cleaves the water, and the whole body flung
after it through space with an intensity of motion
shown in the flight of no other bird, I think. Night
after night they pass, with the long piercing cry that
the north wind must have taught them, and their flight
is always northwards ; but I think they come back in
the dawn when I am asleep, for it is too early for their
migration to begin, and they would fly in different
order and larger bodies if they were starting on it.
We think they have feeding-grounds on the north
side of the town, which they are too shy to visit in
the daytime. The Japanese, however, connect their
migration with the appearance of the early plum, and
the poets bewail them for having to fly away from so
much loveliness. The plum's own bird is the *uguisu*,
the Japanese nightingale, the sweetest of singers ; but
I have not heard her yet this spring, and last year
she did not sing till May, when we arrived.

There are so many kinds of plum trees that one or
other of them blooms from now to midsummer. To-
day's snow blossom will be followed by double white
ones and pink ones, deep crimson too, that never
bear a fruit ; some are long trails of blossom growing
obediently in a perfect bell shape round a gnarled
morsel of trunk in a pale-green porcelain pot ; others
make a mist of whiteness waving against the sky
from the black branches, stiff and knotted, which the
Japanese consider characteristic of the plum, and culti-
vate with extreme care. The show plum-gardens take

PRESENTING THE TREE WITH A POEM IN PRAISE OF THE SPRING.

rank according to the age and ruggedness of their trees, which furnish a sharp contrast to the delicate snowy petals of the flower. This contrast seems to me to lie at the root of many theories of beauty of the Japanese, and is so desirable in their eyes that they obtain it by means of almost dishonest artificiality. The knotty bark of the plum is emblematic of old age, and the year's first bud is the symbol of extreme youth; therefore the tree must be made to look as old as possible, and the true enthusiasts go to view and rave over the blossoms while they are still hard little buttons with scarcely a touch of white.

This is the condition in which the gardener brings them to decorate my rooms; and when I expostulate and say that I want flowers, not sticks, he shakes his head and draws in his breath, and bends double in a bow, all of which is meant to hide his disappointment at my impatience and want of artistic feeling. The worst of it is that I fancy he is right and I am wrong! He would give me the pleasure of watching the little brown sheaths burst and shed themselves, of seeing the closely crinkled petals unfold to the daylight like a new-born baby's hand, of breathing in the first whiffs of the faint fine scent, so sweet and distinctive that the Japanese say the nightingale can find the tree in the dark by its perfume; all this I should lose if Naratake Ginsemon, the gnome of scissors and string and brown mould, brought me masses of ready spread bloom. So I take patience, and we add warm tea to the water in which they stand, and in a day or two the

long hall and the sunny drawing-rooms are a bower
of bloom, more beautiful even than the groves of the
" Recumbent Dragon " at Kameido, where the old
trees almost creep on the ground, and look, in their
moonshine mist of blossom, like a withered old witch
in a bridal veil.

There is a feast called " The First Rabbit of January,"
which is celebrated in this same temple at Kameido,
chiefly associated in European minds with the splendid
show of wistaria blossoms later in the year. Here
the memory of a great scholar, Sugawara Michizane,
is venerated. He lived some sixteen centuries ago,
but is still believed to take so much interest in literature
that ambitious youths write poems in large characters
on paper and burn them at his tomb. Anxiously they
watch the whirling ashes ; and if they are carried
high in the air, the scholar may go home satisfied,
for his great aspirations will be fulfilled.

People here have carried the power of will and
imagination to such completeness that they have succeeded in limiting the winter to a few short weeks,
which end on December 22nd, when the shortest day
is past, and theoretical spring begins. Then the last
chrysanthemums are still hanging on in our warm
rooms, and seem to look askance at the jonquils,
propped with pebbles in their flat dishes, brought in
by the gardener, who has been nursing them in some
dark corner of his house until they were ripe enough,
in his eyes at least, for drawing-room decoration. To
us they still look cold and raw ; but in the first night

A MOONLIGHT PICNIC.

their grey silk envelope is broken, and morning finds them all staring about the room as if just awakened from sleep. It is thought lucky to have them open for the New Year, an easy matter when New Year's Day was a movable feast, falling near the end of January or even later, as it did formerly in Japan, but involving some effort since the introduction of the European calendar.

Although winter is thus shortened in theory, no one dreams of leaving off winter clothes until April, or even May, for the cold is apt to return at any time, and nobody cares to have brightly coloured garments ruined by a sudden storm. The thick wadded clothes worn make it possible for people to have winter picnics, when they sit in open verandahs, making poems to the moonlight on the snow. The pictures of such entertainments generally give the guests an expression of concentrated melancholy, each looking away from his companion as if he would say, " I refuse to see how miserable you are. It might unnerve me ! "

The first acknowledged day of spring in old times depended on the weather, and perhaps on the mood of the ruler of the land. It was understood to mark the division between severe cold and milder airs, and generally fell towards the end of January. On this day the head of the family (or his chief servant) took a basket of white beans, and, going through the house, scattered some in every room, crying, " Evil spirits outside, good fortune within ! " The ceremony probably took its origin in an offering to the higher powers, and a prayer for their protection; but at last it came to be looked upon as a kind of household carnival, and was accompanied by games and laughter, which resounded from house to house along the streets of

A RICE-FIELD.

the town, or in the little huts, just within calling distance of each other, along the dykes by the yet empty rice-fields—empty because the rice is growing still in its first nursery, blade by blade, as thick as moss. In a month or two it will be removed one root at a time from the small bed, and placed in a larger one, to feel its feet; and yet again, as the summer grows, the precious shoots will be lifted from the half-liquid soil and spread in rows down the great wet fields, until they shake their full-grown tassels in the sun, yielding the harvest which is so eminently the chief wealth of Japan that rich men's incomes are reckoned, not in dollars, but in *koku*, or bags of rice.

Surely there have been many Methuselahs in Japan! Nothing less than the leisure of eight or nine hundred years could have induced people to undertake such tasks as the division of every month into twelve zodiacal parts, each presided over by a reptile or animal and subdivided among elements and minerals. The system may have simplified the casting of horoscopes or the choosing of a site for house or camp; but even with the spare time of a thousand years and the entire absence of preoccupation as to a future life, it must have taken much patience to divide one month into sixty-one parts—and then remember what day it was when one sat down to write a note!

This custom has left its impress on the Japan of to-day; for when a man reaches the age of sixty-one (at which point the old numeration starts again), he is congratulated on having taken a new lease of life. The family drink his health in full assembly, new clothes are made for him, and he is no longer expected to work, if he has done so till then, but may depend on his sons and grandsons for his maintenance.

Many are the popular festivals during these first months of the year. February the 9th is marked by a touching ceremony, when the Emperor, dressed in

antique State costume, performs a service of homage
to the spirits of his ancestors. The loving recollection

ANTIQUE STATE COSTUME.

of the dead is deeply rooted in the hearts of the
Japanese, and has often smoothed the way for Catholic
teaching. Even tiny children will keep gifts of cakes
and flowers, and lay them on the grave of father or
mother in the pine-shaded resting-place of the family.
No violent manifestations of grief are made, but the

dear one is never forgotten in his silent shrine. The Buddhist priests mark the 9th of February as the " Feast of the River's Farther Shore." The name alone seems to constitute a tie between the thought of East and West. Life and death, and life's renewal after death —these are the undying and indivisible inheritance of the children of God wherever He has placed them.

CHAPTER XVI.

*The Girls' Month.—Origin of the Dolls' Festival.
—A Wonderful Show.—The Japanese Girl and
her Upbringing.—Wives and Mothers-in-law.—
O'Sudzu's Divorce.—" Flame is the Flower of
Yedo."*

CHAPTER XVI.

THE month of March, in which falls the girls'
festival (the third day of the third month), must
make up in a great degree to the little Japanese maiden
for the secondary place she occupies in the family
councils during the rest of the year—secondary, at least,
as compared to the one filled by that all-important
personage, her brother. His especial festival comes
later, when the year is nearer its summer glories, and
the sun, low now, will be riding high and hot in the
heavens. But March, with its camellias and cherry
blossoms and toys, belongs to the girls ; and they queen
it royally in the midst of their double family, their
adoring relations and their submissive doll subjects.

Long before March the 3rd has come, the elaborate
preparations for the doll festival have been begun in
the families of the nobles and the princes. Away
from the house with its inflammable woods, in a safe
part of the grounds, stands the *godown*, or store-house,
where all the precious things are kept safe from thieves
and fire. It is generally an ugly little building of
white-washed brick, in two stories, heavily clamped
with iron, and having iron doors and shutters often ten
or twelve inches thick. Fires are the curse of Tokyo,

and have been raging frightfully of late, the wood and paper and mats of which the houses chiefly consist leaping into flame at the first spark that falls upon them. So the rich people keep their treasures in fire-proof store-houses, which I have often seen standing untouched when the rest of the home was reduced to ashes.

European children would be surprised to hear that they were expected only to see their favourite toys for one month in the year, and to consign them to fire-proof safes for the other eleven ; but the dolls brought to light on March the 3rd are mostly heirlooms, triumphs of the art of a day which worked as if its sun would have no setting, which took no account of labour or time, but only of the passionate straining after perfection for its own sake.

And now March is here, and the girls' festival is being celebrated from Hakodate to Nagasaki. In great houses the store-rooms have been opened, and hundreds of wonderful doll families brought to light, to be displayed in all their glory in a special room prepared for them. From generation to generation the dolls are handed down and preserved with that unquestioning reverence which the Japanese bestow on everything they love. Little children are called the treasure-flowers of life, and that which ministers to their happiness is never considered trivial, but regarded as a necessary part of the family occupa-tions. They themselves do not look upon their delicate toys as things to be knocked about in rough

ARRANGING THE DOLLS.

play; seeing that the grown people handle them with care, they do the same, and do not repine when valuable dolls are put away in boxes in the *godowns*, and only brought out for this, their special festival.

The origin of the celebration lay in the devotion of the people to an always invisible sovereign. For many centuries the Emperor and Empress were never beheld by any but a few favoured courtiers who shared the seclusion in which they were kept by the all-powerful Regents. So their loyal subjects made images of them, dressed in State garments, and surrounded by all the pomp and luxury due to their exalted rank. In the flowery springtime the images were displayed and worshipped throughout the land with the most eager homage. Even the language retains the impress of this loyalty; for the expression invariably used in regard to beholding the sovereign is not to *see*, but to worship.

I have been paying a visit to the little daughter of one of the great nobles. It was her mother's reception day, and beside the tea-cups on the pretty tea-table stood small bottles of a thick white wine, only used for this festival; I had only been in the room a few minutes, when she said, " Would you like to see the dolls ? Pray forgive me for putting you to the trouble of going to another room." Then the heroine of the moment, a tiny girl of five, stepped forward and offered to lead me in. She was dressed in sapphire-coloured crape, shading from pale blue at the foot to dark purple at the shoulder, embroidered in gold in lovely patterns, and girdled with royal scarlet and gold; her hair, gathered in a shining knot on the top

MY LITTLE HOSTESS.

of her head, was held in place with jewelled pins; and there was a distinct touch of rouge on either round cheek. With perfect gravity she took my hand, and led me into the farther room, where a wonderful show met my eyes. On rising shelves, covered with crimson damask, several hundreds of dolls were arranged, with all the furniture and belongings that the most ambitious doll-lover could dream of. In most instances an emperor and empress were sitting on their thrones surrounded by their entire court. There were generals, prime ministers, musicians, dancers, all in the costume of a long-past day; the chairs and stools, painted screens, gold lacquer cups and utensils, musical instruments, and weapons of war were all carried out with a reckless expense and patient perfection surpassing the finest antique work of the West. It is very strange to see modern French and English toys among these splendid curios ; but this little lady is cosmopolitan in her tastes, and takes special delight in creatures who will walk or sing when they are wound up with a key. After admiring everything, and congratulating her on the arrangement of the show, I asked which were her favourites out of all the vast collection of dolls. With true

JAPANESE GIRLS OF TO-DAY.

Japanese breeding she at once pointed to a china baby floating in a bath-tub, which she received from me last Christmas, and then, after a moment's hesitation, to a gorgeous Parisienne sent to her by the wife of the French Minister. This precocious tact so took

345

away my breath that it was hard to find words to
express proper admiration of the dolls' country house,
with gardens, farms, lakes, and pine trees all complete,
which she showed me in another room. Real flowers
had been planted round it in light earth brought up
for the purpose ; and her mother, when I returned to
the drawing-room, told me that " Nobu cho " arranged
this part of the show entirely by herself.

The Japanese girl ! She is a creature of so many
attractive contradictions, with her warm heart, her
quick brain, and her terribly narrow experience ; with
her submissions and self-effacements which have
become second nature, and her brave revolts when
first nature takes the upper hand again and courage
is too strong for custom—perhaps it is too soon yet
for me to speak of her to any purpose, and yet I
want to tell you how deeply she interests me, how I
believe in her, and hope for her in the new develop-
ments which the next few years will bring forth.
The books I have read on Japan have always had a
great deal to say about the *musumë*, the pretty,
plebeian tea-house girl, or the *geisha*, the artist, the
dancer, the witty, brilliant hetaira of Japan. I
suppose these are about as unrepresentative of the
normal Japanese woman as a music-hall singer would
be of the European sister of charity. That they
are very much less objectionable than the corresponding classes at home is doubtless due to the innate
refinement of the Japanese woman ; but what a gulf
is set between them and the girls of whom I would

A QUIET HOME.

speak—girls surrounded with punctilious care, and brought up with one inflexible standard always kept before their eyes, the whole law of Duty! Inclination may never govern their conduct after they have arrived at years of reason, early reached in Japan; and if they are the brightest children, the most faithful wives, the most devoted mothers, always serene, industrious, smiling, it surely is because Duty is justified of her children.

I think that the simple unfettered life led by the little children here gives the girls a happy foundation to start on, as it were. There is no scolding and punishing, no nursery disgrace, no shutting away of the little ones day after day in dull nurseries with selfish, half-educated women, whose mere daily society means torture to a sensitive well-born child. Here, children are always welcome; they come and go as they like, are spoilt, if love means spoiling, by father and mother, relations and servants: but they grow imperceptibly in the right shape; they mould their thoughts and expressions on those of the sovereigns of the home; and one day, without wrench or effort, the little girl is grown into a thoughtful helpful woman, bent on following the examples of good women gone before her. Very gently but persistently one lesson has been preached to her ever since language meant anything in her ears,—" Give up, love, help others, efface thyself"; and in the still atmosphere of the home with its ever-repeated round of necessary and unpraised duties, in that quiet sunshine of humility, high motives grow and are not pulled up by the roots to be shown to admiring friends, the young heart waxes strong and pure, and should the call to heroic sacrifice sound, a noble woman springs forward to answer it ; should it never ring in her ears the world is none the poorer, for a true sweet woman is passing through it, smiling at every duty that meets her on her unnoticed way, leaving a train of gentle, wholesome memories behind her when the journey ends. In real womanliness, which I take to mean a high combination of sense and sweetness, valour and humility, the Japanese lady ranks with any woman in the world, and passes before most of them.

Her lot as a child and as a young girl is an exceptionally happy one ; but it cannot be denied that marriage often brings distinct hardship with it. The mother-in-law is apt to be exigent in the extreme, for, by the time she has reached that dignity, a woman's duties are considered over, the young people must provide for her comfort and amusement, and, in the lower classes especially, it does sometimes happen that a woman who has worked hard all her life and suddenly finds herself comparatively unoccupied, becomes fretful, difficult, and makes the young wife's life anything but a happy one. Also, mothers are mothers all the world over ; and where is the woman who ever thought her son's wife good enough for him ? It seems hard that the person who really has most to do with the young wife's fate should be, of all others, the one who will certainly depreciate her qualities. I have spoken of the lower classes, because it is there, I think, that the burden is most heavily felt; but the possibility of it exists in every class, family life being always shaped on one traditional model, and human nature, alas! often producing some fretfulness and selfishness in age of which there has been no trace in youth or prime.

An amusing instance of the clashing of nationalities on this ground took place when, some years ago, an English girl married a Japanese pro-fessor, and, quite unaccus-tomed to the ways of the country, came

AN EMBROIDERED ROBE.

out to live here, in the house of his mother, who received her kindly, but was horrified at what she considered the ignorance and flightiness of her new daughter-in-law. She especially disapproved of Mrs. N——'s having so many dresses out at the same time, wearing first one

and then another, according to the fancy of the moment.
Expostulation had no effect, and the young bride continued to flaunt her trousseau frocks in the old lady's
face. Something had to be done; the Japanese habit is
to carefully fold away the last season's dresses, and never
look at them again till next year brings the need for
them round. In this way the same robes may serve
for ten or twenty years; and if fashions never changed,
there might be a good deal to say for the custom. Old
Madame N—— at any rate made up her mind that it
should be enforced. She waited, generously, until her
daughter-in-law had gone to a garden party in her best
frock, and then she made a raid on her room, emptied
drawers of underlinen and wardrobes of dresses, and
carried everything away to the family *godown*, the
fire-proof store-house which I described just now.
I believe the scene was terrible, when Mrs. N——
returned, and found that she was expected to live on
her garden-party frock and two pocket-handkerchiefs
for three months. The old lady took a strong stand
on her rights; but the high-spirited English girl won
the day. "You got the things back?" I asked, when
she told me the story. "By bedtime!" she replied.
"We had a dreadful scene; but it was the last. She
saw that I must have my way, and we were good
friends afterwards."

I think it would be advisable for Japanese girls to
assert themselves a little more when the mother-in-law
is inclined to be tyrannical, and it is a pity that the
elaborate books which explain the duties of women at

every other stage of life do not contain some lessons
as to how to treat one's juniors when one has arrived
at the envied dignity of having a married son. This
is the time to which every woman looks forward eagerly,
the time when she will be openly honoured, and repaid
for many a silent sacrifice by the devotion of the
necessary daughter-in-law, and by the love of many
grandchildren, the proudest ornament of old age out
here. But the books and teachers are silent on this
point, as far as I can discover, and are entirely taken
up with telling a girl how great and all-reaching her
service to her parents-in-law must be. These rank
before her own father and mother, who expect to see
very little of her after her marriage ; she is completely
absorbed into her husband's family, in which alone will
she be remembered by prayers and offerings after her
death. Her submission to her husband has no limit :
but her husband himself owes entire submission to his
parents as long as they live. He cannot interfere on
behalf of his wife, or at least he very seldom ventures
to do so ; and if he does, the interference is more likely
to do harm than good. There is one bright point
towards which the poor little daughter-in-law can look
hopefully. The moment she herself becomes a mother,
especially if her child is a boy, she is regarded as a
person of some importance, and is treated with much
more consideration by the old people.

I know a charming little woman whose husband is
a Government official. They are Christians, and devoted
to one another ; but all his affection could not protect

her from a kind of persecution inflicted by the selfishness of his mother. Young Mrs. S—— was in delicate health, and needed all the rest and sleep that she could get ; but her mother-in-law would not allow her to go to bed until she herself was ready to retire. Like many elderly people, she slept badly, and sat up regularly, reading Japanese novels till one and two o'clock in the morning. Only when the lights were out, and the venerable O'Bassan comfortably rolled up in her *futons*, might the poor young wife seek her rest ; and long before daylight she had to be on her knees by the O'Bassan's couch, offering her the early tea. It was she who had to undo the shutters, get hot water, help the old lady to dress, and go through all the services performed for us by our maids, but for the old ladies by daughters-in-law in Japan. Rich or poor, it is the same for all ; and if there were an army of servants in the house, it is the weary privilege of the son's wife to attend to these details alone. In this case the result was very nearly fatal. When a son was born, Mrs. S——'s health was so broken down that it seemed unlikely she could survive, and she will all her life be a delicate woman in consequence. Let us hope that she will be merciful to her successors, remembering her own sufferings. Parents of only daughters greatly dread this ordeal for their child, and I am sure it has a great deal to do with the custom of adopting into the family a young man who is willing to take her name and merge his individuality in hers. When this happens, it is done, ostensibly, to carry on the family name and estates; but I believe the dread of a mother-in-law for the petted little daughter has much to do with it, and also the fear in her parents' hearts of having a lonely and uncomforted old age. Although the youth who consents to fill such a position is generally of a class slightly inferior to her own, happy is the girl whose life is run on these lines; her own parents will always be kind and indulgent to her, and her married life is a continuation in a fuller, more perfect sphere, of the sunny years of childhood.

One of the Legation employés married away his daughter this year. When the family came to receive the little present usual on these occasions, I asked the mother if the bridegroom seemed a good and kind young man, who would make O'Sudzu happy. "Oh yes," was the answer, "O'Sudzu will be very happy; her mother-in-law is a good woman, and has taken a great fancy to her." The bridegroom was not even mentioned. As it turned out, he proved to be either very unreasonable or very unkind; for six weeks after the wedding, our poor O'Sudzu was sent home again—divorced! I was dismayed, for we all thought that she was making a good marriage; and although she was plain, we knew that she was a good girl, and well-educated for her class.

"What has happened?" I asked in deep sympathy; for a divorce is a great misfortune to a girl, and marks her as having some distinct defect, bad temper perhaps, or clumsy hands with a habit of dropping the china, or something equally undesirable. But it turned out that poor O'Sudzu was not accused of anything so serious. Her husband came into the room one day, and found her sewing ; and as he watched, she threaded her needle, holding it up to one eye as women do.

" Why do you do that ? " asked the man.

" Because I see better so, honourable husband," she replied.

" Hold it up to the other eye and thread it," he commanded ; and she obeyed. At least, she tried to obey and failed, being slightly more short-sighted on that side.

" Go home," he said, " and return no more. Who wants a one-eyed wife ? "

So O'Sudzu came home, and her parents are now seeking for a less particular husband, who will have to be found in a lower class than the one she could marry into before she was divorced.[1]

There is an old saying in Japan that " Flame is the flower of Yedo " ; that flower has bloomed with terrible profusion of late. The end of last month and the beginning of this were marked by some fearfully destructive fires in Tokyo, and whole districts are still lying bare and black, as if people were almost afraid to rebuild on the same spot. I fancy, too, there is some hesitation in the public mind as to the best material for building under present conditions. These fierce fires have always been the curse of Tokyo, the city of wood and bamboo and paper. In old times

[1] The position of married women has been greatly improved by the new laws which have come into force since these words were written.

they were so much a part of life that a whole code of customs grew up round them, regulated by severe etiquette : there was only one costume in which it was proper to assist at a fire, and this was a particularly showy and elaborate one ; there is a whole nomenclature in which every variety of fire is described by a different name—one word expresses a fire kindled by intention,

A FIRE.

another the accidental outbreak, another the fire caught from the next house, another that kindled by a falling spark, and so on. There was special music, a kind of religious hymn, which was sung by the firemen at their work, and several of their number were told off to stand on the roof with standards on which were painted sacred and terrible symbols, intended to frighten the demons of the flames and arrest their farther progress. Although the fires seem to us both frequent

357

and terrible, the Japanese say that they were still
more so twenty years ago, when some part of Tokyo
was in flames every night of the week. In the old
days there was nothing to quench a fire but hand-
buckets, filled from the nearest moat; now there are
fire-engine stations all over the city, and a constant
watch is kept over each district. One of these stands
on the edge of the moat, very near our own gates. It
consists of a building for the fire-engine, a small guard-
room, and an enormous ladder, set upright in the ground,
crowned by a railed platform, very much like the crow's-
nest in an old man-of-war. On a transverse beam
above the platform hangs a bronze bell, on which the
watchman strikes the first signal of any conflagration.
The climb to this eyrie looks like a thing of peril; but
the wiry fireman runs up like a cat, and then sits on the
top rung of the ladder, swinging his legs with splendid
indifference over the sixty feet of empty air between
him and the ground. When an outbreak is discerned,
he strikes his bell, one stroke if it is in the district of
his station, two if it is in the next, and so on. Often
in the quiet night one is waked up by that first ominous
stroke, and then one sits up, listening breathlessly for
the next. If there is no second one, the household
is astir in a moment; for that might mean fire in our
close vicinity.

An old resident in Tokyo tells me that he witnessed
one or two of the almost historical fires which occurred
here in the early days of foreign intrusion. He and
others were students in the Legation when it was estab-

lished in Takanawa, and, as we have seen, somewhat
ineffectually guarded by Japanese troops. The students,
mere boys of eighteen and nineteen, were forbidden to
leave the compound without an escort, which usually
consisted of four or five native soldiers, and at least
one English mounted constable; but naturally enough
their chief joy was to escape from all this supervision
and constraint by saddling their own horses and slipping
out unseen to wander at will about the picturesque
town. If they met no Daimyo's procession, they were
fairly safe; but once or twice they had narrow escapes,
and were thankful to gallop back to the friendly shelter
of the compound, where nothing worse than a serious
reprimand was in store for them. When great fires
occurred in the city, the students always managed to
see them; and my friend tells me that nothing could
be more impressive than the quietness and order with
which everything was done to save property, to help
neighbours, but, above all, to bring the children into
safety. A certain number of men banded together
for this purpose, and going through the streets of the
district, where perhaps the danger, still unknown, might
at any moment become acute, would knock at every
door, saying, "A fire has begun; give us the children!"
And all the little ones were brought out (the elder
ones carrying the babies), and at once took their places
in the orderly procession, walking nine or ten abreast,
with a man at the end of every fifth or sixth row to
keep the order; and so the small people marched away
in regiments of three or four hundred at a time, singing

little songs to keep their spirits up, and showing no fear
in their perfect confidence that they would be protected.
There would be no risk of losing a child, since each
one wears a label with its name and address hung round
its neck, in case of accidents. When the children
were gone, it was an easy matter for the parents to
collect their household goods into bundles and carry
them away if necessary. The most precious objects
are the tablets of the ancestors in the household shrine.
These must be saved before any other properties, and
there is a saying that if the tablets are saved all is saved,
but if they are lost nothing will be rescued. I have
seen people sitting on their doorsteps with everything
portable tied in cloths or piled on a hand-cart, ready to
go if the flames or the almost equally destructive hose
came too near, but unwilling to leave their houses till the
last moment. The furnishings of a Japanese house are
so few and simple that they are easily transported ; but
the delicate wood, the dainty mats, and treasured screens
always suffer in these unexpected journeys. If the fire
is very sudden and near, there is an indiscriminate rush
to save property the moment the children have been
removed ; and thieves come sometimes in the guise of
neighbours, to help themselves to valuable things, which
are never seen again. But in general, great kindness
is shown to the sufferers, and a whole quarter will
open its houses to shelter the people who have been
deprived of their homes, and large subscriptions are
got up to help repair the damages. The Emperor and
Empress have sent a thousand yen, and Prince Haru

two hundred, in aid of the sufferers from the late fires here. There is a common saying that these catastrophes occur when the carpenters (who are the universal builders) are out of work; but one must hope that this is a calumny, merely inspired by the fact that

CARPENTERS AT WORK.

they are the only class who benefit by the misfortune. The ground is hardly cold before the carpenters are at work, rebuilding the dwellings which have been destroyed; and it is useless to try to get any carpentering done in other ways at that time; the Kinoshita San is better employed, and I must wait for my wardrobe or table till he is free.

All this consumption of wood must entail a serious
drain on the timber resources of the country, and
must also mean very heavy expense to somebody. I
believe it is possible to insure; but the premium is
so high that it puts such precautions quite beyond
the reach of the masses, who are, as it seems to
me, extraordinarily careless of fire-risk already. The
hibachi, a box lined with iron, or fire-proof clay, and
filled with glowing charcoal rising out of a bed of
fine white ashes, serves for tea-making and pipe-
lighting chiefly. It is carried from place to place as
it is wanted, and has often been the cause of accidents
through some end of paper or drapery which floats
into it unnoticed and causes an instant flare. The
stationary fire in the floor of the room is less dangerous,
being deeper and larger. This is called the *kotatsu*,
and is used for cooking; an iron pot hangs over it on
a chain in the poorer houses, and it forms a centre of
warmth round which the family spread their beds at
night. A fruitful source of fire is the kerosene lamp, a
cheap and brittle thing, so universally used that there
is hardly a house in Tokyo without it. One of these
flimsy glass lamps is often placed on a bamboo stand,
quite a yard high, and so slender that the slightest
touch will send it over. Round this the whole family
gather closely, so as to get light for the work which
they often carry on till very late at night. Just as
they are all intent on the task in hand, perhaps an
earthquake shock is felt, and in five seconds every
one is in the street, half paralysed with terror, quite

forgetting the lamp on its frail stand. The earthquake has overturned it, and by the time any one gathers courage to return, everything is in a blaze.

I find that here, as in South America, the worst damage done during an earthquake is generally caused by its follower,

A FIREPLACE IN THE FLOOR.

fire; and in the constant shocks which enliven our existence we always fly to the lamps first, and put them out if the vibrations continue. Were it not for the earthquakes, Tokyo would soon be a city of bricks and mortar, and the picturesque, inflammable, wooden houses would disappear; but the earthquakes will keep the old fashion in dwellings long alive, I fancy. The brick house behaves far more violently during the shocks, and does more harm when it is injured. The wooden one can toss and shake a good deal before being really shattered, and there are many instances on record when, the wooden pillars having given way,

363

the peaked roof sank on the ground, enclosing the inmates as in a hen-coop.

It has often been said that the more one sees, or rather feels, of earthquakes, the less one likes them; the Japanese take every other catastrophe with calm philosophy, but the earthquakes really cause panic to every class of the community. It is said that many of the rich people who have built themselves beautiful stone houses, furnished with every possible luxury, steal out of them after dark, to sleep in some old pavilion, nearer to the kindly ground.

CHAPTER XVII.

The Spring Manœuvres.—Opening of the Uyeno Exhibition.—Ancient and Modern Art in Japan. —Ivories and Enamels.—The Duke and Duchess of Connaught.

365

CHAPTER XVII.

I HAVE greatly envied the chiefs of missions who were invited by the Emperor to attend the Spring Manœuvres, the first that have been carried out under his own eyes. A great deal of enthusiasm was manifested, when it was announced that the Emperor intended to witness the sham fights himself. It is still and always will be here considered a miracle of graciousness, when he condescends to show himself to his subjects; and there is no mistake about the fervent loyalty of all classes to the person of the sovereign, however opposed they may be to one another. The arrangements were in consequence made on a much more important scale than usual, and a larger number of men were employed, fifty thousand being massed near Nagoya, besides those on board the battle-ships.

The Emperor left for Nagoya on March 28th, and the Empress and Empress-Dowager both accompanied him to the station to see him off. The plan of the manœuvres was based on the supposition that an enemy, crossing the Pacific, had struck at the coast between the two points of Kii and Izu, thus attempting to separate the country's forces and resources. The attacking body in consequence landed at Wakayama at the mouth of the Inland Sea, and tried to penetrate to Osaka and Isé. To turn them aside was the task of the defending force, called the Eastern Army; and a great deal of very smart work was done, which—I could not have understood, but simply longed to see!

AT THE MANŒUVRES.

The weather was awful; but the various battles were fought out with zeal and perseverance, the organisation and commissariat appear to have been excellent, and if the gallant Army of the East was beaten, it had the consolation of knowing that its conquerors were brothers and compatriots. Prince Arisugawa, who framed the official report of the manœuvres, was not sparing of either praise or blame where he thought it was deserved; but the report was sufficiently favourable to give the Emperor grounds for pronouncing himself wholly satisfied with the conduct of the troops and the ships, adding a little word at the end of his speech to the effect that he hoped they would do even better in time to come. Among the battle-ships the *Takachiho* and the *Naniwa* seem to have carried themselves extremely well, and the torpedo-boats did very good service.

Before the Emperor went to the manœuvres, he had inaugurated the great Exhibition at Uyeno, in order that on April 1st it might be thrown open to the public. There was rather an imposing ceremony for the opening, all the Court as well as Japanese and foreign officials assisting ; but it was amusing to find that the exhibits were in no way ready to be looked at. They were still lying about the galleries in packing-cases, and it seemed probable that weeks must pass before there could be much pleasure in wandering through the huge courts. Much to every one's surprise, however, the Emperor's visit and the accompanying ceremony (conducted in a temporary pavilion outside the Exhibition building) seem to have given an impetus to the work, and in a few days after that time a really splendid show of Japanese art-work was all in order to be admired, and—for rich people— acquired. It is a great pity that so little announce- ment or advertising of the Exhibition was done abroad ; for many art-lovers would, I am sure, have taken great pains to see this collection of the modern produce of Japan. That it is modern is perhaps its most characteristic feature, and shows conclusively that Japan has not lost her cunning ; for the enamels and carvings, the silks and the embroideries, are as fine and perfect as any of the recognised models of the best ancient periods. There are only two things in which the old work seems finer than anything the best modern artists can produce, and these are lacquer and sword-blades. I am in the minority in my opinion of modern lacquer, for such judges as Captain Brinkley consider the modern as quite equal in merit to the old. But there is hardly time to notice this among the exhibits at Uyeno, which are so many, and, alas! so unsatisfactorily arranged that it takes several visits to get a good idea of them. The thing which seems to strike the strongest note in the whole is the new school of painting which has been growing up here, on a battle-field, as it were, so violent was the opposition it encountered from the conservatives, who cling tenaciously to the old school, while their work seldom shows any of the vigour and freshness which made the work of the old masters in Japan so admirable. The warcry of these Eastern pre-Raphaelites is that nothing can be good which departs in any way from the models created and the canons laid down when Japanese art stood at its highest. Of course this involves both a philosophical contradiction and a confession of weakness. That which is stationary in art, or science, or morals, is already on the decline ; and the advance party of Japanese artists refuse to admit that the present cannot equal and outdo the past.

A FARM AND CORNFIELD WITH PAPER FLAGS FOR SCARECROWS.

From a painting by Yuangi.

The use of oil-colours, for instance, is condemned by the purists, because their predecessors have never made use of them ; the new school of painters delight in the richness and freedom of tint thus placed at their command, and are producing works which would take a respectable place in modern exhibitions in Europe. I have a series of little oil landscapes by an artist called Yanagi which I should never wish to part with. Fresh and clear and truthful, they put the more simple effects of landscape in Japan absolutely before one, and compare more than favourably with a number of paintings by European artists which hang beside them on our walls.

But strongly as I sympathise with the artistic courage which thus comes forward and asks to be judged by European standards, I confess that where mere private taste is concerned I prefer the original Japanese methods for many reasons ; the chief one being that they express ideas and deal with subjects that no other art has touched, and which cannot be even approached through the rich and heavy medium of oil-colours. The transparency and spontaneousness of the old paintings on silk, where perhaps one wash of thin dryish water-colour had to express unfathomed perspectives of cloud or depths of forest, are to me true portraits of the spirit of Nature here ; the heavy materials of oil and canvas can only produce her exterior lines, a faithful likeness of a body as it were, with the informing soul left out of the picture. Please do not accuse me of talking nonsense. Nature has both body and spirit like our other friends, and she is not always pressing the spirit on our notice, nor do we always wish to see it ; sometimes we are more in the mood for the opulent beauty of matter than for the delicate half-expressed secrets of soul, which imply and command a certain silence and peace and humility before they can be understood. But there are times, thank Heaven! when we can really close the doors of our mind to racket, and emulation, and all the noises of the century ; and then—the sweep of a single grass blade on the breeze suffices for our direction ; the sight of the blossom shedding its petals softly on the running water that carries them away soothes sorrow into peace ; the glory of blown autumn leaves against a golden sunset warms a chilled and tired heart ; panting with the dustiness of our daily road we are suddenly cooled and refreshed by the view of a forest glade veiled in wet mists that seem to fall on the brow like holy water from holy hands ; and all these things, I venture to say, can only be expressed and brought before us by the old spirit and the old methods of Japan.

There hangs a little scroll picture in my sitting-room which I would not exchange for a Claude if mere love turned the scale. It has helped me through many long hours of enforced idleness, and has often made pain lighter to bear. It shows a woodland stream overhung by the branches of a wild cherry tree, in bloom and past the blooming ; for the flowers are raining down on the stream, blown sideways by the breeze that is shaking the bough. Beyond, a point of rock stands up, and makes a swirl in the stream, and a few of the petals are washing against it like the froth of a ripple. That is all, but it is much. I can almost hear the tinkle of the stream, the delicate hum of the flowers and water against the stone; and when day falls and the evening comes on warm and languid already, the breeze that is shedding the blossoms seems to be whispering through the room.

There is a new art in Japan in which these ethereally delicate effects are well worked out, and that is in the cut velvet pictures which, little known till a very few years ago, have reached great beauty and perfection. The fabric is of extreme fineness, and lends itself well to such details as the plumage of birds or the foliage of trees. I have seen some charming snow scenes worked in this, and groups of wild duck,

DRAWING BY KYŌSAI.

where the colours were a pure pleasure to behold. My feminine appreciation, however, goes out to the embroideries, which far surpass any that I have ever seen, although we have been collecting them for years. There are, among other things, two *portières* in the Exhibition, about ten feet long and four or five feet wide. The whole of the ground is worked in a warm fawn tint, the stitches consisting of threads of silk laid close together in damasklike patterns, which only show themselves when the surface breaks in the light ; these threads are held in place by stitches of a much finer silk at intervals of a millimetre apart, and alternating, so that they make the effect of a slight mottling of the whole background. On one is worked a maze of pine-tree branches, so full and strong in design, so tender and

DRAWING BY KYŌSAI.

deep in colouring, that they do not affect one like pictured branches, but as the real tree, with all its significance of strength and ruggedness, its friendly needles that do not hurt, its resinous odour and sticky bark. The other curtain, against the same background, pictures a mass of tiger lilies and chrysan-

themums, tossing over a bamboo lattice gate in the
sunshine, while at the foot of the hedge grow docks
and common plants ; the stitches vary according to
the surface and thickness which they are intended to
portray (and splendid effects are produced by merely
changing the direction of the thread), and from end
to end the great curtain is one stretch of patient
perfect work.

It would only weary you, if I went through a list
of productions which you can never see. There is a
quality in Japanese art which cannot be conveyed by
description. When I speak of ivory-carving, people
at home think of Hong Kong glove-boxes and brush-
backs, or of the Chinese pagodas under glass in the
houses of our grandmothers. Here it is used for the
figures of men and women, birds and beasts ; and it
lends itself to the most subtle shades of expression,
to the closest imitation of nature. I saw a group the
other day, the figure of a young woman turning to
smile at a child who had just run to catch at her robe,
and was holding up a bunch of flowers towards her.
The thing was what we have seen a thousand times,
a young mother moving through her house, arrested
by an eager little one with an offering to make. One
almost heard the cry of the child as he caught at her
robe and held up his flowers, half withered in the
little hot palm ; her face was so lifelike that it seemed
to change expression as one looked at it ; the mouth
was serious, but the eyes were smiling down on the
boy in affectionate amusement. When I say that the

figure was not more than twelve inches high, you will understand how fine the work must be which can

DRAWING BY KYŌSAI.

convey such completeness of expression in these miniature proportions. The ivory, when used in this way, is slightly coloured (warmed would be a better word) where face and flesh tints are needed, and the finely wrought fabric of the draperies sometimes flushes into pink or pale primrose; but if there is colouring, it is so delicate that one hardly realises it at first, so imperceptibly does it melt into the warm paleness of the ivory.

The enamels are many and beautiful, and there is no shadow of doubt that modern enamel in every way surpasses the old. There are two very distinct styles in the modern enamel, the Kyoto makers preferring to work the true cloisonné, where the design is laid on in gold or copper wire in geometrical (or at any rate purely decorative) patterns of bewildering fineness, the colour being applied to the interstices, and often showing the gold surface of the foundation through its shimmering and jewel-like tints. This is the most costly form of modern enamel, and large sums are given for small pieces of it, while the larger ones can only be bought by very rich people. The surface of the finest cloisonné is so perfect that I think I should know it in the dark by the touch alone ; and there is no more trace of the original workmanship than if the elaborately patterned surface were the bowl of a spoon.

The Tokyo enameller works on different lines, and produces panels which look like fine paintings on porcelain (landscapes, birds, or animals are the favourite subjects for these), or monochrome vases and dishes, which are a triumph of workmanship, but convey at a little distance no more than the impression of delicate china which carries no par-ticular value. Of course on close inspection the brilliant quality of the colour and its perfect surface proclaim the identity of the piece ; but on the whole I care more for the Kyoto than for the Tokyo enamel. Of the latter, how-ever, I have two pieces which I greatly prize. They are rather tall vases, in the deepest sang-de-bœuf enamel, orna-mented by heads of grass (those tall crimson grasses which smother the meadows in the Tyrol) growing up from

DRAWING BY KYŌSAI.

the base, and hovered over by shadowy butterflies. Our old Chinese cloisonné looks heavy and laboured beside

379

all this easy perfection and smoothness ; and I think the only piece I still care about is a very ancient bowl, where the *cloisons* were cut deep in the original copper, and then filled up with enamel. It is strange that the chief artists in Kyoto and Tokyo both bear the name of Namikawa, though I believe they are not related.

I have turned out of *Ichiban*, and am inhabiting one of the smaller houses in the compound during the visit of the Duke and Duchess of Connaught, who arrived here from Shanghai on the 15th, and came at once to Tokyo as a convenient starting-point for their excursions. They brought a good many people with them, and we thought it better to give up our house entirely to them, since, although it looks large, the number of guest-rooms is limited, and there is absolutely no accommodation for foreign servants. I took this opportunity to do away with the horrible English wall-papers with which the Board of Works had disfigured the rooms, and covered the walls with Japanese papers, slightly embossed with free flower patterns, warm white in tint and with a satinlike surface, which made the rooms look fresh and gay. I brought out a quantity of English cretonnes when I came ; but I have never been able to look at them after seeing the Japanese cotton fabrics with their pure colours and true designs, so the cretonnes have disappeared, and are replaced by cool-looking crapes. The Duchess's room was very pretty, all the draperies being soft pink crape showered with cherry blossoms, the carpet dove-colour, and the silk quilts and cushions pale pink lined with robin's-egg blue.   And the cherry blossoms came out to greet the visitors; the gardens were forests of pink, roselike blooms, and I had all the house filled with the branches, so that every place was a bower.   The

BRINGING HOME THE BLOSSOMS.

Duchess was delightfully enthusiastic about them, and said that her blossom bedroom was the prettiest she had ever slept in.

Yes, the cherry blossoms are here; and I hope you will not think me wanting in loyalty if I say that they have been almost more of an excitement to me than the royal visitors. I have been very ailing all the spring, and I suppose flowers mean more to me than they do when I am running about and constantly occupied. And this is my first sight of the glory of Japan; for the crown of the year has come at last, and the country greets its beloved Empress's birthday by an outburst of bewildering beauty such as no words can convey to those who have not seen it for themselves. Tokyo is the city of cherry blossoms; every avenue is planted with them in full, close-set rows; every garden boasts its carefully nurtured trees; over the river at Mukojima they dip to the water, and spread away inland like a rosy tidal wave; and the great park at Uyeno seems to have caught the sunset clouds of a hundred skies, and kept them captive along its wide forest ways. In their capricious glory, the double cherry blossoms surpass every other splendour of nature; and it seems but right and just that, during the week or two when they transfigure the world, people should flock, day after day, to look at them, and store up the recollection of their loveliness until next year shall bring it round again. There is a tall grove of cherry trees in my garden, and as I look from my upper window I see the soft branches moving against the sky, and far away, rosy white as they, Fujiyama, the queen of mountains, flushing in the sunset. Then life seems full of promises and peace. The peace will remain; and if the promises are not all fulfilled, it will be because our life is a beginning whose end is the summer of another clime, and therefore, like the spring, it must be here " no perfect thing."

But I must return to my chronicle, which will probably interest you more than cherry-blossom metaphysics. Everybody except myself (I was too ill to travel) went down to Yokohama to meet the Duke and Duchess. The *Ancona* got in half an hour before she was expected ; but warning of the arrival was given by the guns of the forts and those of the battle-ships in port. The visitors landed at the Admiralty Hatoba (or quay), where they were met by those of our people who had not gone on board ; but they were officially received at the station, where the British residents presented an address of welcome, and a bouquet from the Yokohama ladies was given to the Duchess by Madgie M——, the beautiful child of whom I wrote you last winter when I had seen her at the children's fancy ball.[1] The Duchess was much struck with the wonderful little face. As the royal visitors had been rather overwhelmed with entertainments given them in Shanghai and Hong Kong, the English people here wisely refrained from taking up their time in that way, and they were left free to devote it all to sight-seeing, as of course they wished to do.

The Duchess, indeed, is an ardent sight-seer, and seems to have only one dread ; namely, that she should miss some interesting experience which the ordinary traveller would ferret out for himself. Before the party arrived, word was sent that they wished to travel quite unofficially so as to have all possible freedom for sight-seeing ; and this desire of theirs tallied with H——'s

---

[1] This letter has been omitted.

feeling that it was better for them, in the excited state
of the country, not to accept any very pompous Imperial
or official hospitality which could attract the unwelcome
attentions of the fanatics and the *soshi*. The Emperor
would have wished them to be his guests during the
whole of their stay, and proposed to put them up in
the Enryō Kwan Palace ; but in view of their own desire
to move about freely, and because of one rather embar-
rassing misunderstanding in the past, it was thought
better that they should not accept the gracious invitation
in its entirety. The misunderstanding rose from an
event which has never been explained, but which made
a most painful impression in Japan. At the time of
the Queen's Jubilee in 1887, Prince Komatsu, the
Imperial Prince nearest to the throne, went to England
to take the Grand Star of the Chrysanthemum to the
Prince of Wales, who unfortunately never returned
the visit, though Prince Komatsu stayed some time
in England. The Princess accompanied him, but very
little attention was shown to the Emperor's cousin ; and
this was the more deplorable because when the Duke
of Clarence and the Duke of York had visited Japan
some time before, they were received with open arms,
honours and kindness were showered upon them, and
nothing was left undone which could add to the pleasure
of their stay. All this added to the kind significance
of the Emperor's invitation, but seemed to point towards
declining to put our royal family under still heavier
obligations to his Majesty while those already existing
had not received ordinary recognition.

At all events the Duke and Duchess have made the most of their liberty, and from the moment they arrived in Tokyo refused to have anything to do with the Court carriages which were sent every morning to carry them about. They did consent to come up from Shimbashi Station in these pretty glass coaches, but an hour after their arrival insisted on going out in

INSPECTOR PEACOCK.

jinrikshas, a long procession through the dust, to see the curio shops. Public jinrikshas correspond to omnibuses in London, and official people do not use them. The private jinriksha may be a very dainty and luxurious little affair; but as we ourselves always use carriages, we only keep one such private perambulator for our English servants, and when nine were ordered for the royal party they had to be brought in from the nearest stand in the street, with their dusty bare-legged coolies, who were of course radiant with pride at being employed on such distinguished service.

Two chamberlains and an Imperial equerry have
been detailed off to accompany the Duke and Duchess
wherever they go. One of these gentlemen pleaded
sudden indisposition, and disappeared in the direction
of the Palace when the jinrikshas were ordered; the
others meekly took their places in the procession with
an expression of resigned despair. The Court coachman
looked on in profound amazement, and drove slowly
after the disappearing chamberlain; and even Inspector
Peacock,[1] the head of the escort, the Chief's right hand
in numberless ways, shook his head disapprovingly, and
was heard to say it was "most unusual," the strongest
term of disapprobation in his vocabulary.

From that moment the visitors have been flying
from one sight to another with an energy and per-
sistency which are rather surprising when one considers
that they have been for so long in what is supposed
to be an enervating climate. Everything that could
be "done" from Tokyo has been done thoroughly—
Kamakura, Nikko, Hakone, Miyanoshita, Atami; from
Miyanoshita the Duchess walked most of the way to
Atami over the route which we took in the heavy
snow last December. To be sure the road is easier
in coming from Miyanoshita than in going to it, since
the worst part of the stiff climb up to the Ten Province
Stone is an easy drop if one is coming down from

---

[1] Inspector Peter Peacock is a beloved and familiar figure in the British
community in Japan, and has seen long service there. He joined the escort
in February, 1867, and has served under Sir Harry Parkes, Sir Francis
Plunkett, Mr. Hugh Fraser, The Hon. Le Poer Trench, and Sir Ernest
Satow.—1898.

it; but a respectable walk of nearly sixteen miles remains, and the Duchess used her chair and coolies very little. I think she rather surprised the small foreign community by the extreme plainness of her dress, generally a light flannel coat and skirt (made by her sewing-maid) and a serviceable sailor hat. She is daintily neat and trim, and when she clicks her little heels together and bows straight from the waist reminds one irresistibly of a smart German officer. Soldierliness is in the blood after all, and the daughter of the Red Prince has an honest right to her share. She is not exactly pretty, but holds herself admirably, and looks so young that her rather shy stiff manner seems to suit the light girlish figure and the erect little head. She is everything that is kind and pleasant, and has the happy gift of getting amusement out of all the vicissitudes of travel, even rough inns and bad weather, and has managed to see more in her short visit than hundreds of people who have stayed months and years in the country.

CHAPTER XVIII

Danjuro, a Great Actor.—His Position in Japan.—A Foundation Stone.—The Destruction of Japanese Ideals by English Education.—Prince Komatsu and Two Imperial Orders.—Departure of the Duke and Duchess of Connaught.—A very Sad Story.

CHAPTER XVIII.

May, 1890.

IT is a year since we landed, and I am sure I have not yet seen half the things which our energetic visitors managed to " do " before they left. That which most amused the Duke was, I think, a Japanese play, or that part of it which it is possible to see in one afternoon. Danjuro Ichikawa was acting one of his great parts, in which he assumes four or five characters of men and women, youth and age, all of which he personates so entirely that it seems impossible to believe that he is anything but what he appears to be at the moment. He is a remarkably tall and gaunt-looking man, about fifty years old, rather like Henry Irving in his general appearance ; and yet he personates a dancing-girl, an old woman, a boy, a court lady, with the most bewildering realism. All the women's parts are played by boys or men, in Japan. The Japanese practice of wearing a mask, or a partial mask, on the stage is of course a notable help towards the perfection of the disguise ; but it would be easier to make up the face of a *geisha* than to imitate her dancing, with its curious flowing movements like the curves of a pennon on the wind, its sudden agile turns, changing the point of gravity with such rapidity and precision that the dancer's body seems to vibrate like a bow-string whence the shaft has but now sped.

A great actor in Japan is courted and flattered even as in England, openly and secretly. Many a girl in the seclusion of an aristocratic household is never allowed to make acquaintance with a man who is not a near relation; but she is taken to the theatre perhaps once in her life to see some exceptionally moral play, and sits through the whole day in the open box with her father and mother, drinking in all the speeches of the hero on the stage, admiring his courage, his beauty, rejoicing in his triumphs, weeping for his misfortunes. Who can be surprised when the poor child falls in love with the actor, writes to him, bribes her maid to carry presents to him, presents of flowers and fruit and poems, all significant of the most profound devotion and admiration? Love is such a strange thing here. It passes by nine hundred and ninety-nine women, and singles out one poor little creature, who suddenly becomes a heroine, an ideal, a canonised saint of love, throwing the world and life and honour at its feet in a kind of glory of self-annihilation, and as often as not obtaining such martyrdom as death for its sake can give. It is whispered that Danjuro has been much loved; however that may be, he is wonderfully kind and good to his family, maintaining a whole tribe of relations, who keep him poor in spite of his great popularity, and who live on his bounty with kindly indulgence, as is

THE DUKE OF CONNAUGHT.

the manner of people here when one member of the
family is earning large sums of money.

The Duke was delighted with his acting and
dancing, and sent for him to thank him for the pleasure
he had given. Danjuro was much gratified, especially
by being compared to Henry Irving, of whom he
said he had heard much and greatly desired to see.
The Duke told him that he ought to come to Europe;
but Danjuro replied rather sadly that he should never
have time for that, and of course he deprecated his
own attainments, as polite people have to do here.
Shortly after the interview he sent a present to his
Royal Highness, consisting of two plants of rare
chrysanthemums in full bloom, a costly offering at this
season, and in Tokyo, where valued plants command
a price unknown in Europe.

The Duke has bought some beautiful things at
the Exhibition, notably two splendid vases to take
to the Queen. As nothing may be carried away until
the Exhibition closes, there was some little trouble
to induce the authorities to allow the fairings to be
packed; but all has been made right now. He collected
also some beautiful embroideries, *kimonos*, and *fukusas*
as presents for various relations; and both he and the
Duchess have spent so much on curios in both Tokyo
and Kyoto that their visit will long be remembered
by the curio-dealers. The record buyer of last year
was Mr. Liberty, who is reported to have spent £25,000
in Japan, and whose influence was felt in a more
elevating way; for he had the courage to tell the

Japanese that in certain products, especially in their brocades and silks, they were following debased models and losing their sense of beauty by attempting to Europeanise the designs and colours. They seem to have taken his words to heart, for those shown in the Exhibition are purely satisfactory.

The laying of one foundation stone was asked of the Duchess; and I think she felt that the loyal Britishers had on the whole been pretty forbearing. The stone was the beginning of a kind of Cottage Hospital connected with the Anglican Mission School of St. Hilda's. The ladies who keep the school have one or two dispensaries in the town, which are widely resorted to by the sick poor; and it is thought that much good may be done by this little hospital, which is to start with twelve beds. I do not sympathise greatly with the objects of the school, which only receives girls of a class who can pay very highly, and gives them, in secular teaching, only that which they could have, on a very much higher scale, in the various high schools where the best foreign teachers are employed. The Christian element, although enforced by Bible and catechism lessons, appears most strongly in a kind of rough contempt for all the devout traditions of the Japanese. Ancestor worship, which is such a tremendous factor in Japanese life, instead of being transformed into tender and prayerful remembrance of the dead and a desire to imitate their virtues, is stigmatised as idolatry, and the Protestant dogma regarding departed spirits is put forward in all its brutality as

THE DUCHESS OF CONNAUGHT.

the only recognised truth. No one who has not lived among them can imagine how shocking this is to the feelings of the Japanese; for with them parental and filial devotion rank as the chief virtues, and make the harmony of the family. Minor prejudices and refinements, the duties of hospitality and of friendship, the thousand gentlenesses which give so much beauty to the family life of the Japanese—these, instead of being wisely utilised and encouraged, are pushed aside, ridden over rough-shod, in the attempt to transform the shy, quiet Japanese maiden into the healthy, selfish, rough-and-tumble school-girl of our own clime. The education seems to have little to do with the life which awaits the pupil as soon as she returns to her own home. As for morality, consideration for others, scrupulous cleanliness, duty, economy— all these are as strongly insisted on in Japanese education as in our own, and I think more successfully instilled than in any ordinary English school. I hope I am not being unjust to people for whom I have the greatest personal respect; but I must say that the manners and appearance of girls living in the English and American schools here do not compare favourably with those of girls brought up at home and merely attending school for a few hours in the day after the present Japanese fashion. I was painfully shocked in going over the dormitories at St. Hilda's by the dirty and untidy appearance of the cubicles where the girls slept, contrasting strangely with the expensive finery which they are encouraged to wear; and, system for system, the Anglican one, costly as it is, compares badly with

that adopted in our convent schools, where the most
rigid economy has to be practised, and considerations
of comfort must take a secondary place. A room built
full of small cubicles, with barely space to pass along
the passage into which they open, gives an impression
of stuffiness and darkness very different from the huge
upper space at Tsukiji, for instance, where one whole
wall is a window opening on a verandah as long as
the house, where only white dimity curtains divide
the beds, and the air is fresh and sweet on the hottest
day. Also, pagan or Christian, I think the girls are
glad to see, the first thing in the morning when the
sun strikes on it gaily, and the last at night when the
little lamp burns low, the figure of the Mother with
the Infant in her arms, and the pictured angels, who,
as they are told, stand by every white bed all night
long, to keep harm away. It would be strange, indeed,
if the desolate untidy cell without a single symbol of
prayer or sweetness proved a better growing ground
for a young girl's heart and soul.

But the Hospital is a different matter, a thing in
the management of which Englishwomen usually excel;
and I wish it God-speed with all my heart. I am sure
the fact that the Duchess of Connaught laid the first
stone and said so many pleasant things about it will
help it on with its subscriptions. That ceremony took
place in a pause between a flight back from Nikko
and one off to Kyoto, whence the Duke and Duchess
returned here and stayed a day or two, then went to
Miyanoshita and Kamakura. At Kamakura they spent

one night at the Kaihin-in, and left everybody delighted by their pleasant kind ways. There is very little to do at the Kamakura Hotel in the evening ; and the Duchess asked if a band could not be found to play after dinner. There was none in the vicinity ; and the

A CORNER OF THE DRAWING-ROOM.

nearest place where a band could be procured was at Yokusuka, the naval dockyard a little farther down the coast. A Japanese naval officer who was by chance in the hotel wired to Yokusuka, and the band was immediately sent up. The Duke was very much pleased with the promptness and goodwill shown, and insisted upon inviting all the other guests in the hotel to come and enjoy the music, which helped to pass an otherwise dull evening.

They got back to Tokyo in time to meet the Emperor, who came up from Kyoto on the 6th, and gave a dinner at the Palace on the 7th. Various other entertainments had been given for the royal visitors by the Princes and the Ministers. On the morning of the 8th, Prince Komatsu arrived at the Legation to return the Duke's visit, the Prince taking the place of the Emperor, who cannot pay a visit in a foreign house in his own dominion. When the Duke of Clarence and the Duke of York were here nine years ago, the Emperor called on them in person; but they were staying at one of his own palaces, the Enryō Kwan.

Prince Komatsu came, without warning, at a quarter to nine, and neither the Duke nor the Duchess was quite prepared for such an early pleasure. It was, however, the only time which could have been chosen, since they were to leave for Yokohama before eleven o'clock. Fortunately H— — was dressed, and Prince Komatsu, always the kindest and cheeriest of royalties, took everything in very good part. He brought many messages from the Emperor and Empress, and two gifts of another kind—the Grand Star of the Chrysanthemum for the Duke, and a most lovely little decoration, the Grand Star of the Crown, for the Duchess, who was very much pleased. Then all the good-byes were said, and any number of people accompanied them on board the steamer, which sailed at one o'clock for Vancouver.

In Japan they have left a charming impression, if

one can judge by the outbursts of enthusiasm in the
local newspapers, and by all the pleasant things said
about them by the Court people and officials here.
One paper says that "they showed the same kindly
and courteous mien to high and low, and that people
forgot the honour and only remembered the pleasure
of meeting such gracious personages."

There is a sad story which illustrates a very different
side of life in Japan, and which for that reason perhaps
ought to be told in these letters. I do not want you
to think that existence is one long series of cotillon
figures out here ; it can be very sad and very bitter.
I do not think I was ever more sorry for anybody in
my life than for a poor Canadian lady whose husband
was murdered in a most horrible way a little while
ago. Mr. L—— was assistant teacher at the Tokyo
Eiwa Gakko, a Canadian Methodist School for boys
and girls. The two divisions were quite separate, and
Mr. and Mrs. L—— lived in the girls' section, as did
one or two lady teachers, young Canadian girls. The
school has been established a long time, and is rather
a popular one, and Mr. L—— was much beloved by
the scholars. They went up to Miyanoshita for the
Easter holiday, and returned on April 4th, a day sooner
than they had intended, owing, I think, to bad weather
at Miyanoshita. The fees of the pupils had just been
paid in, and there were some hundreds of dollars in
a safe on the ground floor, the keys of the safe being
kept by Mrs. L—— in her room. A watchman, such
as we all employ, was supposed to make his round

every hour through the night, to see that all was right.
Only a few girls had returned, as the 5th was the day
fixed for reopening after the Easter holidays, and the
boys' building was entirely empty. The L——s, tired
with travelling, had gone to bed early, and so had the
two girl teachers, all occupying rooms that open into
the same corridor. Mrs. L— has a dear little girl,
a tiny thing, who slept beside her. The watchman
had gone back to his room at eleven o'clock, after
making his rounds, when he was terrified by the sudden
appearance there of two young men, tall and strong,
wearing masks over their faces, and having their gowns
drawn up through their girdles as people do here
when they are preparing for rough work. They were
dressed like labourers, and carried heavy sword-blades
fastened to bamboo sticks. They seized and bound
the man, and then asked him where the money-box
was kept. He told them at once, and also where the
keys were, in Mrs. L——'s room, where she and her
husband and child were asleep. The watchman's account
of the occurrences seems suspicious in many ways; but
all the inquiries point to his having only been guilty
of the worst of all crimes—abject cowardice.

The next part of the story was told me by Mrs. L——
herself. Awakened out of her first sleep, she sat up
suddenly in bed, and saw that her door was open,
and that in the light of a lamp which shone in from
the hall two poorly dressed men were making their
way round the foot of her bed. "Nan deska?" (What
is it?) she cried out; and a voice, which she says she

knows, answered, "We have business here." She saw what she thought must be sharpened bamboos in their hands, and in sudden fear clasped her baby closely to her. Mr. L— — had been awakened by the quick words, and without an instant's hesitation jumped out of bed and rushed at the robbers, though he had only his naked hands to attack them with. Although they were armed, they

"EVIL SPIRITS WITHOUT."

retreated to the door; but poor Mr. L——, as any other brave man would have done, followed them, and, as I think, must have attempted to wrest their weapons from them. After all, he was the only man in the house, and it contained girls and teachers committed to his care. Being what he was, he could hardly shrink back into his room and let these murderous burglars have the run of the house. So he followed them, and at the door a fierce scuffle took place. Mrs. L——, till then divided between her fears for the child and her fears for her husband, heard the quick rattle of blows, and ran to help Mr. L——, who by this time had followed the men into the narrow corridor outside. He seemed to be unconscious of having received any wounds, and was attacking them desperately; and they were raining blows upon him with those awful blades. Mrs. I.—— realised that the men were using sword-blades, and threw herself between him and them; she was frightfully wounded in the struggle, but she could not save her husband, who at last fell, quite dead, at her feet. Then the robbers went as they had come, untracked, undisturbed, except by one of the school-girls, who, poor child, came running from her room at the noise, and meeting them on the stairs took them for house-coolies, and asked them what was the matter. When Mrs. L—— saw her husband at her feet, she gave one terrible scream, which brought out the teachers from their rooms. They saw that he was dead; but she could not believe it, and made them carry him to his bed, since her own hand was useless, two fingers having been severed by the sword-blades, while a gash on the eyebrow had laid her forehead open. She was unconscious of being hurt, and with her left hand quickly dashed water again and again over her husband's face, washed it tenderly, and did all that she and the girls could do to restore him to consciousness. Just think of those three women and that poor dead man, and not a soul to do anything for them! It is surely one of the most pitiful stories I ever heard. Suddenly Mrs. L—— realised it all: her husband was dead, her only child

lay beside him, a tiny helpless thing that needed her,
and she was bleeding to death as she stood. So
very quietly she explained to one girl how to make
a tourniquet on her arm, and sent the other to reassure the school-girls in the dormitory; and then,
as she told me afterwards, she felt that a terribly
decisive moment in her life had come. Unless grace
were given her to forgive her enemies fully now, even
while her murdered husband lay before her, she knew
certainly that she would never be able to do so later;
and so, with an intense effort, she forced herself to
say, "God bless the Japanese," and she told me that
from that moment she never felt rancour or hatred
or any desire of revenge.

The watchman is in prison, but no trace has been
obtained of the two burglars, although every kind
of machinery has been put in motion to find them.
That they were burglars seems evident; robbers here
constantly supply themselves with swords, which they
use freely when attacked. But poor Mr. L—— is the
first foreigner who has been killed in Japan for twenty
years, and the outrage has excited an intense feeling of
anger and apprehension among the foreigners, and one
of humiliation and profound regret among the Japanese.
Mrs. L—— has had almost a miraculous recovery
from her wounds; but she looks terribly shaken, and
will not be able to use what remains of her hand for
a very long time. A brave woman—the widow of a
brave man!

CHAPTER XIX.

Kamakura, To-day and Yesterday.—The Strange Adventures of Yoritomo. Masako's Mirror and a Wonderful Dream.—Yoritomo's Triumph.— " Death has conquered."— A Moonlight Pilgrimage.—The Great Buddha. Kwannon, the Lover of Humanity.

CHAPTER XIX.

WHEN the excitement of the royal visit was over, it was rather pleasant to leave the smaller house, and come back to our own dens, and sit on our verandah in the May moonlight, talking over what has been of late an inexhaustible subject of interest-- the building of a Japanese house far away in the hills, where we hope to pass our summers in future. The question of six- or eight-feet wide verandahs, of glass or paper *shoji*, of how few trees need be cut down from the pine grove in which the nest is built—all this has been a constant amusement to me during the spring. At the end of this month I hope we shall be able to take possession of the little home, and then you shall have a full description of it. Meanwhile I have had a pleasant change in spending a fortnight at Kamakura, a little place an hour from Yokohama, very sheltered and quiet, close to the sea. Like Atami, it lies between two spurs of hills, which seem to be carrying it down to the water ; and a plain, far wider than the Atami one, stretches inland, covered with rice-fields, and crossed here and there by some ancient avenues of pines—sad old pines, crippled and scarred, and standing at irregular intervals, because their comrades in arms have fallen in

413

the ranks and lie crumbling at their feet. In the day-time a few families of peasants work at the rice-tilling, standing up to their knees in the horrible liquid dressing which nourishes the precious crops; here and there an

OUT FOR A WALK.

empty hut, kept only by the family dog, stands close to the road; everything is poverty-stricken and desolate; sand-dunes rise near the sea, and are planted with scattered pines, which seem holding out their arms as if to warn the waves not to come and gaze too near on the desolation which has swept over the site of one of the most splendid cities in the world. The Kamakura Plain, wide as it is, the foot-hills, and the valleys running up into them were all covered once with streets and temples, and full of the clash and the colour of the Daimyos' processions. The air must be thick with ghosts (if ghosts can walk unwearied for six hundred years), and—how one would love to see them! For Kamakura has witnessed some of the most stirring events in Japanese feudal history, and was the very centre of the power of Yoritomo, that strange man, indomitable, ruthless, astute, a mediæval Napoleon, who took his country into his own hands, and made his history hers while he lived.

In the struggle of two great families for the military power, the Taira (or Hei) had overcome the Minamoto (or Gen).[1] Both the families had originally been called into service by the Fujiwara Regents, to do their fighting for them, when they themselves had become too effeminate to attend in person to military matters. It was thus that the immensely powerful military class came into existence : as soon as its strength was, so to speak, full-grown, its members turned on each other, and on the Shoguns, who had been the cause of their greatness. In the year 1159 of our era, the Taira, headed by Kiyomori, took possession of the Imperial Palace in Kyoto (the reigning Emperor was Nijo, a boy of sixteen), and overcame all their enemies, notably the Fujiwara, and the rival military

[1] The monosyllables are merely the Japanese pronunciations of the Chinese characters in which the names are written, and which are the nearest equivalents to the true Japanese names Taira and Minamoto.

clan of the Minamoto, led at that time by Yoshitomo, who fled after his defeat, and was assassinated by the orders of his conqueror, Kiyomori. When Kiyomori was dying, long years afterwards, he said to his heir, who stood by his bed: "I have but one regret: it is not that I must leave life and power, for these I have had in their fulness. I have served greatly and ruled widely; but it is bitter to die without seeing the head of 'Minamoto no Yoritomo' [Yoritomo of the Minamoto]. After I am dead, say no prayers for me, but hang up the head of Yoritomo before my tomb."

Yoritomo, the son of Yoshitomo, was thirty-five years old when Kiyomori died. At the time of his father's defeat and death, though only thirteen, he was called the demon warrior; but if he was brave in battle, he was none the less quick to catch at any chance of saving his life, and both his courage and intelligence served him in good stead. From childhood he seems to have had that strongly magnetic personality which always made people anxious to serve and please him.

After the contest at Kyoto, he got separated from his father and brother, and lost his way, wandering alone through the night in very evil plight. His noble appearance attracted the attention of a poor fisherman, who disguised him as a girl, wrapped up his sword, the "beard-cutter," in matting, and brought him to the house of a lady called Yenjiu, who had been greatly loved by Yoshitomo, to whom she had borne a daughter, called Yasha Gozen, now twelve years old. Yoritomo would not stay with her, however; but left her his sword to take care of, and started out alone to try and pass into the Kuanto, the eastern territory, consisting of eight provinces, still wild and independent, and the home of thousands of outlaws. He doubtless expected to fall in with his father and some of their adherents, but was recog-

A LONELY PINE TREE.

nised on the road by Munékiyo, a Taira lord, and taken prisoner. When he was led back past Yenjiu's house, his little half-sister saw him, and burst into tears, exclaiming, " I can hope for nothing but disgrace hereafter; let me die with my brother ! " She was prevented from following him, but found means to commit suicide by drowning herself.

Yoritomo was brought to Kyoto, and a day was fixed for his execution ; but the Taira lord who had captured him seems to have felt pity for the boy, for he asked him whether he wished to live. Yoritomo's answer shows his astuteness even at that age. " Yes," he said ; " if I die, who can pray for the souls of my father and brother ? " thus suggesting the possibility of retiring to a monastery. The Taira lord then begged Kiyomori's step-mother to intercede for the boy, because he resembled a son whom she had lost in early youth. Her heart went out to Yoritomo; and she persuaded Kiyomori to spare his life, and only banish him to a distant province. When he was on his way there, all the people who met him said, noting his noble and resolute countenance, that to spare his life was like letting a tiger loose in the fields. Kiyomori lived to repent his clemency even in his dying moments, when he seems to have foreseen that Yoritomo would take to himself the power and place enjoyed by the Taira family.

The boy refused to shave his head and become a monk, as all his retainers but one entreated him to do, thinking that thus his enemies would no longer dread him. He waited patiently, living in the family of one of the two chiefs of Idzu, to whose custody he had been confided. Most of his father's retainers revolted, and abandoned him; none dared to communicate with him in any way. He lived a double life, inwardly full of hopes and ambitions of which he never spoke, and outwardly peaceful and resigned; so that he was described as "never showing any emotion in his countenance; of a quiet, hardy, and enduring nature, respected and beloved by all." A violent love affair with the daughter of his guardian does not affect this estimate of him in Japanese eyes; but it made it necessary for him to leave the house, since he was discovered and betrayed by the girl's step-mother, and her father threatened to take his life.

He fled to the house of his other guardian, Hojo Tokimasa. Here, too, there were daughters; but they were jealously secluded, and Yoritomo could not even catch sight of them. So he asked many questions of one and another, and learnt that the elder, Masako, was a very beautiful girl; the younger, not fair, but the daughter of the second wife. He determined to have the mother on his side this time, and sent his faithful servant Morinaga to the younger sister with a love letter. Morinaga was surprised at his master's choice, and after much consideration decided to put the matter straight; so he destroyed Yoritomo's letter, and wrote another in its place addressed to Masako, the beautiful elder sister.

The night before he did this the younger girl had had a wonderful dream, the dream of a pigeon flying towards her with a golden basket in its beak. When she told her sister of the dream, Masako's heart was wrung with envy; and she said, " Honourable younger sister, let me buy thy dream of thee! Thy dream and all that it foretells shall be mine, and thou shalt have instead my mirror for which thou hast so often longed!" Now the mirror was exceedingly rich and beautiful, and the younger girl had often wished to have it. As Masako held it out towards her, and she saw how clearly it reflected all things, she thought, " The dream may be a delusion, but the mirror is real"; so she said to her sister, " Take my dream, Masako, and

give me thy mirror that I have longed for." And
Masako gave her the mirror gladly, being a devout and
pious maiden, who did not scoff at the invisible gifts
of the gods. And the next day Yoritomo's messenger
came, with the forged love letter. Yoritomo was glad
when he found that, after all, Morinaga had taken it
to the beautiful Masako, and he had cause all his life
to be thankful for the fraud practised on him. Masako
was not only fair, but wise, courageous, and devoted,
and helped him greatly in his after-career.

The lovers kept their affection secret at first;
and Masako's father, who was away at Kyoto, meanwhile promised her to another man, the Governor of
Idzu. When he came home and found how matters
stood, great was his perplexity; but he insisted on
keeping his word to the Governor. And Masako kept
hers to Yoritomo, for the very day her father married
her to the Idzu man she rode away with her own
true love, and never left him more. Every one seemed
to feel that honour was satisfied; and Hojo Tokimasa
espoused Yoritomo's cause, and, as I think I said
before, did much to restore that hero to his rights,
and to those of many people, which he made his
at last.

In 1180 Prince Moshihito, the second son of the
Emperor Go Shirakawa, who was then living in
retirement, took up the cause of the Genji or Minamoto
clan, and sent messengers to Yoritomo, requesting
him as head of the family to collect men and lead an
expedition against Kiyomori and his Taira adherents.

THE NIGHT BEFORE A BATTLE.

Yoritomo, assisted by his father-in-law Tokimasa, collected an army, and after one or two checks, met with his usual calmness and courage, was joined by many chiefs of rank, and took possession of Kamakura, which he established as the seat of a military government. Soon after this Kiyomori died, having lived just long enough to see Yoritomo, the son of his old enemy, rise to the height of power and splendour.

It is rather sad to read of how Yoritomo rewarded those who had helped to win his battles for him. His younger brother, Yoshitsune, who had fought valiantly for him, was sacrificed to Yoritomo's jealousy of any power but his own, and was forced to commit suicide, after killing his own wife and children to prevent their falling into Yoritomo's hands. But this did not shake the power of the elder brother, who little by little established a far-reaching system of government and taxation, and placed his relations in high and lucrative posts. Kamakura was the heart of the country in those days, and its pulse was felt in the most distant provinces. Yoritomo became Shogun in 1192, and died from the effects of a fall from his horse in 1199. His two sons who succeeded him were both murdered, and little by little the Hojo family whence he had taken his wife absorbed all power into their own hands as Regents (*Shik-ken*—Holders of Power) of the Shoguns. The extraordinary complication of Japanese feudal history, with its two or three contemporary retired Emperors (some of them were children still), its " shadow " Shoguns (children, too, as often as not, and, if they were lucky, deposed before they were murdered), and its Regents of Shoguns who themselves fell under the power of ambitious guardians—all this makes a bewildering army of names and dates impossible to place clearly in one's mind. But here and there a great figure stands out ; strange heroic stories group themselves around it ; the splendid ghosts take their places in triumphal processions ; and old Japan is suddenly before us, with all its pomp and chivalry, its hot heroism and cold cruelty, its love of life and gay contempt of death.

Death has conquered at Kamakura. Yoritomo's gorgeous capital was burnt, and only its ashes remain to mingle with the dust and sand of the plain. Tidal waves have helped in the ruin ; and now the sea rolls in, empty of ships, to the deserted shores, and the pines along the broken avenues seem to be dying willingly, for branch after branch drops with a crash in the wind that is sweeping the dunes to-day as if seeking for something still left to destroy.

But I was wrong in saying that no trace of the old glory remains. There is one which fire and storm and tidal wave have torn at in vain : shorn of its old surroundings, bared of its temple roof, the great Buddha still meets the moving seasons with a front of eternal calm.

It was a mild May night, and the moon rose round over the heaving sea. The wind had fallen, the sighing pine trees were at rest, though one stretched out an arm here and there as in sleep, throwing a twisted shadow across the road where our footsteps fell muffled in the sand of many storms. We passed in silence by the empty fields, the darkened huts,

BUDDHA.

and up the village street, touched to a square of soft dull gold where here and there a light still burned behind the *shoji* for birth or death or unfinished toil, the three strings of our life's lyre. Then the village was left behind, we turned in at an embowered gate, and before us, in a wide temple, roofed only by the sky, lighted only by moon and stars, rose the great Buddha, the monument of peace.

Peace! In the hush of that flood of moonlight, the very mantle of peace seemed hanging round him in the silver air. All daylight reds and greens were washed to one luminous grey in that transforming haze; all sounds consoled, fulfilled, harmonised in that vibrating silence.

"Venit pax in die una, quæ nota est Domino; et erit non dies neque nox, sed lux perpetua, claritas infinita, pax firma, et requies secura."

The monk who wrote the words knew the well-springs from which such peace may flow to the humble in heart. The artist who moulded the calm face of Buddha must have been his brother in this land of

425

the sun-rising, having attained to that wide spiritual enlightenment which is the reward of all who, under whatever skies, of whatever race, have done the best, the highest, the purest that they could see to do. And there are few higher, more perfect works of art in the world than this representation of Amida Buddha, the incarnation of a humanity which, after long struggles to break free from earth, is enthroned in irrevocable peace, but is not deaf to the cries of those who are still stumbling along the thorny road he too has known. The countenance, full of inscrutable majesty, seems only still by the soul's command; behind the deep eyes and the quiet mouth lies a smile gentle and calm, as if rising from the very heart of knowledge. "Having attained," is what the beautiful lips would say, were speech needful. On the brow a silver boss draws the moon-rays to itself; the breast is bare to the kiss of the wind, the feet and hands folded in profound repose. All around, at regular intervals in the pavement, stand the old stone bases of wooden pillars, long ago swept away with the splendid roof that rested on them, with the gates and steps and altars that once surrounded the image and helped to make this temple one of the wonders of Japan.

Yoritomo before his death was inspired by a desire to have in his own city a great Buddha like the one at Nara; but he died before he could carry out his idea. Some lady in the Court, for love of him, collected money to have such an image made, and in time it was completed, cast in bronze, and set up here to replace a wooden one which had stood for a few years and had been destroyed by fire. No fire or water could injure the fifty feet of towering bronze of the new Buddha; but the sea seemed jealous of its greatness, and broke over it twice, in 1369 and 1494. This last tidal wave carried away everything, except what we see to-day. The temple was never rebuilt, and for four hundred years the sun has shone and the rain has wet the image, which stands like a symbol of the soul, outliving all the trappings of this earthly life.

No farther than the home of Amida Buddha did we go on that night of our moonlight pilgrimage; but there is another temple near, to be seen by daylight— the shrine of the goddess of mercy, Kwannon, every- where loved and worshipped in Japan. I knew her in China as Kwan-yin, and possessed once a most beautiful figure of her in soft white *pâte*, a lovely mother-woman standing with a babe nestling in her arms, a *mandorla* of blown flame enshrining them both. Here, in her temple on the hill behind Daibutsu, she holds no child in her arms, but stands, a great golden image in the darkness of a jealously secluded shrine, with hand raised as if to bless, and a smile of love and tenderness on her face. It is as if the other gods had thought her too lavish, too spendthrift of her favours, and had enclosed her here, and set a guardian to keep the gate and to count those who go and come, for fear that all mankind should enter into paradise through her intercession; for Kwannon has a great and faithful love for the human race, and, having already attained to Nirvâna, put eternal joys aside, and returned of her own free will to this world to save and comfort men and women. Sometimes she is represented as having numberless arms, each of which reaches out some good thing, some desired grace; she never refuses a supplication, except when invoked a second time under one especial title, "Hito Koto Kwannon" (the Kwannon of a Single Grace), for it is not lawful to pray to her twice by that name, although the first use of it compels her compliance. She is the mother to whom all mothers pray in the land, she sends children, and she protects children; and Jizo Sama, the god who tends the children's ghosts, does so at her command. Even the animals she loves, and there are shrines where the peasants bring their horses and bullocks to receive her blessing, and perhaps get the promise of a higher reincarnation when they return to this weary world. Such is the Buddhist picture of Kwannon, the faithful, loving, powerful mother, the type of all womanly grace and holiness. Except by divine revelation, could the heart conceive a more perfect ideal?

CHAPTER XX.

CHAPTER XX.

A S one looks out from the verandah of the Kai-hin-in, the one hotel of Kamakura, the sea only shows itself as a blue or grey line made narrow by high sand-dunes, and half hidden by a pine wood which grows in the hollow behind the protecting crest. This wood is just now carpeted with thin green grass, pushing up its way through the pine needles. A few hardy wild flowers swing on the wind, and here and there the tree roots make inviting seats, where one can rest awhile and listen to the cool sibilant talk of the branches in the breeze overhead. A scrambling path leads across the dunes to the wet firm sands, marked with long rosaries of little footprints, undulating as the ripples which break lazily a few yards farther on. Numbers of children come here at low tide to gather the delicate shells, which they sell to the shell-workers of Enoshima, the island which lies behind the promontory to the right.

The children are laughing, communicative little people, who walk up and down beside me when they catch me on the sands, and evidently take me for a shell-gatherer too; for they insist on my buying their little basketfuls of shells (generally for a sum too small to be translated into English), and then they run away

to their homes among the fishermen's huts, delighted at
having earned their money without taking the long walk
to Enoshima in the burning heat. I can only understand a few of the things they say, just enough to make
out how many brothers and sisters have been left at
home, or the age of the baby on the little shell-
gatherer's back ; but my stupidity seems not to diminish
the pleasure that one at least of them takes in my
society. She is a bright-eyed little creature of ten or
thereabouts, with a very solid baby on her back, to
whom she pays less attention than I do to my parasol.
She jumps about, slides down sand-hills, hops on one
foot, plays little games of " chuck-farthing" with five
pebbles in a circle of friends and contemporaries, all
without the faintest reference to the solemn baby, who,
safely tied to her back with strips of blue linen, falls
asleep and wakes up again, cries or laughs, sucks a
sugar-cane if he is happy, and bangs his nurse's head
with it if he is cross, all without influencing her any
more than we can change the weather by grumbling
at it.

The children gather in numbers to see the nets
hauled in, and it is a sight I seldom miss if I can help
it. When the sun is getting low and throwing red
reflections along the water and the sands ; when the
trees on the promontory towards Enoshima are visibly
falling asleep in a haze through which they look almost
black,—then a light boat rows to shore, leaving a larger
one some way out from land, and moving slowly from
point to point, where dark objects like human heads

ON THE SHORE.

are bobbing up and down on the water. They are not heads, but lumps of tarred cork, to which the upper edge of the huge net is fastened. Below, it hangs with weights attached, in many a turn and snare in the water; and now the time has come to draw it in and count the take. All the men but two have come ashore in the smaller boat, and form a line pointing inland, each man holding the rope with both hands: the bare limbs are firmly planted on the sand, and all the brown bodies gleam like bronze in the sunset. Then at a word of command from the first on the line a measured chant breaks out, and a long swinging pull brings the rope some yards farther up the shore. Passing it quickly from hand to hand, the men run down again to the water's edge, never changing their relative positions, and again the toil-song sounds along the beach, as more of the heavy length is retrieved from the sea. The net is sunk so far out that often the men must work three-quarters of an hour before its real mouth is brought to shore; and meanwhile their comrades in the fishing-boat row from point to point where it shows above the water, pushing it gently towards the land. When at last its black drifts are creeping up the rippled shallows close in shore, the rope-draggers leave the piled cable, and, wading into the water, seize the web in armfuls and bring it farther in, to separate mesh from mesh with extreme care, and to catch the leaping fish, who flash their live silver from side to side with a curious rattle and snap against the cords of their wet prison. It is a beautiful sight as the brown men, their loins girded with twisted blue cotton, stand in the water, stretching out the lengths of the net full of dancing silver fish, behind them the sunset sea, and before, the dusky velvet sands. This is the time when the children glean their harvest ; and not the children only, but poor widows, who have no man to send a-fishing, and very old people, whose sons are dead, all gather round the fishermen, holding out little bowls and baskets for what they will give ; and all that is fit for food and yet not good enough for the market goes to them. When the catch has been a good one, the suppliants go off with their begging-bowls full ; when, as sometimes happens, nothing has been taken, then there is no supper for anybody, the fishermen's pensioners separate sadly, and the men themselves, without a word of complaint, pile the net on the boats and row out to sea to drop it all into place again. Once I saw them draw it in long after dark, and lanterns had to be lighted to sort the fish, while the children and old people, waiting eagerly, kept peering forward into the ring of light. It is good to see that there is never a rough word said to the beggars, who, though as poor as the grey grasses on the dunes, do not look despairing or dirty or unhappy. The thanks are simply and duly said, be the gift great or trifling ; and there is no grumbling or wailing if it is withheld.

In the first half of the fourteenth century the Hojo Regents (*Shik-ken*) took the entire control of both Shoguns and Emperors, after the short-lived dynasty of the Minamoto Shoguns came to an end with the

murder of Yoritomo's second son. Several
generations later, by some oversight of the
Hojo, an Emperor thirty years old, and

NITTA THROWING HIS SWORD INTO THE SEA.

having some sparks of independence in him, was
allowed to come to the throne. He chafed secretly
at his wretched position, and took advantage of a
famine which wasted the land to excite his few
partisans to rise against the reigning family, already
greatly hated on account of its avarice and cruelty.
A noble who immediately espoused his cause was
Nitta Yoshisada. A powerful and resolute man, he

succeeded in raising a large army in a very few days, and came to attack Kamakura, Yoritomo's city, then the seat of the Hojo power.

But Kamakura, lying safe in its bay, with rocky spurs easily fortified running down to the sea on either hand, was a place hard to take. Nitta found the small stretch of beach under the sheltering promontory bristling with improvised fortifications ; beyond it, a huge fleet of war-ships stretched out in long lines, barring the approach by sea. As he gazed down from the cliff, he saw that only supernatural help could enable him to take the great city which stretched out at his feet, filling the plain and the lower valleys as rice fills a bowl. So Nitta prayed very earnestly to the gods of the sea, and then, in sacrifice to them, and also to show his army that not his own prowess but the grace of Heaven must win this battle, he threw his sword from the cliff far out to sea.

Then he came down, saying to himself, " To-morrow Kamakura will be given into my hands"; and he went into his tent in the camp on the beach, and lay down and slept. And early the next morning, when the sun rose over the sea and Enoshima, a great cry of joy was heard in Nitta Yoshisada's army, and the general rose and shook himself, and went and stood in the door of his tent. And before him was one great stretch of shining sand, a mile and a half wide, reaching from where he stood right into the forefront of Kamakura city ; far away the useless war-junks floated on the water ; from the defences under the promontory

THE TEMPLE OF HACHIMAN AT KAMAKURA.

near at hand not even an arrow hurt his troops, as they made a wide circle round by the sand and marched straight into the heart of Kamakura.[1] Then came a battle, fierce and bloody, for the Hojos were gallant fighters and their retainers strong and trusty ; but they were vanquished. Many of them perished by the " happy despatch " rather than fall into their enemy's hands, and most of the gay young city was burnt.

As one stands under the pine trees of the Kaihin-in Hotel at Kamakura, the famous promontory lies on the right hand, hiding the strange island of Enoshima. A mile or so to the left, somewhat inland, runs an old road, where the grass pushes up between the grey uneven paving-stones, and hangs undisturbed from low stone walls on either side. Here and there tall pines, battered and crippled now, show that a stately avenue once led to the temple at whose lowest step the road ends, the Temple of Hachiman, the god of war. The steps are grey, and worn with many feet, and very long and wide and steep. A gallant tree, as old as they, springs from a deep court beside them, and towers far above, its enormous body seeming to almost push them aside, while overhead the branches spread out in thick clouds of leafage, brilliant green, polished, odorous ; and this is the thousand-year-old camphor tree of Hachiman, the rival of the one I loved in Atami's temple grove, less great in girth, but marked somewhere in its ringed

[1] The Japanese of to-day explain the story by saying that Nitta took advantage of his knowledge of the tides to work on the credulity of his followers.

strength with very noble blood, the blood of Sanetomo, the youngest son of Yoritomo, and the last of the Minamotos.

The tree was younger, but not less green, when Yoritomo used to come to sit in its shade, and look out over his fair strong city of Kamakura. He loved this spot, and often climbed still higher to the slope of Shira-hata Yama, just behind the Temple, whence he could see his war-junks rolling in the bay, and count the white standards of the guards round his palace wall in the town. It is said that Yoritomo foresaw the weakening quarrels which would undermine the Minamoto power after his death; and it may be that he wondered, as he looked down from this green hill, how long his name would be supreme in Kamakura after he himself should have passed to the "farther shore." His own strength and wisdom kept the kingdom in peace, and great prosperity everywhere followed on his administration; but when he looked at his two sons, he must have remembered that he had calmly sacrificed his brother to his ambition; and—Yoriiye and Sanetomo were not so strong or so wise as their father. The elder, Yoriiye, was only eighteen when Yoritomo had the fall from his horse which brought on his last illness; and when the hero died, this boy, his successor, was far more occupied with feasts and shows and dancing-girls than with the government of the country.

His mother, Masako of the mirror, a woman who had the strongest influence on the history of her time, swore to herself that no weakling should succeed the great man who had been her husband. Though nominally a nun after the death of Yoritomo, she directed the family councils with a strong hand, and insisted that Yoriiye should not be left at liberty to bring ruin on the Minamotos. With her father, Hojo Tokimasa, and other powerful partisans, she attempted to force Yoriiye to resign, and to divide the kingdom between his younger brother, Sanetomo, and his own youngest son, an infant of days. Yoriiye very naturally refused ; and in the contest which ensued he was overcome, banished, and put to death. His son, poor baby, was killed by its grandfather, Hojo Tokimasa ; and so was Yoriiye's father-in-law, who had upheld him in his resistance to the family decrees. Masako triumphed once more ; her favourite child Sanetomo became Shogun at the age of twelve ; and the power seemed likely to remain in her hands and those of her father Tokimasa for many years to come. But at last, Tokimasa himself, a hoary reprobate of sixty-eight, had to be sent away ; Masako finding that he was plotting to oust Sanetomo from the Shogunate, and put the infant son of the step-sister (to whom Masako had sold the mirror) in Sanetomo's place. So this valiant and unscrupulous lady sent her father off to repent his sins in the seclusion of a monastery, the poor unconscious little usurper and his father were murdered, and things seemed safe and quiet for a season.

But while whole families were being sacrificed to keep Sanetomo's inheritance safe for him, a far more

dangerous enemy was growing up almost at his side.
The eldest son of his brother Yoriiye was five years
old when his father was killed, and his life was spared,
for no reason that has ever been explained. Since
Sanetomo adopted him and sent him to a monastery
to be brought up, it looks as if the boy of twelve must
have had some affection for his little playmate of five.
At any rate, no one seems to have regarded young
Kugiô with any suspicion, and he grew up to manhood,
having kept his own counsel well. His purpose grew
strong in silence : he saw a sacred duty before him—the
duty of avenging his father's death.

They made him the high-priest of the great Temple
of Hachiman, where the god of war was worshipped,
where Yoritomo's helmet and sword were kept as relics,
where everything spoke of the pride and strength of
the family whose honours should have descended to
himself. Day by day, as he walked on the Temple
terraces or passed under the three holy gates which
still lead thence to the outer world from which Sanetomo
had banished him, Kugiô would swear deep and strong
by the grave of his great grandfather, by the head
of his murdered father, that Sanetomo's blood should
flow, and Yoriiye's soul enter into peace—avenged.

Now on a cold night in the first days of the year
1219 (1879 by Japanese reckoning), Prince Sanetomo,
who was then twenty-eight years old, and full of the
love of life and the recklessness of youth, called his
people, and said, " Now will I go and worship at the
Temple of Hachiman ; even as my ancestors have

always done." And his old servant came weeping, and said, " My heart is full of fear for my Lord, and I am one that have never feared or wept! Oh, my Lord, if you will go to-night, let me put on you a coat of mail, such as even my Lord Yoritomo did not disdain to wear when he dedicated the Temple at Nara!" And one of Sanetomo's friends, young and headstrong as he, said, " Nay ; great soldiers wear no coats of mail!" Then the servant entreated, " At least, let my Lord go in the day, and not in the darkness and the cold!" And the same young man, whose name was Naka-akira, scoffed, and said, " This worship is always rendered at night."

And Sanetomo sent for his favourite servant Hada Kinuji, and bade him comb his hair before he went, that he might appear at the shrine with all decorum ; and he pulled out one hair, laughing, and gave it to Hada, saying, " This is my bequest to thee!" And then he set out, with a thousand men and great pomp ; but when they reached the Temple gate, Sanetomo bade all his soldiers and his people wait outside, while he passed in alone with his friend Naka-akira, both filled with the pride of life, and thinking no evil. And he entered the Temple, and made his devotions to Hachiman, and returned, passing down the steps with his friend at his side, talking of many things. And as they passed the tree which is by the steps, the tree reached out death to them both ; for a great sword flew out, and a man's hand swung it high once and twice, and one after another the two proud young heads rolled on the steps, and the blood dropped after them and made a little sound in the darkness. And Kugiô leapt out from the tree, and called in a loud voice, " Thus does the high-priest avenge his father !" Then he took up Sanetomo's head in his hand, and fled away through the night, stopping to rest at the house of a retainer, where he broke his fast, never letting go of that on which his soul was feasting—the head of Sanetomo.

But he was pursued, and dropped it at last, and was killed himself, and the head of Sanetomo was never recovered ; so they buried his body without it, and his power passed in name to his infant son, and in reality remained in the strong hands of Masako until her death. But the end of the Minamoto Shoguns came under the great tree on these steps of the Temple of Hachiman, where I sit to-day, and hear the grasses shiver, and the gulls cry out at sea ; and blind insects crawl dustily where the blood made a little sound in dripping from stone to stone. The place is lonely and empty as a rifled grave.

Printed by Hazell, Watson, & Viney, Ld., London and Aylesbury.